DEATH-BLINDER

The swords met again. Omund felt a sudden stinging pain on his left forearm from Hather's deflected blade. His eyes grew wide and wild with desperation. Close-quarters combat was impossible on the ice . . .

Allfather lowered his head. 'My choice is made, Mother Skuld,' he muttered sadly.

The combatants turned to face each other across the long, narrow lake. For the last time they dug in their skates and pushed out towards the centre, their legs moving in sweeping strides to build up speed. With the distance between them diminishing rapidly one of Omund's skates caught an irregularity in the frozen surface. With a scream of fear he crashed to his knees whilst Hather swept towards him, his face a mask of merciless determination.

Omund scrabbled up to regain his balance. With Hather almost upon him he extended his sword, holding it at arm's length . . .

Also by the same author and available from NEL:

STARKADDER
VARGR-MOON

About the Author

Bernard King was educated at Northampton Grammar School and at teacher-training college in Lancashire. He quickly left the profession and took a variety of jobs, including fitter's mate, foundry-worker, carpet salesman and assistant theatre manager. In 1974 he joined the Northampton Development Corporation as advertising copywriter and Press Officer, and now writes full time. He is married and lives in Northampton. DEATH-BLINDER is his seventh novel.

DEATH-BLINDER

Bernard King

NEW ENGLISH LIBRARY
Hodder and Stoughton

Copyright © 1988 by B. J. H. King

The characters and situations in this book are entirely imaginary and bear no relation to any real person or actual happening.

First published in Great Britain in 1988 by New English Library Paperbacks

An NEL Paperback Original

This book is sold subject to the condition that it shall not, by way of trade or otherwise, be lent, re-sold, hired out or otherwise circulated without the publisher's prior consent in any form of binding or cover other than that in which it is published and without a similar condition including this condition being imposed on the subsequent purchaser.

No part of this publication may be reproduced or transmitted in any form or by any means, electronically or mechanically, including photocopying, recording or any information storage or retrieval system, without either the prior permission in writing from the publisher or a licence, permitting restricted copying. In the United Kingdom such licences are issued by the Copyright Licensing Agency, 33–34 Alfred Place, London WC1E 7DP.

British Library C.I.P.

King, Bernard, *1946–*
 Death-blinder.
 I. Title
 823'.914[F]
 ISBN 0-450-48490-4

Printed and bound in Great Britain for Hodder and Stoughton Paperbacks, a division of Hodder and Stoughton Ltd., Mill Road, Dunton Green, Sevenoaks, Kent TN13 2YA (Editorial Office: 47 Bedford Square, London WC1B 3DP) by R. Clay

To Auld Nick, Winnock-Bunkered i' the West.

Deyr fé
deyja frændre,
deyr sjálfr it sama;
en ordstírr
deyr aldregi
hveim er sér gódan getr.

Cattle die, and kindred die,
One day we die ourselves;
but the praise-song never dies
Of a man who has won fame . . .

HAVAMAL – The Words of the High One (Odin).

Contents

Prologue: The Burning Stones — 1

THE FIRST PART: THE FEAR OF THE HIGH KING — 9
1. Son of the Vargr — 11
2. The Master of Sudrafell — 22
3. The Mortality of Kings — 31
4. The High Tower — 39
5. Harbard at the Grave-mound — 49
6. The Disappearance of Svipdag Hathersson — 57
7. A Killer at Uppsala — 66
8. A New High Queen for Sweden — 75

THE SECOND PART: OF DANES AND SORCERY — 81
1. Answers to Some Questions — 83
2. Hanni of the Dane-Lands — 90
3. The Contents of Another Mound — 97
4. The Tunnels of Trollheim — 108
5. Confrontation with a God — 117
6. Discoveries at Uppsala — 123
7. The Shifting of the Stars — 133
8. Into the Whiteness of the North — 145

THE THIRD PART: THE WIZARD IN THE WASTES OF FINNMARK — 151
1. The Shape-Shifter — 153
2. The Circles of History — 163
3. The Victims — 171
4. Divination by Death — 179

5 The Burrowers in Darkness	188
6 Sorcery at the Burning Stones	197
7 The Death-Blinder	208
8 Blood Upon the Ice	214
Epilogue: The Ending of a Saga	223

Author's Note

Throughout the surviving Sagas of the Dark Age north run hints of the daemonic, malevolent powers of Lapp sorcery. That the Vikings and their forebears feared little is evident from their behaviour, yet the nighted, brooding gods of the forests of Finnmark might bring even the hardiest warrior shaking to his knees.

For Hather Lambisson, the Champion of the Yngling Dynasty, Lapp magic and sorcery were grim realities. His fate as the so-called slayer of Starkadder had been foretold by runes cast from a Lappish hand. His battle against the *vargr* at Skroggrmagi was presaged by a sign from the dark lore of Lapp shamanism. Now the gods and Norns were trying a further test of his prowess, a test that was to take him north into the wastes of Finnmark to face the greatest sorcerer the Lapps would ever own.

This is the third and final episode of Hather's Saga. It is the last adventure of a man who never wanted to be a hero.

B.J.H.K.

Prologue

The Burning Stones

Deep in the snows of Finnmark, from the midst of a snow-shrouded forest, a column of steam rose high above the treetops to a point where it merged with the luminous clouding of the impassively threatening sky. The ancient crone had seen it first from a high ridge on the far side of the valley, had looked towards the place of mystery and legend waiting for her, and smiled beneath the heavy veil she wore . . . so that none might read the secrets of her face. Then she climbed down from the ridge to make her way across the forest floor. Her progress was slow, impeded as it was by a tangle of fallen branches and rotting bracken.

It was a slow journey to the stone circle which was the source of the rising column of steam. Each step had to be tested to ensure that it concealed nothing which might cause a fall.

Mother Skuld smiled again at the thought. A fall, indeed. Wasn't that what it was all about? Wasn't that the reason for her journey into the wastes of Finnmark, to this place of rumour and legend which some said lay beyond even the dominion of the Norse gods? To bring about a fall?

'Let Odin follow me here if he can,' she muttered. 'Let him hear what we shall say to each other, Vultikamian. Let him hear, and know that we plan the fall of his beloved Ynglings.'

Her voice was dry, and beneath the veil her eyes narrowed as she spoke her thoughts to the listening forest.

Ahead of her the trees began to thin as she approached the clearing where the Burning Stones stood. Not once did she doubt that Vultikamian would be there. The Lappish magic of which he was master might be outside the ken of the Norse gods, yet there were certain similarities, details of ritual and invultuation, which linked them, not to mention the promise of personal power which would guarantee the legendary shaman's presence.

The trees parted suddenly, and were gone. Before her, the ancient Norn saw the edge of the column of steam she had first seen from the ridge. It rose high above her into the snow-laden air, ringing and shrouding the hot stones. Awesome, forbidding, the steam created a terrifying barrier between the world of the forest and the grim, otherwordly circle of runestones it concealed.

She stood for a moment and gazed through her veil at the rising steam, but only for a moment. Mother Skuld had seen much stranger sights than this during the course of her long life. It would take more than a wispy vapour of melted snow to turn her from her purpose.

Testing the Allfather, marking the limits of his power and intentions, that was all that concerned her. Whether the burning stones had any power of their own, whether Vultikamian was human, animal, or something between the two, didn't matter to her.

Skuld stepped forward, feeling her feet sink less and less deeply into the snow as it became shallower.

Then she entered the column of steam, and was briefly hidden as she walked towards the centre of the circle.

'I've been waiting for you, Mother Skuld,' said a voice that was little more than a whisper. Yet even in that whisper there was something that suggested it was either more or less than human.

Before replying to his greeting Skuld paused to survey her surroundings. She stood within a circle of standing stones, each one taller than the tallest warrior and carved with the mystical characters of the old rune-run, like the uneven teeth of some monster's gaping maw.

Beneath her feet the grass was fresh, green, springy,

unnaturally summer-like for the snow-bound wastes of Finnmark, yet towards the centre of the circle a ring of snow persisted between the outer stones and the massive slab which served as an altar at the middle. Here, beyond the inner ring of snow, a ring too broad for any to cross without leaving signs of their passage yet unmarked by the foot of animal or human, Vultikamian stood waiting.

He was tall and cadaverous, clad in a loose robe of pallid, dirty white. No trace of features showed beneath the hood, but Mother Skuld knew that he was grinning, salivating in anticipation of her request.

'What are you, Vultikamian?' she demanded.

He shrugged and leaned back against the altar-stone. 'I am he who has been waiting for you, Mother Skuld,' he answered in a disturbing whisper. 'You asked me to be here to meet you. Well, Norn, here I am, to speak with you. I am Vultikamian. I am Death-Blinder, Giver of Immortality.'

'You know that *Death-Blinder* is one of Odin's titles?' Skuld asked. 'Only one so certain of his power that he knew there would be no revenge would dare usurp one of Allfather's titles.'

'Perhaps he usurped a title that was properly mine,' Vultikamian replied calmly. Although Odin the Allfather was the most powerful god in the north, as powerful as the Norns themselves, the Lappish sorcerer showed no trace of fear.

This time he's met his match, Mother Skuld thought to herself. This time even Odin won't be able to save his precious Yngling dynasty.

The Ynglings had ruled Sweden for hundreds of years. A legend fostered by Odin himself suggested that the line had sprung from his own loins, that he was the primogenitor of the kings who even now, in the person of High King Omund Olisson, were responsible for bringing man through barbarism to the threshold of civilisation.

Even so, both Mother Skuld and Allfather knew that the dynasty was doomed, that it had reigned too long and was fated to crumble and decay. Already a taint of madness had been introduced, a taint which had sealed the fate of Omund's father, Oli the Great, and had caused Omund to ally himself with a *vargr*, a fearsome outlaw almost more than human, before his plans were brought to nothing by the dynasty's champion, the petty king Hather Lambisson of Ostragotland. And the doom which had for so long threatened the Yngling dynasty was growing closer with every moment. The time was coming when Odin would no longer be prepared to defend his chosen blood-line.

What Mother Skuld desired more than anything was a time when she and her sisterhood might rest, freed by the demise of the Norse gods before the advancing banner of the White Christ who was storming northwards out of the south.

And that was why she was here, to prepare a test for Odin's support of the crumbling Yngling line.

And for that she needed the help of the wizard called Vultikamian.

She opened her mouth to speak, yet before the words could leave her throat it was as if Vultikamian had divined her very thoughts.

'You want to know how strong Odin's precious Ynglings are,' he hissed. 'That's why you need my help Mother Skuld. You want to set a trap for them, and see if they will fall into it to their deaths. That's why you've come to find me, because you know that Vultikamian is more powerful than any in the north.

'Well, listen to me now little Norn. I shall play your game. I shall help you destroy Odin's precious Ynglings. I will even bring about the *Ragnarok*, the doom of the gods themselves, if that is what you want. I've lived too long, become too certain of my own power, Mother Skuld. That is why I accept the challenge you bring to me. That is why I shall work the deaths of all the Yngling brood, and that of their champion Hather Lambisson. You want to sleep, to rest, veiled Mother. I shall give you that rest, that sleep. And, in return, you will leave the north to me, for my dominion and my plaything. That's all I ask.'

My dominion and my plaything. The words sent shudders down Mother Skuld's spine. Was it for this that she and her sisters had cherished their domain for uncounted centuries? For an unseen Lappish sorcerer to take it from them as the payment for the fall of the Ynglings?

She sighed beneath her veil. What did it matter? The house of Yngling was already doomed. The one they called *Hvitakrist*, the White Christ, already held the southern lands in the nail-pierced palm of his hand. His fingers were stretching out to touch the northern realms. The end was coming, slowly but with unremitting certainty, for gods and Norns alike. And what could even the power of one such as Vultikamian do before the advancing might of the White Christ?

Her eyes scanned the sky through her veil. No dark, circling shapes of Odin's ravens wheeled above her. Why should they? She smiled to herself. Perhaps Allfather knew of her plans, but she had journeyed here, to a place on the very edge of his realms, to a place feared in legend, ruled by a sorcerer possibly even more powerful than he.

No, Odin wasn't watching, not this time. This time she might complete her scheming alone.

'You think Odin cannot stop you?' she asked the sorcerer at length.

His laughter, in reply, was soft, almost musical; it bubbled from beneath his hood like wisps of steam. Then he said: 'I am less than a god, Mother Skuld, yet I think you will find me a match for one who has grown old and tired, and yearns for rest almost as much as you do. Listen to me, Norn. If you doubt my power, then set your hand against one of my runestones.'

Mother Skuld shook her head. I can see their heat, she thought. I can see the snowflakes melting into vapour even before they settle. Shall I burn myself to prove to this creature that I disbelieve him?

She felt Vultikamian smile beneath his hood.

'Choose a stone, then,' he bade her in his insidious whisper. 'Any one.'

He reminded her of nothing so much as a magician at a feast, bidding the revellers gamble on the shell-game. Three shells, a dried bean under one of them. Which one hides the bean Mother Skuld? Go on, choose.

But it was more sinister, more potent, than that.

If I did not believe in his power I would not be here, she thought. Yet he doesn't know that. He thinks he has to convince me. Very well. Let him show me what he can do.

'That one.' She pointed.

'So shall it be.'

A covering of snow began to form upon the surface of the stone and upon the ground about it. The stone was cold. Its neighbours to either side, and the other runestones in the circle, continued to burn, but the stone Skuld had chosen paled beneath its covering until it stood white and shapeless in stark contrast to the others.

'It has not lost its power,' Vultikamian told her. 'It simply sleeps for a little while. Now watch it, Norn.'

The white shrouding glowed softly pink. Then, in an instant the runestone erupted into a thousand flying, glowing, red-hot fragments, each trailing vapour as it flew into the steam-laden air.

And then the pieces came together again.

Briefly the re-made stone stood red-hot against its fellows. Then it slowly dulled, and resumed its former colour.

Skuld nodded, more to herself than to the sorcerer. 'A clever trick,' she muttered.

'If I can impress a Norn,' Vultikamian sneered, 'then how much more will I impress a human, even one of the house of Yngling? You see what I can do, little Mother. Now, do you accept our bargain?'

The north for his dominion and his plaything, until the

White Christ came up from the south. A heavy price, but that was the price he was asking.

'Your power will not fail you, Vultikamian?' Skuld demanded.

He laughed again beneath his hood. 'Only when these stones grow cold will my powers fail me, Mother Skuld. I am Death-Blinder, the Giver of Immortality. Should I not be able to ensure that immortality for myself?'

'Then we have a bargain, sorcerer. When the last of the Yngling line is dead, the north is yours.'

'I thank you for coming to me, Mother Skuld,' Vultikamian said.

There was no doubt, from his tone, that he was dismissing her. As she turned away to leave the circle of burning stones the Norn felt ill at ease. She had cheated, of course, on the bargain. As soon as the last Yngling died, the White Christ would bring his priesthood in their stead. There would be no time for Vultikamian to work his will upon the realm he had bargained for. Yet this wasn't what disturbed her.

Somehow, Mother Skuld felt certain the sorcerer knew of her cheating as well as she did herself. The trick with the runestone had been impressive, yes. But it was still no more than a trick and, she knew, hardly the limit of the sorcerer's power. So what did he *really* want in payment? The chance to try his strength against the coming *Hvitakrist*? The Norn knew that sorcery bred insanity, but could even Vultikamian, whoever, whatever, he was, be so insane, so *sure*?

As she left the circle for the snowy waste beyond the shrouding column of steam, Mother Skuld was less content with her bagain than she had been before it was struck. It was her turn, she felt, to be cheated.

She turned to look back at the burning stones for a few moments, then continued on her way to the south. Only as she was about to re-enter the forest did she see the two black shapes circling in the sky above her, and hear the distant crying of the wolves.

The Norn smiled to herself as she felt the single eye

watching her. She smiled. The pieces were being set up upon the *tafl*-board once again. A new game was beginning.

Allfather had been watching after all.

THE FIRST PART

THE FEAR OF THE HIGH KING

1

Son of the Vargr

Time was beginning to exact its price from Omund Olisson, High King of Sweden. The whites of his eyes were beginning to rheum, and his face was seamed with fine wrinkles. Beneath his cap with its gold circlet, he was almost completely bald.

He smiled, his thin lips curling to display time-discoloured teeth. Then he said: 'It was certain that one day you would come to me with such a request, Vermund Bjarnisson.'

His voice was thin and weak, unlike the strong, gruff tones which answered him.

'There is little of my choosing about it, King Omund. We're all growing old. For my part, I've served the Ynglings for over forty years. I'll be seventy-two before next Yule. That's a good age for a man to reach, especially one in my profession. Now my jointy parts are getting stiff, and some of them refuse to work at all. It's time to resign myself to a straw-death.'

'There will always be someone to cut the spear-rune for you, Marshal Vermund,' Omund replied. 'It is my regret that there will not always be a Vermund Bjarnisson to lead my forces. Tell me, have you given any thought to your successor? Hather of Sudrafell, perhaps?'

The High King's last words were mocking, and they both knew it. Hather Lambisson of Sudrafell was one of Omund's petty kings, and as such was excluded from holding overall command of the armies without surrendering his rank and title. While he would have been prepared to do so in the service of his king, he would have left his own kingdom of Ostragotland without a ruler. His eldest son, Svipdag, was himself king of Tiundaland, the district surrounding the High King's capital at Uppsala, and it would have been grossly improper for him to take control of his own father's province as well, while his younger brother Olaf was yet too inexperienced for Hather to surrender Ostragotland to him.

'Not Hather, sir,' Vermund said flatly. 'Apart from anything else, he'd not be comfortable at court here in Uppsala.'

The plain statement concealed a wealth of hidden meaning. Hather and Omund, whilst mutually careful never to become actual enemies, could never be true friends. The High King's dislike of Hather Lambisson had begun nearly forty years before, when they were both little more than boys. Hather, together with the legendary and accursed warrior Starkadder, had rescued Omund from certain death at the hands of his father King Oli, setting him upon the throne in his father's place. Omund had never forgotten that he owed his life to Hather Lambisson, but, far from feeling gratitude, Omund resented his obligation to Hather and had conceived a plan to destroy him.

For thirteen years Omund Olisson ruled quietly and well. Then he became greedy, as the strain of madness inherited from his father began to manifest itself. He had leagued himself with a *vargr*, a supernatural outlaw of awesome fearfulness, and sent Hather off to be destroyed by it whilst he planned to increase his territories by invading the Danelands to the south. Far from being destroyed, Hather had discovered that the *vargr* was his own wife, long believed dead, who sought to bring down Omund and to slaughter Hather and her own son Svipdag. Hather had killed the *vargr* with the help of Vermund Bjarnisson and Saeunna, who became his third wife, before thwarting Omund's plans for invasion and forcing the system of vassal kingdoms upon him to keep the real power out of the hands of a king bound for madness.

All this was behind Vermund's words, and both the ageing King's Marshal and the High King knew what he meant.

'Then whom would you choose to succeed you as King's Marshal, Vermund Bjarnisson?'

'I've given it a deal of thought, King Omund. More than that, I have spoken to someone whom I hope will meet with your approval.'

'And who might that be?'

'Svipdag Hathersson,' came the reply. 'He would deem it an honour to serve you. In order to do so he is prepared to give up the kingship of Tiundaland.'

Omund pursed his lips. Svipdag was now thirty-four and a noted warrior. He was also the ideal candidate to succeed Vermund, for many reasons. As vassal king of Tiundaland he spent a great deal of time at court in Uppsala and had always shown himself a loyal friend and adviser to the High King. The fact that he was prepared to give up his kingdom for the service of the realm weighed greatly in his favour.

Svipdag was also acceptable, Omund was sure, to the other vassal kings who would meet to elect his successor, and to his father Hather Lambisson. Also he was well-qualified for the position, having become Vermund's own foster-son after the death of the *vargr* and Hather's marriage to Saeunna.

There was, from Omund's point of view, one more fact which made Svipdag an ideal candidate to replace the ageing Vermund. He was married, the father of three young sons, any one of whom would make a perfect hostage to ensure his father's loyalty to the High King.

'Your opinion is noted,' Omund muttered, removing his hand from his beard long enough to gesture for Vermund's withdrawal. The old warrior bowed his white head, his single eye never leaving the High King's face as he left the royal presence.

Later, when he reflected upon the interview in the privacy of his own quarters, Vermund Bjarnisson found it had left him uneasy. There had been something in the

High King's manner throughout their discussion which made the old warrior believe that the old Omund of the days of the *vargr*-moon had returned, that some new scheme was being hatched behind his outwardly-amicable features.

King Omund sat upon a wooden dais, raised above the rush-strewn floor of the longhouse which served as his audience-chamber, and watched as the old warrior left his presence. Stationed about the walls were members of his personal guard, picked men dressed in mailshirts and plain surcoats of black leather, each armed with a halberd and a broadsword, their faces hidden behind the back-curling noseguards of their polished metal helmets. Omund signed to the nearest, and the soldier approached.

'Find King Svipdag,' Omund commanded. 'Bring him to me here. And, if you can, do it without being seen.'

The guard bowed and left the audience-chamber. Omund stroked his beard again, a quiet smile playing about his lips. Yes, Svipdag Hathersson was the ideal choice, for many reasons. Unlike his hero father Hather Lambisson, Svipdag was an obedient henchman who would not question orders. And that was vital if the half-formed plan in Omund's mind was to stand any chance of success.

Some minutes later the guard returned to Omund's longhouse, accompanied by a tall, slim man in his early thirties who wore his long dark hair uncropped and unplaited. His clean-shaven face, with its small nose and dark eyes, held traces of almost-feminine beauty.

Svipdag's clothing, like King Omund's, was cut from the finest silk and brocade, his boots of fine kidskin, and his cloak of white bear's fur was held at his shoulders with a magnificent pair of of byzantine box-brooches glimmering with the dark fires of garnet and emerald.

If anything, Svipdag's appearance was even more elegant than that of the High King himself, but beneath the peacock show was a seasoned fighter with a quick, able and sometimes treacherous mind. His looks came from his mother, Hather's first wife Astrid, who had sought so desperately to sacrifice her son to make herself truly *vargr*. Although only a child of ten in those far-off days, Svipdag had from that time been fascinated by things sorcerous.

Now he stood before the throne of the High King. His grim eyes looked up into Omund's. 'You sent for me, King Omund?' he asked, his voice deceptively quiet, his tone gentle.

Omund's smile persisted. This was the son of his old enemy and his *vargr* wife, a runemaster in his own right, a sorcerer, a warrior, a killer. Thirty-four years old and one of the most powerful men in Sweden. He was also one of the few men at his court that the High King was prepared to call his friend.

'I think we should have a little talk, in my apartments,' Omund replied, rising. He stepped down from the dais and placed his arm about the younger man's shoulders. Signing to the guards to remain where they were, he led Svipdag out of the audience-chamber and across to his own longhouse at the centre of the palace enclosure. Together they passed through a vestibule where more guards were stationed, and entered a hall hung with elaborate tapestries, the exposed timbers carved into the intricate, serpentine forms so beloved by the craftsmen of the age.

They sat down either side of a low trestle table and Omund poured pale gold wine from a glass flagon into fine crystal goblets. His face broke into a grin.

'Your foster father's been to see me,' he said, triumphantly. 'He wants to relinquish his position and pass it on to you. If you will surrender the kingship of the Ten Lands, that is.'

Svipdag smiled in reply and tasted the Rhenish wine in the goblet. 'You know I will,' he said. 'I can serve you much better as King's Marshal than as King of Tiundaland. With my help you can become the most powerful ruler the north has ever known. That's what you want, isn't it?'

Omund nodded. 'That's what I want, Svipdag. But tell me, what do *you* get from helping me? Why surrender your kingship?'

The younger man drained his wine and set down the goblet. He shrugged. 'Escape, perhaps.'

The High King's brow furrowed. 'Escape?' he queried. 'From what?'

'From the shadow of my famous father.'

Omund laughed. 'Are you not content to be the famous son of the national hero, Hather Lambisson, the man who killed both Starkadder and the *vargr*? The champion of the Yngling dynasty?'

'To be the son of such a man is one thing,' Svipdag countered. 'To spend my life denied any lasting fame of my own because of his prowess is completely different. You of all people must understand that.'

Indeed Omund understood. His father, mad King Oli the Great, had united Sweden and held it together beneath his tyrannous sway. Omund had merely succeeded him. Even his attempt to enlarge his domain by invading the Danelands had been thwarted, by Hather Lambisson.

'No man is remembered for simply keeping the peace,' the High King muttered. 'Kings are remembered for breaking the peace, for restoring it, or for some mighty deed of their own. I've heard the skalds sing of your father, Svipdag, and of mine. But for us they have no songs or sagas. Not yet.'

Svipdag's handsome features remained impassive, though inwardly he was smiling to himself. *Not yet*, Omund had said; but there would come a time, not too far distant, when the name of Svipdag Hathersson would be greater than that of the man he now sat with, greater even than that of his *vargr*-killing father.

'You will be the greatest of us all King Omund,' he lied. 'And I shall command your forces.'

'Good. Very good. And Vermund Bjarnisson?'

Svipdag shrugged. 'A quiet retirement. He'll leave the court and go home to his estates. He's bought some land near my father at Sudrafell. They can visit each other and relive past glories. You know my father will only come to Uppsala in obedience to a direct summons.'

'Or by invitation, to witness his son's installation as King's Marshal. He will come for that.'

'Of course.'

Omund stood up, grinning broadly. 'Then it's decided,' he said. 'Now all that remains is to decide a date for your installation and Vermund's retirement. That shouldn't be too difficult.' His face suddenly became serious. 'Let's allow Hather his moment of pride. Then he'll go home to Sudrafell and leave us to our intentions.'

Svipdag rose and bowed. 'I await your proclamation, King Omund. And now, may I withdraw?'

'Indeed you may. I thank you for attending upon me, King Svipdag. Or should I say *Marshal* Svipdag?'

'I am honoured, High King Omund.'

Svipdag Hathersson left the High King's apartments and returned slowly to his own. About him the life of the palace compound, the longhouses ranged in rectangles within the circular stockade, continued at its usual leisurely pace. It was a fine day in late spring and the sun, nearing its noontide zenith, slanted down past the high wooden ramparts from which Omund's guards looked out upon the town outside the gates. Cooking fires burned beneath pots slung from tripods in the open air. Children ran playing from shadow to sunlight and back again. The warm, comfortable, comforting smells of peace wafted between the buildings, as they had done throughout Svipdag's reign as king of Tiundaland, the Ten Lands surrounding the High King's court at Uppsala.

Naturally, there had been occasional risings and incursions; once there had even been a band of roaming outlaws to suppress. Sweden was at peace, though, and Svipdag had been forced to set the deck of a longship beneath his feet and travel to foreign lands to gain his experience as a fighting man. It was twenty-five years since Svipdag had been taken by his *vargr*-mother to the dwarfish citadel at Skroggrmagi. He had been drugged for much of the time and could not remember much of his experience in the stone-built fortress beneath the frozen waterfall.

Now, at last, the years of planning and patient waiting were coming to a close. Now at last, with old Skeggja's help, he would take his rightful place in history and saga.

To die unknown is not to have lived at all, he thought to himself as he passed through the vestibule and entered his longhouse. Servants approached their king but he dismissed them with a wave. Then he stopped and called one back.

'Where's Skeggja?' he demanded.

'In her room, sir,' came the reply.

Svipdag's servants never named the old Lappish woman, referring to her always as *she* or *the lady*. If ever it became absolutely unavoidable to speak her name it would be done with one hand concealed, forming a protective or propitiatory gesture in secret.

He passed through the partition at the end of the hall. As a mark of his regal status his personal longhouse, like that of the High King and those kept as guest-quarters, had a second storey reached by a plank-ladder. The servants' fear of Skeggja made them unwilling to see more of her than they had to, and this suited the old witch well. She preferred the privacy this afforded her and, by Svipdag's consent, had made a domain for herself in the upper room of his longhouse. Time was beginning to work on her frail body and she left her quarters only by Svipdag's command or to journey into the forest to that place where her greatest sorceries were performed.

Svipdag ascended the wooden steps slowly. He always felt a thrill of expectancy when he climbed out of the world of servants and underlings and into that arcane room where he almost felt that he was a servant himself. His father had been too concerned with rebuilding Sudrafell and satisfying his new wife when old Skeggja had arrived. The young Svipdag had been left alone with the Lappish nurse and her secrets through the formative years of his adolescence, imbibing her dark wisdom as if he had been a babe taking milk from her age-wrinkled dugs.

A cackling laugh floated down to him. 'Is King Svipdag coming to see his old friend?' she called, her voice hoarse and cracked. 'Has he something to tell old Skeggi?'

It was for others to call her Skeggja. She always referred to herself as Skeggi. The word had two meanings, either *rough* or *of the forest people*, and only Svipdag was permitted to use the name back to her. Otherwise he called her by the name she had first given, and so, when they were forced to name her, did everyone else.

'Does King Svipdag want to tell old Skeggi who the new King's Marshal is to be?'

'You know that already, Skeggi,' Svipdag called up. His head came level with the opening in the floor at the top of the ladder. 'Is there anything you don't know, old witch?'

Herbs for salves, simples or poisons hung drying from the rafters, together with fragments from a variety of once-living creatures, including men. A strange, sweetish odour pervaded the air, almost the sweet rot of decay but redeemed by the woodland scent of dried plants which hung fragile, almost forgotten, amongst the dust and cobwebs of the roof.

Old Skeggja sat upon her bed, a simple box with a straw-stuffed mattress. Before her stood the drum which she stroked, rather than beat, with age-crooked fingers, the knuckles knotted like the boles of the world-ash Yggdrasil. The stretched skin of the drum was traced with strange shapes which might once have been as red as blood, shapes emblematic of the stick-forms of men and animals. Her *runakefli* lay scattered on the decorated skin, the forms of the magical letters being marked on bones rather than on chips of wood.

The walls were hung with rugs and tapestries bearing symbols similar to those upon her drum. Bottles and jars in all shapes and sizes were ranged on the floor along the walls, and to Viking eyes it all held the strangeness of a world not their own, a world closer to the forbidding gods of the snow-wastes than to the bloodthirsty, lecherous deities who peopled Asgard. Yet of all the strangeness in that upper room, the strings of dried red and white caps of fly agaric, the carven fragments of wood and bone, the knives and wands and the rolled-up ox-hide in one corner, the strangest, most sinister thing of all was the old Lapp herself.

She was dressed in reindeer hides, once brightly painted in earth colours but now faded and wrinkled into formlessness. Her ears were hung with earrings of gold wire and bone, her neck with a loop of holed flints spaced with brightly coloured beads. Over all she wore a heavy cloak of bear's fur, hooded so that only her face and a few strands of snow-bright hair showed beneath it.

And what a face it was. Eyes the hue of nightshade berries, their whites long rheumed to amber, burned beneath white eyebrows slashed across a wrinkled brow almost the brown of bare, baked earth. Her nose was long and sharp, her mouth a thin gash. The chin had once jutted sharply, but was now sunken back into the dewlaps which folded into the neck of her dress. Between nose and mouth a fringe of white hair stood out against the seamed flesh.

'Anything I don't know, my Svipdag?' she asked. 'You know me in a way that no-one else does. Tell me, child of my old age, tell me if you believe that there could be something I don't know?'

He wanted to shudder at her words, but he smiled instead. It was she who had first taught him to dissemble, and he had learned his lessons well.

'I can see everything, King Svipdag. Old Skeggi looks out across the world and sees the past, the future, all.'

He knew little of her gods, the dark gods of the frozen forest wastes. He worshipped Odin, as was befitting a warrior and a king. Somehow he felt that it wasn't fitting to know so much, that only Odin, the Allfather, sitting upon his high throne Hlidskjalf, should be able to look out over the world and know the fates which the Norns had decreed for men.

Instead of showing weakness by betraying his misgivings, he asked: 'So you know that Omund has agreed. Very well, Skeggi. What shall we do now?'

'Why,' she cackled evilly, 'we'll ask your father to a feast. And that wife of his, and your half-brother, Olaf. And you'll all sit down and stuff your silly faces. And then we'll go to work. We'll give Omund and all his kin to my master. Then his realm can pass to you.'

Her master. Svipdag had often heard her speak of the one she called her master, but had never heard her name him. All he knew was that old Skeggja's master had taught her and sent her south into Sweden. Obviously he was powerful, perhaps even more powerful than his pupil if he could send her out to do his bidding. But who *was* he?

He hadn't asked her for a while. If he kept asking her, perhaps she would tell him who this great magician was. Perhaps even today. So he asked her again.

'Who *is* your master, Skeggi?'

She grinned at him, displaying uneven, discoloured teeth. Then she said: 'The one who taught me, King Svipdag.'

She wasn't going to say any more, and he knew it. This far south of the Finnmark wastes, the name was just that, a name. Only in the frozen depths of the far north, and to a certain veiled and ancient Norn, did the name of Vultikamian have any meaning.

He would know her master soon enough, though. Before the summer was out, King's Marshal Svipdag Hathersson and the one called Vultikamian were fated to stand face to hooded face.

2

The Master of Sudrafell

The town was a sprawled mass of wooden dwellings. Down by the jetties, where native traders tied up their *knorra* and bolder seamen anchored their longships, warehouses had been built to hold merchandise of every kind. Further from the sea, between the blue waters of the Baltic and the proud wooden walls of Hather's palace, were the homes and shops of those who served the port and the royal stronghold which was the capital of the province of Ostragotland.

The messenger dismounted to walk his tired horse towards the distant stockade. On either side of the dirtroad, its surface dry in the sunlight though rutted by cart-wheels and the feet of many travellers, rose the grave-mounds and runestones which the king had set up to those he had loved. Here a mound rose to his parents, to Lambi Nef, his father, killed when he challenged Starkadder in the berserk fury of betrayal, and to his mother Hervara, who pined and died because she could not love the living as well as she loved the dead. There was the mound to his second wife, killed when the *vargr*'s outlaws burned his home and kidnapped his son. Beyond it a runestone commemorated old Tisti, his Lappish nurse, whose dying warnings had helped him destroy the evil which threatened both Sweden and his son. A little way off, unmarked, were five smaller mounds, where lay the bodies of those who had sought out the man who had killed Starkadder to make a name for themselves, and had paid for their folly with their lives.

Even though he always denied the killing of Starkadder, claiming it as the work of the dwarf-forged sword Tyrfing, Hather Lambisson of Sudrafell, king of Ostragotland and Odin-appointed champion of the House of Yngling, was a legend in his own lifetime, a man whose exploits, told in saga and sung by the skalds, were known throughout the length and breadth of his native land, a man who many felt should have ousted and supplanted the Ynglings instead of offering them his loyalty.

During the twenty-five years since the institution of the vassal kingdoms, Sudrafell had grown from a small stronghold to become a provincial capital. The old stockade, little more than a family home, had been rebuilt as a palace compound only slightly smaller than that of the High King at Uppsala. Here Hather lived with his wife Saeunna and his younger son Olaf. Their daughter Gudrun was at court in attendance upon Omund's queen, Aud. Here also Hather maintained and quartered a small army of local soldiery and foreign mercenaries, which in time of need could be strengthened by levies from among his own people.

Omund's messenger passed by the burial mounds and continued up through the thriving seaport towards the palace. The wooden gates of the stockade stood open, so that any one who wished to speak to the king might freely do so. He entered and was approached by a sentry. Briefly he stated his business and a man was called to take him to the king's apartments. He waited in the vestibule to be announced, then was shown into a hall only a little smaller than Omund's and arranged in a similar fashion. Against the partition wall at the far end, upon a raised dais, King Hather Lambisson sat upon his high seat, while petitioners waited to state their business. At his right hand, occupying a slightly smaller seat, sat a young man with a strong, open face, his yellow-gold hair plaited to either side at the front to keep it clear of his face in combat. This was Olaf Hathersson, learning the business of keeping the kingdom of Ostragotland content, settled and safe.

The messenger had never before seen Hather Vargr-Slayer, as the king was known throughout Sweden, and was faintly surprised to find himself in the presence of one who, despite his immense fame, was still only a man.

There could be no denying that in younger days Hather Lambisson had been a handsome man. He was still, at fifty-three, a distinguished and imposing figure. His ice-blue eyes were still clear and bright, lighted with interest as he listened to those who spoke to him. He was possessed of an intelligent, questioning mind which could be both devious and decisive as circumstances might demand. His skin was dark from the weathering of half a century of northern wind and sun, though his hair still showed, through its whiteness, traces of the same yellow-blond as Olaf's. Like his son he wore his hair long and plaited, while a gold circlet of serpentine design further confined it at his forehead. His nose was slightly large for his face and somewhat accentuated by the heavy moustache he wore. His clothing was fine enough to befit his rank, and beneath it his body was still muscular, though the years of peace had brought a thickness and a heaviness to his frame.

He might only be a man, this King of Ostragotland, the messenger thought, but what a man he still was. Fifty-three and still alive, despite the odds. King Oli, Omund's father, had ordered Hather's death at fifteen, and he had offered his own life in battle countless times since then. He had defied the *vargr* and its outlaws at Skroggrmagi, marching boldly to almost certain death up the frozen river which led to the dwarfish citadel. Yet still he lived, working for peace and safety for Saeunna and Olaf and Gudrun, and for all his people.

The petitioners drew aside for the High King's messenger, who wore the black surcoat of Omund's guard.

'Greetings, King Hather Lambisson of Ostragotland, Master of Sudrafell and Champion of the Ynglings, from Omund Olisson, High King of Sweden.'

Hather had been popularly dubbed *Champion of the Ynglings* by the people, but it was a title he had neither sought nor been officially offered. King Omund would never have included it as part of a formal salutation. The messenger was adding a tribute of his own.

'I thank the High King for his greeting,' Hather replied, permitting himself a brief smile. 'It must be some weighty matter to bring word from Uppsala to Sudrafell. I hope you've not brought me bad news?'

'My news is good, King Hather,' the messenger said. 'I bear a request from King Omund that you attend a feast at Uppsala three weeks from tomorrow, yourself and all your family.'

Omund's clever, Hather thought. He's given me time to check his intentions before I leave. He wants me reassured before I set out. That's why he sends me a *request*.

'This is not a feast-tide, so far as I know,' he replied. 'Am I permitted to ask the reason for this celebration?'

'Indeed, sir. It is to celebrate the installation of Svipdag Hathersson, former King of Tiundaland, as Marshal of the High King's forces.'

'But what of my old friend Vermund Bjarnisson?' Hather asked, an edge of concern to his voice.

'Marshal Vermund has chosen to step down by reason of his age,' the messenger said. 'I understand that he will retire to his estates after your son's installation as King's Marshal. When I left the court he was well and in good spirits.'

Hather nodded. It took the better part of a week to travel from Uppsala to Sudrafell, but little enough would have happened to his old friend in that time. As for Svipdag's decision to relinquish the kingship of Tiundaland, that was easily explained. Svipdag had always been off on some Viking expedition or other, always fretting for action. As King's Marshal he would at least have the opportunity to keep Omund's fighting men in shape. It might not be war, but it was the closest to war that he was likely to come in a time of peace.

Olaf, beside his father, watched and listened carefully. He knew better than to interrupt, and he deemed it wisest to suppress the twinge of jealousy he felt on hearing that his half-brother was to be chief officer of the High King's forces.

'You've ridden long and hard to bring me this message,' Hather said to the messenger. 'I know that you will want to return with my reply without undue delay. But first, rest and refreshment will not go amiss. Join me at dinner this evening and let me hear news from the court. For now, though, take your rest. This man,' he continued, gesturing to an attendant, 'will show you to your quarters and provide whatever you need.'

The messenger bowed and withdrew. Hather and Olaf continued to hear petitioners throughout the afternoon. As the last of them left the hall, Hather turned to his son. 'Fetch your mother,' he said simply.

Olaf went immediately to Saeunna's quarters. Hather's queen sat with her attendants at a stone-weighted vertical loom, working at the same tapestry she had been engaged upon for almost a year. She looked up as he entered.

Eleven years younger than her husband, green-eyed and with only the merest hint of grey in her red-gold hair, the queen was, in maturity, still as beautiful as when Hather rescued her from the *vargr*'s men, and as brave as when she walked with him into the gorge at Skroggrmagi to save Svipdag from butchery at the hands of his mother.

'Father has asked for you,' Olaf said. 'There's been a messenger from Uppsala. Svipdag's to be King's Marshal.'

Saeunna rose and walked with her son to the audience hall. Olaf had told her exactly the message that Hather had received. What he couldn't tell her was what lay behind it. For the early years of her life Saeunna had known Omund only as a name. Only when she was seventeen, when she travelled with Hather to Skroggrmagi to avenge her murdered family, had she begun to know what a wealth of treachery the name of Omund might signify for those she loved, and that knowledge had never left her. She knew how little love there was between Hather and the king he was sworn to protect. Now that king had sent for them to come to him. Silently she reflected that such word could be the beginning of some new treachery.

Hather sat alone, except for a single attendant. He had never feared for his life in his own kingdom and did not bother to ring the hall with armed guards as Omund did at Uppsala.

'Olaf tells me that Svipdag is to be King's Marshal,' Saeunna said. 'Is Vermund ill?'

Hather shook his head. 'Just tired,' he answered. 'And he has every right to be. He must be over seventy, and that's a better age than any of us have a right to expect to see.'

'Hather, do you suspect Omund of some trick?'

There was so much to learn about being a king, Olaf thought, even a vassal king like his father. It was almost unthinkable that the High King of Sweden might be using Svipdag's advancement as the basis of some plot, yet his mother suspected that it might be so, and clearly his father also thought that such a thing might be possible.

'I don't know,' Hather answered. 'Perhaps, but I doubt it. Omund and Svipdag have been good friends ever since Svipdag began to grow up. And I don't believe any son of mine, and our good friend Vermund's foster son at that, would work with Omund against us. However, I've asked the messenger, who's one of Omund's guard, to join us for dinner tonight. We'll ply him with ale. That way we'll find out what's happening at Uppsala. He's already in awe of me,' Hather grinned. 'He greeted me as Champion of the Ynglings.'

Seunna smiled back at her husband. Hather Lambisson might be the wrong side of fifty, but he was still as sharp as ever, still the wise and mighty warrior who had first won her heart.

And so it was. The messenger sat with Hather and Saeunna and Olaf that night and enjoyed their hospitality before his return to Uppsala on the morrow. He ate well off pig roasted in the new fashion and fresh fruit and vegetables and bread freshly baked in the royal kitchens.

And he drank well of home-brewed ale and mead and wines imported from the south. His tongue loosened.

Hather and Saeunna eventually retired to the warmth of their bed-closet. As they lay in each other's arms the King of Ostragotland said: 'If Omund's planning anything, then he's keeping his plans well hidden.'

Saeunna snuggled closer. 'The messenger told us that the court has become a haven for sorcerers and the like. They wouldn't be there without Omund's permission. Sorcery's a foul thing at best. If you link Omund and sorcery together you get a dangerous combination. You know he's never loved you. He owes you his life and his kingdom. That's a heavy debt for any man.'

'I know,' Hather grunted.

'Do you think old Skeggja has anything to do with all this?'

'Svipdag's nurse? I know she's a Lapp, but old Tisti served me well, and I have no reason to suspect that Skeggja isn't doing the same for Svipdag. He's sensible enough. He'll know that sorcery never brings any good. That's why he's prepared to surrender his kingship to take Vermund's place. He knows that a good sword is the best answer to witchcraft. I must have taught him that, even if I didn't teach him anything else.'

'I hope you're right,' Saeunna said simply.

'Saeunna, what would Omund have to gain from all this, except the best possible man to replace Vermund?'

She sighed. 'I wish I knew,' she answered. 'If I could tell you, we might all sleep easier. But Omund's devious, Hather. You of all people ought to know that. Besides, he's left us alone here for nearly twenty-five years. He's left us in peace so long. *Too long*. From what we know of him you can't blame me for worrying about what he might be planning. Can you?'

Hather kissed his wife fondly. 'No,' he said. 'I share your misgivings. If for no other reason I share them because Omund has never bothered with sorcery before. That alone makes me think that you might just be right. But wondering isn't going to get us any more than a disturbed night's sleep. I've agreed to go to Uppsala. After all, it would be churlish and discourteous not to be there when my son is made King's Marshal.

'And now, wife, good night.'

He settled back under the covers, and was snoring softly long before Saeunna was able to fall asleep.

That night she dreamed as she had dreamed only once in her life. She stood alone in a snowy wasteland, watching a column of steam rise to merge with the distant sky. Twin ravens flitted and circled in the snow-laden sky. In the distance two unseen wolves called raucously to the coming night. The sky was reddening into sunset. There was no sound of a footstep, no sign to tell her when she ceased to be alone. Yet one moment she had no one with her and the next a one-eyed man with a grizzled-grey beard stood beside her. The stranger, though he was not such a stranger really, wore an iron-bound helmet and a light-blue travelling cloak over his mail-armour. For some moments he watched the distant column of steam with her. Then he asked: 'Do you remember me, Saeunna?'

She nodded. 'I remember you, Harbard.'

The name meant *greybeard*. At least she remembered that much, though the other details of their former meeting were blurred and distorted into forgetfulness by the years.

'Did I tell you true the last time?' he asked her.

She smiled and remembered. He had promised her a husband, and the one called Hather Lambisson had come to her.

'You told me true,' she answered him.

'Then hear me now, Saeunna. Hear me and, when you wake, remember. This is what I have to say to you.

'It is time to choose, Saeunna. The Ynglings need their champion again. You are right to distrust Omund Olisson. Were his birth any other than it was he would have fallen long ago. The House of Yngling is doomed. It has always been doomed.'

For a moment it seemed to Saeunna that a single tear was flowing from his eye down into the grizzled beard.

'We are all doomed,' he continued. 'Man is born but to die. Only the manner of his living distinguishes him from his fellows.'

'I don't understand you, Harbard,' Saeunna answered.

'You didn't understand me last time, Saeunna,' he muttered. 'Still,' he continued, raising his voice, 'you did well enough then. I don't doubt that you will do well enough this time as well.'

Harbard turned away. 'You know,' he whispered, his voice almost breaking in the stillness of the waste, 'I have loved you all, Saeunna, in my way. You and Hather, and your children, even Omund. It will all end soon enough, but not just yet. It isn't over yet.'

He turned back to look at her. There was such sadness in his single eye. 'This is not of my choosing, Saeunna. Remember that.'

3

The Mortality of Kings

They set out for the court of the High King at Uppsala, Hather, Saeunna, Olaf and their retainers, arriving two days before the feast in honour of Vermund's retirement and their son's assumption of the old man's office. Omund provided them with the best guest-quarters in his palace, and they settled into their opulence unashamedly. After all, Hather reasoned, if there was some betrayal to come, they might as well take their ease whilst the chance presented itself.

Oh yes, thought Saeunna. We'll pay for this, sooner or later. We'll pay. Possibly even with our lives.

That evening they dined with Omund and Queen Aud. Omund had three sons, each of whom was now grown and married with children of his own. That the future of the Yngling dynasty was assured for years to come only a fool or a wise man would have doubted. And the distance between wisdom and folly, Hather knew, was but an inch of darkness in the world of night.

The feasting finished, they drank the cup for Allfather and the cup for Thor, and they drank the cup for Bragi, god of poetry and storytellers. The ladies of the court retired and left the men to their boasting and man-talk.

Saeunna was still awake when Hather climbed in beside her. 'It's not so bad here,' he said, his voice betraying mild surprise.

She feigned sleep. It wouldn't do to answer him. What could she say?

I've seen Harbard again, Hather. He warned me there was something evil brewing, but didn't tell me what.

No, she couldn't tell him that. She had to know more before she said anything. And at present there was little to know.

They awoke and broke their fast early. Servants were still clearing the remains of their meal from the trestle table when a familiar figure pushed its way unannounced into the hall of their guest-quarters.

'So you came, did you?' came a growl.

Instinctively Hather's hand touched the hilt of his sword as he stood up. Then his face broke into a grin when he saw who it was, and that he was grinning as well, despite the gruffness of his greeting.

Saeunna stood back, smiling as her husband and Vermund embraced each other. The old warrior's hair was now completely white, but his frame had not run to fat, and a spark of the same old fire burned in his single eye still. She could see by his grinning that he'd lost some more teeth and that those which remained weren't particularly good, and by his lumbering gait that his joints were stiffening after so many years of use on a great many battle-fields, but despite the ravages of time he was still their old friend Vermund Bjarnisson.

He raised Saeunna's hand to his lips. 'You're as lovely as ever, Queen of Ostragotland,' he smiled. Still holding her hand, he stepped back to arm's length to appraise her fully. 'And so young. If you'll kindly tell me how you do it I might be able to stop myself rotting quite so quickly.'

'*Very* dear friend,' she replied, kissing him. 'At least I will never need to give you lessons in flattery.'

The old fighter laughed and let go of her hand.

'I'll leave you two together,' Saeunna smiled. 'You must have a great deal to talk about. And I have a great deal of preparation as well, if Omund is to see something other than a travel-stained crone later. Besides, I want your foster-son, when we see him again, to be proud of me.'

She withdrew with her maids, to prepare for a full audience with the High King and Queen Aud.

'Lovely as ever,' Vermund repeated, watching her go. 'A treasure, Hather. I hope you're taking good care of her?'

Hather smiled and nodded. 'As good as I can. Now, let's have a seat and take care of some talking,' he said, steering Vermund towards the trestle. 'How is everything here at court?'

The single eye shone brightly into his own. 'You mean, what's going on?'

'That's what I mean.'

Vermund shrugged and sat down. 'I just woke up one morning and felt I'd had enough of rattling around like a raw recruit. It's time for a younger man to take over, Hather. Next Yule I'll be seventy-two. That's too old for the sort of thing I've been up to all my life. I thought I'd retire to that estate you gave me and call for you when I want the spear-rune cutting.'

Hather smiled. 'Some chance of that for a few years yet,' he said.

He was wrong.

'You know,' the old warrior continued, 'Svipdag's the best choice Omund could make. I've taught him all I know of battle-craft and he's had plenty of experience on his travels.'

Hather remembered. Svipdag had taken a small fleet south out of the Baltic and along the Norwegian coast to raid in the far north. During *strand-hogg*, which meant pulling in to shore to raid for provisions, he'd become separated from his men. Loyally they searched for him for two days, braving hostile Bjarmalanders and some of the foullest weather they'd ever encountered. Just as they were ready to abandon the effort and make sail without him he'd stumbled out of the mist, more dead than alive.

They asked him where he'd been for those two days. He could tell them nothing. All memory of his experience was gone for ever. And there was something else.

Before he'd vanished, Svipdag's eyes had been the clear

ice-blue of his father's. Yet when he returned they were the purple-brown eyes of his *vargr*-mother, Astrid, and of his Lappish nurse, old Skeggja.

Hather suppressed a shudder. Wherever his son had been for those days, whoever he'd met, whatever he'd seen, had been dangerously unwholesome. Still, it was nearly ten years past, and apart from his different-coloured eyes Svipdag showed no ill-effects from the experience.

'And he's not self-seeking. He'd never have agreed to relinquish Tiundaland if he'd been power-greedy. No, your son's the best, Hather. The very best.'

The old warrior smiled contentedly. Reassured, Hather turned to other matters.

'And our High King?' he asked.

'Now there's a shifty one,' Vermund smiled wryly. 'He's as trustworthy as ever he was, and that's not saying much. Still, he likes Svipdag, which is a good thing. There's something else: that old nurse of Svipdag's. What's her name? Ah, Skeggja . . .' Vermund's voice dropped noticeably as he named the old Lappish woman.

'What about her?' Hather asked, remembering that Saeunna had wondered about the old Lappish witch.

'Omund seems to have taken a liking to her as a sort of pet. No official feast can be considered complete unless she's uttered a prophecy or two. And Svipdag seems rather to encourage the High King than discourage the old witch. Personally I'll be only too happy when she crawls off into her grave-mound for good.'

They continued their reminiscences through the morning, talking of old friends and old battles. Hather owed Vermund his life from the time at Dalalven when he and Starkadder and Omund had been awaiting execution on the orders of Oli the Great. It was Vermund's decision to abandon his service to the mad king and free them that had eventually set Omund on the throne of Sweden. Hather reflected ruefully that Starkadder had tried to stop Omund succeeding to the kingdom. The accursed old warrior must have known what lay ahead.

And then there was the fight against the *vargr*. They'd fought hard battles against impossible odds, losing old friends and new ones. Grim old Thorvald had died at the ferry where he met Saeunna. Horsetail and Leif Half-Foot had met their deaths in the gorge at Skroggrmagi, defying the *vargr* to the end. Whilst it was Hather they called *Vargr-Slayer*, it had been Vermund's blow that had finally decapitated the evil monster.

During the afternoon they joined High King Omund and Queen Aud in the High King's apartments. Aud was a distinguished matron, only slightly younger than her husband. Her hair, once as black as obsidian, was now a hard, iron grey, and the marks of ravens' feet had dug deep into her once smooth skin.

Later the company was joined by the one in whose honour the next day's festivities were being held: Svipdag Hathersson, son of Hather and his first wife Astrid. Svipdag embraced his father warmly and bestowed a kiss upon his step-mother. Slightly distant, but ever courteous to his equals and superiors, he looked fit and well, with only those brown eyes to remind those who knew of his mysterious disappearance years before.

They talked and laughed, congratulating him on his new position, Hather nodding with the sage contentment of middle age and pride in his eldest son. For the time being any misgivings were kept in check.

The feast to celebrate Svipdag's installation as King's Marshal was duly held upon the morrow. The following day the council of vassal kings was to meet and elect a new ruler for Tiundaland. The eldest of Svipdag's sons, Fulke, was only eight, and whilst there might be tacit acceptance of the fact that one day Fulke would take his father's place as king, a regent would be required for at least a decade to come.

Platters of every kind of meat and fresh bread were brought to the tables. Enormous aurochs' horns, silver and gold mounted, were filled with ale and mead and, at the high table, with the pale wines of the German lands and the darker, blood-red wines imported from the empire of Charlemagne to the south. They were beginning to lose count of the healths they had drunk, to the gods and to each other, when the hall grew quiet as by some signal. Hather had been shouting across to Vermund, but his voice, the last to be heard, died away with his words incomplete, paying homage to the silence which had gathered about them.

She was there, in the centre of the hall, beside the log fire. None had seen her come in. The guests sat as if turned to stone in the presence of one who inhabited a different, more sinister, more terrifying world.

Hather struggled to focus his wine-misted eyes, fought to pierce the shadows and make out her features, seeking the changes which time must have wrought. Only the faint moustache, now whiter, showed the passing of the years.

Old Skeggja grinned. About her hardened warriors, even Vermund, were making protective signs under the tables.

Hather Lambisson forced a smile of welcome. It was only fitting that the old Lapp should be there to witness her charge's triumph. Skeggja saw him and grinned back mockingly.

Omund leaned forward from his high seat. 'Greetings, *volva*,' he said. 'You are welcome here.'

Vermund cast his eye over the assembled guests. From their expressions and hidden gestures the old warrior concluded that the High King was speaking for himself alone.

'Greetings, King Omund,' she croaked in reply, 'and to your guests also, greetings from old Skeggi. My, what a worthy reception is assembled here to do *my master* homage.'

My master. Only Svipdag knew that it wasn't him she was referring to, that the witch's master was unknown to all save herself. His brow creased. The old sorceress was up to something, and he had no idea what it might be.

'Give us your words, prophetess,' Omund invited her cordially. 'Let us have the benefit of your wisdom.'

Saeunna dug her fingers like claws into Hather's arm.

Vermund growled softly, then forced a cough to cover the sound.

With a slowness born more of age than deliberation Skeggja lowered herself to sit cross-legged on the rush-strewn floor. She drew the hood of her cloak up over her head, then down to cover her face. There was something frightening and evil about that huddled shape, something that whispered of coming death.

'*Ibmel-Jumala*,' she began, her hoarse voice seeming to come from anywhere but beneath the hooded cloak, 'Thou who sent Maddar-akko down to earth, Thou who art Acce the Father, speak through me. Thou who sendest Biegg-Olbmai across the face of the tundra, speak through me. Thou who sent Leib-Olbmai for his purposes, speak through me . . .'

Svipdag felt himself stiffen in his seat. He'd heard the name of Leib-Olbmai before, when he was in Bjarmaland. Its meaning was chillingly sinister. It meant *blood-man*.

Old Skeggja fell silent. Her clawed hand fumbled with the pouch which hung from her belt, loosening it, and brought out a dried red and white cap of the poisonous fly agaric. The hand moved up beneath the hood, then dropped away, empty.

Her breathing became stertorous, and her hunched body shuddered at each new intake. Hather heard the thudding of his own heart in the silence between her breaths, a silence he felt he could have reached out and touched. Saeunna's grip upon his wrist became torturingly hard, but he didn't notice.

'Hear me,' said a voice out of the air. It must have come from the old Lapp, but it was not her voice. It was a deep, seductive whispering, the sound that Mother Skuld had heard in the circle of the burning stones.

'Hear me,' the voice repeated a second time. 'Omund Olisson, High King of Sweden, this is for you.'

Vermund glanced across at the High King. Omund was no longer smiling. He was ashen, bolt upright in his high seat.

'Death is a little thing for such a king as you,' the voice

continued. 'Fear it not, for it is beneath you, O last and greatest of the Ynglings. Last, for you shall outlive your progeny. Greatest, for your reign will be so filled with the glory of your age that all who came before you will be as chaff before the wind . . .'

Suddenly sober, Hather shook off Saeunna's grip and began to rise in his seat, his hand straying towards where his sword would have been had all not come unarmed to Omund's feast.

'Sit down and keep quiet,' Omund hissed to him.

'And you, Hather Lambisson,' the voice continued. 'You, who are called Champion of the Ynglings, your task is over. Your world is passing into other hands. You have no work to do here.'

From the other side of Queen Aud, Saeunna's daughter Gudrun stared at her father, fear plain on her face. Olaf too wished he had a sword to lop the old Lapp's head off. He'd never liked her, and at this moment he hated and feared her.

'There is mortality amongst even kings,' the foul whispering continued. 'Cattle die, men die. All things die in the season of their passing, be they Hather or Vermund or Aud or Saeunna. But Omund is above such simple deaths. He shall conquer them all, outlive them all. Hail, Omund Olisson, the last and greatest, and the longest-lived, of all the House of Yngling.'

The echoes of the whispering began to die away. In their place the silence flooded heavy and oppressive. Skeggja remained where she was, unmoving. Vermund, recovering from the shock of hearing himself named by the prophecy, found himself hoping that the ancient crone was dead.

But she wasn't. The season of her passing had not yet come.

4

The High Tower

They rode out in silence through the palace gates and along the side of the still, deep lake towards the forest on the skyline. Vermund's expression was set and determined in the morning sunlight.

Beside him Hather was occupied less with curiosity as to their destination than with reflections upon the prophecy uttered by old Skeggja. He had been named before Omund as Champion of the Ynglings, and told that he had no useful role to fulfil any more. That he could accept, if he could only trust the High King. Yet he couldn't. Omund had always been devious, and this revelation that he was to be the last of the Yngling kings, outliving even his own children and grandchildren, was hardly calculated to allay the suspicions of a man like Hather Lambisson. The short hairs at the nape of his neck were prickling, and not without good reason.

Omund live for ever? The man was a weakling, though not a fool. Once before he'd gambled for lasting fame and lost, despite an alliance with a *vargr* and the raising of the greatest army Sweden had ever seen. This time, though, there was no army, no *vargr*, only a prophecy spoken by an old Lapp woman he'd made his son's nurse almost twenty-five years before.

Yet it hadn't been her voice that spoke. Someone, *something*, had been speaking through her, and he knew that, whatever it was, it was going to face him with the greatest challenge of his life.

He recalled an old Viking proverb. A slave's revenge

comes at once, but a coward's, never. Omund was no slave, at least. Coward he might be, otherwise he'd not have waited twenty-five years to devise some means of taking revenge. No, the High King wasn't looking for revenge. He was looking for something more than that. And it would be dangerous for all of them. Of that Hather had no doubt at all.

And then Vermund, his oldest and closest friend, the man he had chosen to foster his eldest son, had come to him that morning and said, without Saeunna hearing: 'I'd hoped I wouldn't have to do this, Hather. After last night though, there's something I must show you. Will you ride with me, out to the forest?'

'What is it?' he'd asked.

'There are some things that can be explained,' Vermund replied. 'Others, though, need to be seen for themselves. This is one of the things you have to see. Yes, I can tell you, but it won't mean anything to you. Anyway, I think this is important.'

He'd had no choice but to agree, so they rode out across the plain which led to the distant forest, in silence.

It's just an old woman's madness, Hather tried to tell himself. Omund asked her there to entertain us, and the best entertainment for a man like that is to hear fine things about himself. She was simply playing his game, nothing more.

But he didn't believe it. Tisti had never played such games, and deep within himself Hather felt that old Skeggja wouldn't either. No, it wasn't a game. And it wasn't just some casual flattery to stop Omund feeling aggrieved at the feast he was holding for another. There was more to it than that.

In her upper room the ancient Lapp stared into the lump of polished, silver-mounted obsidian she cradled in her withered hands. She was drooling.

It's all as my master told me, she thought. All as he said it would be. It's the beginning. They don't know it yet, none of them know it yet, but it's beginning. The prophecy came first, and now we shall start to see the deaths. So many deaths, she grinned.

Hather and Vermund left the plain behind them and rode into the forest, bowing under low branches, leading their horses across the uneven, tangled ground. Eventually they came across a place where the way had been cleared into a path, not so much by deliberate effort as by long usage.

'We follow this,' Vermund muttered, his voice little more than a whisper.

The tall evergreens towered above them, their branches forming a thick, uneven canopy which denied the morning sun all but an occasional glimpse of their progress. As they travelled deeper into the darkness Hather heard fewer sounds of birds and animals in the undergrowth. This made him wary. The further they came from the habitations of man the more wild things they should hear and see. Here, however, it was as if they were descending into the earth-muted silence of a grave-barrow.

The sounds of their feet and the horses' hoofs, the beating of their hearts, the rustling of their garments, became almost thunderous.

Not a squirrel stirred. Not a bird sang.

And then they saw the mist.

Low and yellow-grey, weaving its tendrils about the boles of the ancient trees, the mist hugged the ground, writhing as if in torment. To Hather and Vermund it seemed to follow some invisible boundary marked out upon the forest floor.

Hather shook his head. 'That's not right,' he frowned. 'Ground mist doesn't behave like that. Nor have I ever seen any mist that colour.'

Vermund agreed. 'I've lived longer than you, but I've never seen such mist anywhere else. Only here. I followed Svipdag and old Skeggja once. They came here.'

'Through *that*?'

'No, *into* it. I didn't want to tell you this, Hather. It's the one reservation I have about your son Svipdag. I think that ancient Lappish witch has tainted him with her own vile sorcery.'

'I think it would take more than seeing them ride into a patch of mist to convince me of that. Is there more, Vermund?'

Vermund beckoned. 'Follow me,' he said, tethering his mount and setting off towards the mist. For a moment Hather hesitated, then followed. His feet seemed to vanish as he stepped into the dense mist. At first he found himself imaginging that they were gone, stolen from him by some evil magic, and lifted them high every few steps to make sure they were still there. Then, with a struggle, he dismissed his fears as childish and continued after Vermund Bjarnisson, his left hand slipping the retaining loop on the scabbard free of the hilt of his sword.

The old warrior stopped and waited for Hather to catch up. Then he stretched out his arm and pointed. 'There,' he growled.

Hather strained his eyes in the gloom. For a few moments it seemed as if Vermund was simply pointing to a group of trees exactly the same as the others that surrounded them. There was nothing to see but trees, their branches radiating from the trunks that rose towards the distant sky . . .

Except for those four. They were different. Whilst they were indisputedly works of nature they had also been worked upon by man.

He drew his sword and strode through the carpet of mist towards them. Now he could see more clearly that some of the branches had been sawn away and beams set between the four towering trunks to support a sort of tree-hut close to the tops, far above their heads. Branches had also been stripped from the further side of one of them and a ladder built against the trunk in their place.

By its position in the forest it was impossible for such a structure to have any military purpose. A sentry tower would simply have been a high platform with open wooden rails about it. That this was enclosed, and that the enclosure was well below the level of the surrounding tree-tops argued for one thing only.

The high tower was used for *seidr*, the oldest and grimmest kind of Norse magic, the kind known as platform sorcery.

Hather snorted disgustedly. That old Skeggja might come to such a place did not surprise him, but Svipdag coming with her did. Sheathing his sword he set his foot upon the bottom rung of the ladder and demanded of Vermund:

'Are you coming?'

With a shrug Vermund moved to join his friend on the ladder.

They climbed slowly and steadily, determinedly making their way up towards the waiting platform. Below them height made the tree-trunks look surprisingly thin and spindly where they met the ground. The thin tips of neighbouring branches slashed at their faces as they neared the entrance to the platform, a trap-door set in its floor.

Their breath was coming in laboured gasps from their exertions as Hather pushed open the trap-door and hauled himself onto the platform. Without pausing to look about him he lay on the floor and reached down his hand to help the panting Vermund. Once they were both inside and the trap was closed again they stood up and looked around.

The walls were daubed with figures and designs which Hather recognised from old Skeggja's tapestries. Another, repeated on each of the four walls and cut into the planks of the floor, he knew only too well, it was on a ring his old nurse, Tisti, had given him at her death. It was a design of eight rays with a trident-shape at the end of each, enclosed within a circle.

Vermund knew it too. They had both seen it before, cut into the ice of the frozen waterfall at Skroggrmagi.

'*The Sign of Ginnir*,' Hather whispered.

Leif Half-Foot, only minutes from his death, had explained the sign which he knew of old. It was set upon the tents where Lappish sorcerers celebrated their mysteries, where gods and darker forces were conjured to manifestation. The sign represented the meeting of the divine and the demonic, the eternal conflict of good and evil.

Hather managed to pull his eyes away and look about the gloomy interior of the platform. A spirit-drum stood in one corner, a *vetjer*, a reindeer-horn drum-stick, upon its painted surface. Beside it, on the floor, badly-rolled, was an enormous aurochs'-hide. Hather walked across to this and kicked it partly open. Dark, straight lines had been burned into it with a hot iron.

'The nine-square skin?' Vermund asked.

Hather nodded. The skin was used for *sitting-out* and other things such as spell-preparations. The large outer square was internally divided into nine smaller ones, in the centre of which the sorcerer or witch sat for particularly dangerous work.

Hather looked up and sighed. 'I think we have the evidence we need,' he said softly. 'The problem now is what to do with it.'

He looked at Vermund. 'Witchcraft is distasteful,' he continued, 'but it's no crime. All that we can do is be on our guard against whatever's going on about us. I'm not happy about this, Vermund.' He shuddered. 'The sooner we're out of this awful place the better.'

Skeggja raised a claw-like hand and wiped the spittle from her hairy lips. The polished surface of the obsidian showed her the two figures climbing down out of the tower.

Her dark eyes sparkled as she heard the whispering within her skull.

'As you will, master,' she muttered in reply.

Vermund and Hather had reached the ground and paused for breath, both aware that they were not as young and fit as they had once been. The yellow-grey mist was still there, clinging like a protective circle to the ground around the high tower.

Hather clapped a hand to Vermund's shoulder. 'We'll rest better away from this place, old friend. Let's find the horses and ride out of here into some purer air. Let's get away from this taint of sorcery.'

Vermund, his chest heaving, began to stumble away from the tower. Hather walked ahead of him, his sword in its scabbard but his eyes bright and alert for any lurking danger. He felt his heart lighten noticeably as he reached the edge of the mist and stepped outside it.

'Ha . . . Hather?'

He turned at Vermund's call. The old warrior was some way behind him, still well inside the circle of mist. Its tendrils seemed unusually agitated around him.

'Hather!'

Slowly, determinedly, the mist crept up his struggling body. With anger in his eyes Hather drew his sword and stepped back towards the formless haze. As he tried to enter it he felt himself flung backwards as if he had encountered an invisible barrier. He struggled to his feet and grabbed for his fallen sword, but the mist had risen to Vermund's shoulders. The old man's face was a pitiful mask of pain and terror.

'HATHER!'

Hather Lambisson scrambled back towards the creeping, moving substance which had Vermund so firmly in its grasp. He proved it with his sword, which seemed to cut it quite easily. Yet when the mist touched his hand the weapon was torn from his fingers and flung away into the distant trees.

The haze reached the old man's face, stifling his cries. Hather could only watch as Vermund's outline began to alter beneath the dreadful, clinging shroud. His figure grew taller and took on the shape of one clad in loose-fitting robes of dirty white. Whilst Vermund's face had disappeared, only the form of a hood showed in its place, a hood with not even the suggestion of a face within it.

'Odin,' Hather groaned, the full horror of the being

which had taken its form from Vermund's body sweeping over him. In that moment he felt himself in the presence of a greater, fouler evil than he had ever known existed.

Old Skeggja felt the spittle running in dribbling strings from her mouth. This time she didn't bother to wipe it away. Her eyes were held upon the surface of the obsidian mirror, watching with the joy of one who beholds a long-sought wonder.

He's here, she thought. The master is here. It's all going to happen, as he told me it would.

The figure laughed, a hoarse, mirthless, *mad* laugh bubbling out from beneath the hood. 'Not Odin, Hather Lambisson,' it hissed. 'No, oh no, never Odin.'

Hather struggled not to flee. His nape-hairs stood up and a cold sweat trickled from his forehead and armpits.

'Who are you?' he demanded with a boldness he was very far from feeling.

'My name will mean nothing to you, yet,' the creature whispered in reply. 'For now, let it suffice that I am the one who is going to kill you, one day soon. And on the day that you die, Hather Lambisson, you will see the last of your beloved Ynglings lying dead in your arms, slain by your own blade. Tell me now, Hather, do you not find that at least a little amusing? Yet I see you do not laugh.'

'I have never found the ravings of the mad particularly funny,' Hather answered defiantly. 'If you're going to kill me, why don't you find a sword and do it now?'

'Find a sword?' the figure mocked him. 'Why, I could stretch out my hand and take your life now, without even touching you. What need have I of the toys of men, little king?'

Hather set his hands to his hips and threw back his head. 'So do it now, if you're so powerful,' he challenged the creature in the mist.

He was nearly frozen with fear, but he knew he mustn't show it. Hather knew that whispering voice. He had heard it before, from the lips of old Skeggja at the feast.

'The stars have to twist about in the sky before the day of your death is due, my little defiant one. You have been called the Champion of the Ynglings, Hather Lambisson. Very well. Let me see what you will do to stop them dying, one by one. You, and your precious Odin Allfather.'

Hather felt his heart chill. Only a fool, or one of enormous power, would dare to challenge Odin's might.

'You know my name. It's only right that I should know yours. Will you tell it to me? Now? Let me know who it is that dares to challenge Odin.'

He felt a smile upon the unseen face beneath the hood. 'In due time, before you die,' came the answer. 'You must suffer first, you and yours. And now, Hather Lambisson, I shall bid you farewell for the time being.'

'Wait! What of Vermund Bjarnisson? Will you restore him to me?'

The outline of the figure wavered. As if receding into an unseen distance the voice of Vultikamian called out: 'He is here, Hather, and he is yours now. What remains of him . . .'

The form dissolved, the yellow-grey mist withdrawing to ground level once again. In its place Vermund stood, outwardly unmarked, unmoving, his mouth open in a silent scream. For some moments he stood completely still, before pitching over onto his face like a length of falling timber.

The mist shook itself and billowed out around him. Forgetting the barrier he had felt during the figure's manifestation, Hather plunged into the haze and drew his old friend's body out beyond its boundary. Only then did he kneel beside it and feel for signs of life.

At first he felt tears start in his eyes as he thought there were none to be found. Then, very faintly, he felt the beating of the old man's heart. Picking him up Hather carried him to the waiting horses and set him upon his mount, using Vermund's belt to bind his hands around the horse's neck. Mounting himself, leading his friend's horse, he made the best time he felt Vermund could stand back to Uppsala.

5

Harbard at the Grave-mound

He laid Vermund upon a bed and sat beside the old warrior, refusing offers of refreshment, trying to persuade his friend to take a little wine.

His family clustered about him, but he offered no explanation. Other things came first. Vermund *had* to recover, and he needed to think, to work out for himself the implications of what had happened beneath the high tower in the forest.

Towards evening Vermund's breathing deepened and his eyes focused once more. His lips began to move as he saw Hather beside him, but no sound came from them. His hands were clasped upon his chest and, slowly and with obvious pain, he unclasped them and traced a single rune over his heart with a fingertip.

↑

Teiwaz. The t-rune. The *geirs-odd* or spear-rune. The rune that one dying on a bed would have cut into his flesh to ensure his entry into Valhalla.

Hather nodded grimly. He tore Vermund's tunic open and took the knife from his own belt. His hand steady, he made the incision upon the old warrior's chest. Vermund stiffened slightly as the cut was made, then looked up at his friend, his eyes moist with gratitude.

Then he died.

Hather threw the knife away. His body was racked with sobs as he took the dead warrior in his arms and pressed his cheek against the spear-rune. He felt the salt moisture of Saeunna's tears as she stood over him, stroking his hair.

He stood up and placed his arm around Saeunna's shoulders. Olaf and Gudrun were there too, weeping.

'He had no family,' Saeunna said softly. 'Yet he loved us, and we loved him. We'll raise a mound for him here at Uppsala, where he served for so much of his life.'

'Take him Odin,' Hather asked. 'Take him for your own. Find him bench-room in your hall. Please, don't let Loki's blue-faced daughter Hel have so good a warrior as he. Hear me, Allfather.'

'He'll hear you,' Saeunna comforted.

Hather blinked back the tears. 'He doesn't always,' he muttered. 'But I think he will this time.'

Olaf handed his father a horn of wine, which was drained and immediately held out for Gudrun to refill.

'How I loved that old man!'

'We all did, father,' Gudrun told him. 'There will never be another like Vermund. There never could be.'

'He saved my life, Saeunna. And when the time came for me to save his, I could do *nothing*.'

He slumped down onto a bench and drained the horn again. Olaf sat down beside him.

'Is there anything I can do, father?' he asked.

'Not just now,' Hather said. 'Though someone ought to tell the High King Vermund's dead. And your brother ought to know as well.'

Olaf laid his hand on his father's shoulder and stood up. 'I'll tell them,' he said, and left the longhouse.

Hather sat alone, lost in thought, whilst Saeunna and Gudrun laid out the body of their old and dear friend. They had come to Uppsala to celebrate Svipdag's new position, and were to leave there after the burial of one they loved. It was almost as if pleasure had to be paid for.

More than that, Hather reflected. It was as if their years of peace and contentment had been bought at the price of their lives. In some ways it was only right that the debt should be paid. He'd had a good life for the most part and if he was going to die trying to defend the House of Yngling then there was at least some justice in such a death. But not those of Saeunna and Olaf and Gudrun. They deserved better. If need be he'd leave the Ynglings to their fate and look after his family, he told himself, though the words sounded hollow.

The fates of those he loved had always been tied to the Ynglings, right from the early days when Starkadder had killed his father in an attempt to keep Omund from the throne. His *vargr*-wife Astrid had tried to destroy the Ynglings and himself and Svipdag.

No, he had to see it through, whatever the future might hold. There was no possibility of separating those he loved from those he was sworn to defend. If the Yngling dynasty could be saved, then so could his family. If not, then at least they would all be united in death.

He found that it was impossible for him to ignore or disbelieve what the figure in the mist had told him. It could have been a figment of his imagination, but figments didn't kill and Vermund lay dead before him. The figure had been brave enough to challenge the power of All-father, and such a challenge would not be issued unless the challenger was powerful enough to make a good try of it.

I'm caught up in their game once more, he thought. Once more the gods and the Norns are playing with my life, and with the lives of those I love. The first time I was too young to know. The second? Well, that time I managed to work out what was happening, but it almost took too long. But this time I know. This time I will be prepared.

He bellowed for a servant.

'Go to the barracks where our escort is quartered. Tell

Haarek I want his best man to take a message back to Sudrafell. Now!'

The man left, alarmed by the urgency in the King's voice. Some minutes later he reappeared with a soldier dressed in Hather's livery.

'Come closer,' Hather ordered. The man obeyed, leaning down to catch Hather's whispered orders.

'This to Thrand Helgisson. Raise levies. I want the best force he can muster standing ready in as short a time as possible. Now, this to my steward Harald. Realise all outstanding debts. I need as large a reserve in coin as he can collect. And say to both of them that they have my authority to do anything else that may be required to secure the safety of the province. Even if I don't return,' he added, darkly. 'Do you understand?'

The man stood to attention, his mouth open.

'Don't repeat my orders,' Hather snapped. 'Just deliver them. Now!'

The soldier saluted and left. There was no possibility of his forgetting what he had been told. The instructions he'd been given were clear and precise. They were preparations for war.

Shortly afterwards Olaf returned to the longhouse. 'I've just seen one of our men riding out, father,' he began.

'Some business at home to be taken care of.'

'I've told the High King,' Olaf said. 'He's ordered a mound for Vermund close to the royal enclosure.'

'Good. And Svipdag?'

'He's not in his quarters. Nor was he with King Omund. I left a message with his servants asking that he come and see you.'

Hather grinned. 'You'll learn cunning yet,' he said. Then he relaxed. 'Son, there are times when a man should get drunk. Let's find a couple of horns and some good honest mead. I'm getting fed up with this piss they call wine.'

Saeunna looked across at her husband and her son. So alike, she thought. And Hather's found as good an answer as he knows for the pain that's burning inside him.

Two days later Vermund Bjarnisson, King's Marshal and for many years the leading warrior of the kingdom, was laid in as fine a mound as any not of Yngling blood had been accorded at Uppsala. His runestone had been ordered by Hather from the finest master-carver of Sweden and would be set in place later, so that all might know who lay beneath that splendid barrow.

The court attended, led by Omund and Aud and their sons, sons' wives and grandchildren. The other vassal kings who had been at the feast, together with their families and retainers, were there too. The townspeople too were there, though maintaining a respectful distance from the splendid and notable assembly about the grave-mound. Even those who had borne the old warrior no love were forced to admit his greatness.

There were tears and praise-songs, and prayers to Odin and Thor to take the old man to Valhalla. There was tribute, as well as his own goods, to be laid in the grave with him.

Only the new King's Marshal was missing from the throng which laid the old one to rest. None had even seen him to tell him that Vermund Bjarnisson was dead.

Once the burial was done Hather assembled his family and their escort and, having received Omund's permission to leave the court, left Uppsala for the journey back to Sudrafell. He knew that whatever was going to happen would take place soon enough. His immediate concern was that his family should be as safe as he could make them, and that meant returning as quickly as he could to Sudrafell and the safety of a palace enclosure manned by his own trusted followers. Svipdag's absence worried him, naturally, but the new Marshal of the High King, he reasoned, would be able to take care of himself.

Their route took them close by the burial mounds, and it was Olaf who first saw and pointed out the shape atop Vermund's. The distance was such that it was impossible to tell what it was. Hather knew, though, that it would be some days before the runestone he had commissioned would be completed and set in place.

'Stay here,' he told the others. 'I want to have a look at this.'

He rode away from the column, towards the mound. As he drew closer he was able to see a figure strangely familiar, standing alone. Behind him, in the sky, two ravens circled.

At the edge of the mound Hather dismounted, hobbled his horse, and climbed up the bank. Wrapped in a blue travelling cloak, the watcher leaned upon a massive spear such as had not been used in battle in the north for centuries.

His mouth was hidden beneath a tangle of grizzled grey beard, and a single eye glinted from beneath the brim of a broad hat which kept one side of his face in shadow. At some time in the past Hather Lambisson had seen that face before.

Saeunna, with Olaf beside her, shielded her eyes from the sun with an upraised hand, heard the distant calling of two wolves. She glanced at her son.

'You know these things better than I do,' she said. 'Have you ever known wolves come so close to any human habitation before, let alone a town the size of Uppsala?'

Olaf shook his head. 'Not this close,' he answered. 'They never even leave the forest if they can help it, and never in daylight.'

Hather reached the top of the burial mound.

'Who are you?' he asked, uncertainly.

The figure smiled beneath its beard. Hather's hand reached for his sword.

'You won't need your weapon, Hather Lambisson, King of Ostragotland,' came the reply. The voice was firm but gentle, significant of hidden strength held firmly in check. 'You've met me before. My name is Harbard.'

His mind reeled. It was as if his brain had been kicked. His thoughts raced back in time.

'Are you Allfather?' Starkadder had demanded before the gates of Trollheim.

Saeunna had said: 'A one-eyed man called Harbard told me to give you a message.' That message had saved

Svipdag, had probably saved all of them, from the *vargr* at Skroggrmagi.

He felt himself falling to his knees. 'You *are* Allfather,' he gasped, his voice threatening to choke him before it could leave his throat.

Harbard's smile widened. 'You know me now, Champion of the Ynglings,' he replied. 'I had hoped never to have to meddle in your life again, my friend. But I have no choice.'

'Odin, what do I have to do?'

Odin sighed wearily.

'Listen to me, Hather. Listen well. Twice now you have done my work. Twice you have saved the House of Yngling from itself. Now I have to ask you to save it one more time. You saw the hooded figure in the mist?'

'The one that killed Vermund? I saw it. It challenged your power, Allfather.'

Harbard nodded. 'I know. Such challenges should not be issued, *are not issued*, unless the challenger is certain of his strength.

'You see, my friend, *Hvitakrist*, the White Christ, has risen in the south. Our world is old, Hather; its gods are tired. Even I am tired. There will come a day, not too far distant when you think how long we have held sway, when we shall have to rest. Whether it will be the Ragnarok, the Doom of the Gods foretold by the skalds, I don't know. Yet the end will come, and when it does we shall go down to our sleep, both gods and Norns together.

'Yet now this . . . *interloper* . . . has ventured into our realms, defying me, defying the White Christ. What he intends I do not know. Yes, Hather, you have heard me, Odin, say that there is something I do not know, and that is what I mean.

'You see,' he continued, 'I *don't* know, Hather. There is the hand of my old lover and arch foe in all this. The leader of the Sisterhood of Norns, the veiled one we call Mother Skuld, has set this interloper against me as some kind of test. Oh, she has her reasons, I don't doubt. Yet the House of Yngling is threatened by her work, as is my power, as is your life and the lives of those you love.'

'Tell me what to do, Allfather. Only tell me what to do and I'll do it, whatever it is.'

The god nodded. 'I know that, my friend. I've always known that. Otherwise I would have called you to join me in Valhalla long before now. I can't tell you, though. I will help you, as I have helped you before, once I know myself what is to happen, but it must be in hints and riddles. The game is mine only to play, Hather Lambisson; I do not make the rules. But I am bound by them. That is why you see me now.

'The next time you see me, old friend, will be when you stand upon the threshold of Valhalla.'

Hather felt his chin upon his chest. He raised his eyes to where Odin had been standing, but there was no-one there. Slowly he rose to his feet and looked about him. Only the distant column, awaiting his return, was to be seen. There were no wolves, no circling ravens, and no one-eyed god to guide him on his way.

I have to see Svipdag, he thought. My son holds some kind of key to these puzzles. I'm certain of it.

He walked down the burial mound and freed his horse from the hobble. Then he rode slowly back to the column, his thoughts jumbled, his heart racing as if he had run for several miles. Urging his horse up to Saeunna's he leaned over and kissed his wife.

'Go back to Sudrafell,' he said simply. 'I have to stay here. Olaf,' he called to his son, 'come with me.'

Father and son watched the column disappear on its way back to Sudrafell. Olaf asked: 'Where are we going, father?'

Hather's face was grim, his expression set in hard lines. 'We're going to a high tower in the forest,' he replied.

6

The Disappearance of Svipdag Hathersson

Hather set the pace, urging his mount determinedly and swiftly towards the forest and its mist-shrouded tower, his face marred by hard, deep lines of concern and anger.

They entered the forest, their pace only slackening as much as the rough ground ahead of them demanded. Hather rode to the very edge of the evil mist before he dismounted and tethered his horse. As Olaf rose in the saddle to follow him Hather called out.

'Stay where you are, son. On your horse.'

'Aren't I coming with you, father?' Olaf asked.

'Not through this stuff,' Hather replied. 'Wait for me here. And whatever happens, whatever you see, don't set foot in this mist. Do you understand me?'

Olaf, still puzzled, nodded. Then Hather stepped deliberately, unhesitatingly, into the mist and began to walk towards the hidden tower.

Though it had proven useless before, Hather's sword was loose and ready in its scabbard. Perhaps an ordinary weapon might not be enough to overcome the powers of sorcery, but it was all Hather had to try with, and his hand swung close to its hilt with every step towards the tower.

By the time he had reached the ladder Olaf and the horses were out of sight, hidden by the trees. Hather's flesh was prickling beneath his clothes, itching with the nearness of a danger that he couldn't understand. He paused, glaring up the length of the ladder towards the platform above. He felt his heart leap in sudden fear.

The trap in the bottom of the platform was open, the opening illuminated by the flickering light of a lamp burning within.

Someone was in the tower.

Skeggja. It had to be old Skeggja.

His hands gripped the sides of the ladder. With grim resolution Hather Lambisson began to climb towards the light.

The forest floor receded beneath him. His feet moved from rung to rung, ever upwards away from the circle of mist which writhed about the trees. The opening above him drew nearer, became brighter. Then finally his head passed through it and he peered into the weird interior of the platform.

'I've been waiting for you, Hather Lambisson,' old Skeggja croaked.

He hauled himself inside and stood back against one of the wooden walls, well away from the opening in the floor. The ancient crone was crouched at the centre of her nine-squared aurochs'-hide, grinning at him, spittle trickling from the corners of her hair-fringed mouth, her claw-like hands idly tracing the patterns on the surface of the spirit-drum, though as Hather watched, almost entranced, he noticed that the apparently casual movements were actually carefully ordered and controlled.

'Come a little closer, Hather,' the witch crooned. 'Come closer to the light. Ah, Hather Lambisson, there is so much that I could show you.'

He felt his feet move, carry him closer to where the ancient Lapp was sitting, closer to the opening in the floor of the platform and the long, bone-shattering drop to the waiting mist beneath.

'That's it, Hather. Yes, Hather Lambisson. Closer to me. Closer, now.'

She watched him set one foot in front of the other, drawing ever nearer to the trap. Her evil grin vanished as

Hather stepped to one side and walked around the open trap, drawing his sword as he approached her.

He came close enough to set its point against her wrinkled throat. Her eyes glittered her fear in the lamp-light as she looked along its length to his hand, then up into his hard and merciless face.

'You have corrupted my son with your sorcery,' Hather growled.

'Did you not learn a little from old Tisti?' Skeggja demanded defiantly. 'When she taught you your runes, were they not the cult-runes of sorcery, Hather Lambisson?'

She was right. She knew that she was right. Yet Hather's sword-point didn't waiver. Neither did the anger in his eyes.

'We're talking about my son, witch, not myself. My son. Svipdag.'

'Ah, Svipdag.'

He pressed the point a fraction deeper. A slow trickle of dark, ancient blood began beneath the blade. Old Skeggja's mocking voice fell silent beneath its vicious threat.

'I'm not a young man any more, witch,' Hather began. 'I tire easily. I tend to lean forward because my legs are less steady. I have less patience with the old and weak. The years pass by me faster and killing has grown easier with each one.

'I shall ask you one question. If your answer has the sound of truth behind it I shall let you live. If not . . .' The sword-point moved a fraction. A fresh trickle of blood began to flow.

'Ask . . . ask what you will, Hather Lambisson.'

'Where's my son, old woman? Where's Svipdag Hath-ersson? He's not at Uppsala or he'd have been at his foster-father's funeral. So, where is he?'

She felt the pain of the pressure at her throat. She saw the hate in Hather's eyes. For a fraction of a second she was ready to lie to her tormentor, but through the years she had come to know him all too well. And he knew her the same way. He'd see the lie. Even if it were a good lie he'd know that it wasn't the truth. And that would cost her her life.

And if she was dead she'd be no use to her master, and unable to exult and take her revenge for this suffering when his inevitable victory was won.

So she told the truth.

'He's . . . gone north. Svipdag has travelled north on an errand for the High King. Omund sent him, not I, Hather.'

'Tell me about the errand.' The sword-point remained resolutely where it was.

'He's . . . he's gone to find a sorcerer for Omund. In Finnmark . . .'

'Sorcerer? What sorcerer? He's a Lapp if he's from Finnmark.'

'He can only be a Lapp if he is human, Hather Lambisson.'

'You speak as if you know him. Was it he who spoke through you at the feast, who made those promises of immortality to Omund?'

She made no reply. The sword nicked her again.

'Was it?' Hather demanded.

'Yes. Very well, yes.'

'The one who killed Vermund Bjarnisson? That one?'

'I . . . I don't know. I didn't see Vermund die . . . I wasn't here.'

Hather snorted derisively. 'I know you, Skeggja. That wouldn't have stopped you seeing if you'd wanted to. What's this sorcerer called?'

'His name would mean nothing to you, Hather.'

'That's not what I asked you, witch. Tell me his name. Now!'

'Vultikamian . . . is his name. At least . . . that's what he's called.'

'And Omund's sent my son Svipdag, the King's Marshal, to Finnmark to find this Vultikamian?'

'Yes. Yesss.'

Hather returned his sword to its scabbard. Skeggja's

hands flew to her injured throat and she glared balefully at her tormentor.

'I see that you remember your promise,' she croaked, ruefully.

With a snort Hather turned away and walked to the open trap in the floor. As he lowered himself towards it a sudden rush behind him made him turn, crouched by the edge. Her face a mask of hate and fury, spittle flying in strings from her contorted lips, the aged Lapp had sprung towards him, threatening to carry both of them to their deaths on the floor of the forest far beneath.

Straightening suddenly, his legs as hard and rigid as dwarf-forged steel, Hather smacked the back of his gloved hand into the old woman's face. Skeggja howled and staggered away from the blow, blood streaming from her nose.

'Your master hasn't told you everything,' Hather snarled savagely. 'I can't die until the last of the Ynglings lies dead before me. Your sorcerer Vultikamian told me that himself.'

He left her leaning against one of the platform walls and started down the ladder. Despite his outward contempt and composure he was deeply troubled as he stepped once more into the mist and made his way back towards where Olaf was waiting with their horses. He could sense the jaws of a trap opening to receive him, a trap which Svipdag had some part, knowing or unknowing, in constructing.

Knowing or unknowing. What *had* happened during those two days Svipdag had spent lost in the northern wastes? It had changed the colour of his eyes; perhaps it had even changed the nature of his being?

Hather scowled at the thought. Svipdag was his son, conceived and born long before his mother had become *vargr*. There was no original taint of sorcery in his breeding, no example of treachery or betrayal . . .

He was almost within sight of Olaf when he stopped suddenly and stared back at the tower amongst the trees. Old Skeggja wasn't following. The trap-door was still open and there was no one upon the ladder, as he had already known would be the case. High above him the ancient Lapp witch would be sitting crooning to herself, trying to stanch the blood from her broken nose. No, there was no one following. That hadn't made him start.

He knew what had, though, even as he tried to fight against it. The example of treachery or betrayal which might taint Svipdag *was* there, buried deep in his memory. Svipdag had been only a year old when Astrid vanished, believed dead. Nine years later he had been captured by the *vargr* his mother had become, captured and held for a ghastly ritual in which his living heart was to be ripped out for her diabolical feasting in a final, bloody sacrifice which would have set her horribly above humanity. Svipdag had been there, his mother's prisoner, at Skroggrmagi. He had witnessed her final defeat and death, though Saeunna had shielded the ten-year-old boy's eyes from the final moments of Astrid's accursed existence.

Mother had betrayed son.

Hather groaned softly to himself, unconscious of the evil mist still swirling about his legs. The most terrible fear a father can know was clutching at his heart, a fear for his child. Until that moment of blinding knowledge it had been inconceivable that Svipdag could be working against him. Now, as he struggled to control his breathing and to keep the tears from welling in his eyes, the disappearance of Svipdag Hathersson had taken on a new and sinister meaning.

As his father approached, his face drawn and his gait that of a tired old man, Olaf asked: 'Father, are you hurt?'

Hather looked up at his son, his gaze glassy and blank.

'There's blood on your glove,' Olaf explained. 'Have you hurt your hand?'

Hather Lambisson stared at his hand for a moment, his mind struggling to dislodge the suspicions it had formed and return to the immediate present. 'Oh, no. It's not mine.'

Then he shook himself.

'Come on,' he said, mounting his horse. 'Time we were away from here.'

This wasn't the moment for Olaf to ask what had happened while he'd waited with the horses. There was an uncertainty mingled with the determination he was used to, on Hather's features. His father was wrestling with some problem which only he could resolve. Yet Olaf was Hather's son and he wasn't going to follow blindly without knowing why.

'Where now?' he asked.

Hather reined in and looked at his son. 'To Uppsala,' he answered.

'We left Uppsala this morning. We halted near Uncle Vermund's grave-mound. You sent my mother home to Sudrafell. We rode here to the forest. You vanished into the mist, then came back with blood on your glove and now we're riding *back* to Uppsala. I'm not a child any more, father. I want to know what's going on.'

Hather leaned across in the saddle and grasped his son's wrist. 'As soon as I know myself, I'll tell you,' he said. 'All I have so far to guide me is suspicion. I can't tell you what's happening, not yet. You see, I don't know myself. I just remember that the last time Omund thought I was out of the way he began to plan what would have been a disastrous campaign against the Dane-Lands. He won't try that again. We broke his power, Vermund and I, by setting up the vassal kingdoms. But Vermund's dead and I'm supposed to be on my way back to Sudrafell. If there's anything behind that gibberish we heard from old Skeggja at the feast, then now's the time to find out.

'I've lived through battles, Olaf. I stood behind Starkadder as he killed King Oli the Great. I duelled Starkadder on the plain outside Dalalven. I fought the *vargr* at Skroggrmagi. I held a sword to Omund's throat and helped to save his life and his kingdom. I'm not boasting. I tell you, each and every time I've spoken of I was afraid. And I'm afraid now. But I can't tell you why because I don't know.'

He released his grip upon Olaf's arm and together they

rode across the plain. Their route took them back through the town and up to the palace gates. The sentries stood aside for King Hather of Ostragotland and his son, and called men to take their horses as they dismounted.

Hather walked determinedly towards Omund's quarters. Olaf followed. In his heart he wished that his half-brother Svipdag was there to talk to. Svipdag was eleven years older and so much better versed in both battle and court intrigue. The age difference made him something of an interpreter between Olaf and his father. Svipdag would know what was going on, Olaf thought. But Svipdag had disappeared, and while Olaf saw nothing sinister in the absence of the new King's Marshal, it would have been both useful and desirable to have his elder brother's help and advice.

Sentries challenged them with crossed spears before Omund's longhouse. Hather scowled and glared, and the weapons were lowered. As they strode into the vestibule they heard the sound of sobbing within the main hall.

Hather's pace quickened. So did Olaf's. Amongst the weeping women within they discerned the voice of Olaf's sister Gudrun.

Hather pushed open the door and they strode through, their hands close by their weapons. In the tapestried interior of the longhouse the predominant colour was red. Hather had seen plenty of carnage and knew well how blood could spray out from a wound, yet the stench of it, spattered across the walls and floor, sickened him.

Gudrun sat upon the floor, her head bowed, her cheeks wet with tears, among the queen's servants and ladies.

At the further end of the hall the leech was shaking and ashen amid a group of weeping servants. Omund squatted on the floor, the savagely-slaughtered body of his wife as limp and lifeless in his arms as a discarded doll.

Hather felt his gorge begin to rise. 'What has happened here?' he demanded.

Omund heard his voice and looked up. For the briefest moment Hather thought he saw the old, thwarted malice in his eyes. Then the suspicion passed.

'I . . . I have lost . . . my wife, my queen,' Omund replied, his voice broken and choked with tears. 'Hather . . . you have ever been a friend when I truly needed one. Will you . . . help me now? Will you find Aud's murderer for me?'

Hather closed his eyes. Odin, he thought, it's beginning. The first moves had been made in the game.

Will any of us live to see the end of it?

7

A Killer at Uppsala

The grave-diggers were busy that season. First they dug for the former King's Marshal, Vermund Bjarnisson. Now they dug a deeper, larger mound for the High King's wife. Five days after her killing she was laid in the earth with her grave-goods and the burial-chamber erected over her before the earth was put back. The rune-cutters, already busy with Vermund's stone, now found they had to break off their work and cut a larger, finer monument for King Omund's dead queen.

Hather stood with Olaf at the burial, as he had stood at his old friend Vermund's such a little time before. It seemed that death was in the very air around them. No plague, no pestilence, could have wrought such havoc as these deaths and what they would lead to.

His face was outwardly calm, betraying none of the showy emotion of the High King. Omund was displaying his grief like a war-trophy, demanding of all who stood with him that it should be seen, noted and remembered. His tears ran freely for his murdered queen, more than those of the children she had borne him.

It was not unmanly to weep. It was a mark of feeling, of respect for the dead, as well as the sign of a well-rounded man, capable of tears as well as laughter. Yet Hather, for all he had known and liked Aud, kept his tears for himself. Olaf remarked upon this, and was told gruffly that Omund was doing enough crying for the whole court; any more tears, and Uppsala would sink beneath a flood of salt water.

In his own mind Hather felt more uneasy than ever. Svipdag's disappearance, possibly linked with sorcery, was bad enough. The frenzied and vicious murder of Queen Aud could hardly be unconnected, though it was impossible to think that Svipdag was in any way responsible for Aud's death, Hather told himself.

Hather growled to himself and shook his head as he watched the closure of the grave-mound. Since Aud's death he had conducted a ruthless and thorough investigation into the murder, questioning any servants and sentries who might have been in a position to witness or prevent it. No one had refused whatever assistance might be asked, for they all shared the loss of the fine lady who had been High Queen of Sweden. Yet to all Hather's questions there were only unsatisfactory answers, or no answers at all.

The maids had been sent away because the High Queen had wished for some reason to be alone. Gudrun, her eyes still red with weeping, suggested to her father that Aud's behaviour had almost been that of a woman plotting to receive a lover. Yet no one was prepared to believe that such could have been the case, and no strangers had been noticed about the court who might have appeared even slightly suitable for the purpose.

The answers of the sentries were even more perplexing. They had been present, in the vestibule and about the longhouse, in their usual numbers. They had changed the watch only a little while before, so the men were alert. Moreover the kindness of the High Queen to all her husband's subjects, bringing her into an almost universal esteem as it had, made those detailed to guard her feel proud of their obligation. They had not fallen asleep. They had not been drugged or rendered unconscious. Neither had they seen anyone prowling suspiciously about the compound.

So if it wasn't murder, Hather brooded, that left witchcraft.

He suddenly remembered the prophecy spoken through old Skeggja at the feast. *Death is such a little thing for a king such as you*, it had told Omund. For the first time Hather began to wonder *whose* death, or deaths, those words had referred to.

It had also foretold that Omund would outlive his progeny, becoming the last and greatest to the Yngling line. That would be magic indeed, Hather scowled inwardly. For Hather Lambisson knew the real truth about the High King, how he had been cowed by his father, Oli the Great, who had destroyed the boy's spirit and left only a scheming weakling to succeed him, how Omund had waited thirteen years to league himself with the *vargr*, and only then because the opportunity had been treacherously presented to him, to be avenged upon Hather for the shame of Hather saving Omund's life and kingdom. Was this to be the last and greatest Yngling of them all? How could a weakling in his middle fifties outlive his children, unless it was by sorcery, or murder? Or both.

Svipdag away seeking a wizard. The queen butchered. Skeggja's high tower casting its evil shadow towards Uppsala. And the monstrous *thing* which had drained Vermund's life from him in the circle of creeping mist. Fool that I am, Hather thought. I saw the first signs and thought it was only just beginning. Oh, but I was wrong.

Beginning? It's nearly done. When death can stalk Uppsala like this, when an unseen killer can take life without a single witness, when a worm like Omund can aspire to greatness and immortality, then things are further progressed than I could ever have suspected.

A growing certainty crept into his brain. Sorcery and murder *was* the only way that Omund could outlive his children. There was some plot, some devious scheme, which linked Omund and Skeggja and the thing in the mist and . . . *Svipdag?*

He shuddered at the idea. Olaf looked enquiringly at him.

'It's nothing,' Hather answered. 'Just a chill in my bones.'

But what a chill. Omund had three sons, all married,

and seven grandchildren, four of whom were boys. There was no reason for the succession to be in doubt, no reason to suppose that all those sons and grandsons would die before the High King, except for the prophecy which the thing had spoken through old Skeggja at the feast. Nor was there any reason not to believe any one of those children would be a better, stronger ruler than Omund, for Aud's blood ran in their veins, balancing the weakness, the strain of insanity, which tainted the Yngling line.

The *thuls*, the high priests of Thor and Odin from the great temple, were supervising the sealing of Aud's grave-mound. As the mourners began to turn away Hather and Olaf moved with them, walking slowly back towards the town and the royal enclosure.

Apart from Omund's personal guards, none of the party were carrying weapons. This was the custom at burials, as it was in council, imposed to prevent disputes becoming deadly conflicts as tempers rose in grief or disagreement. It was a custom which Hather approved of, although he had lived such a life as never to feel properly dressed or at ease without a weapon at his side. Now, as the mourners returned to the court, Hather strode directly to his quarters to arm himself. Olaf went with him, finding his own weapon a comfort in this strange world of intrigue and violence he had been suddenly thrust into, a world so different from the quiet, well-ordered ways which prevailed at Sudrafell.

Upon discovering Aud's death Hather had sent a rider after his party to tell them that he would be remaining at Uppsala for some days, and also to recall some of his personal guard, preferring to have his own men about him rather than ask the use of soldiers loyal to Omund. As was customary, these shared with the other guards the barracks-quarters which were built into the stockade wall, when they were not on duty. When they were, they were stationed within the vestibule of the longhouse forming Hather's guest-quarters, rather than outside. This gave them shelter from the weather and also made it more difficult for them to be surprised by assailants following the line of the walls to get behind them.

Even as he approached the longhouse Hather knew that something was wrong. His men were there, all right, standing within the shadows of the vestibule, but their positions were unnatural. Their hands were limp at their sides and their heads lolled to the side, as if they had fallen alseep standing up.

And their weapons were gone.

To a casual observer the sentries would have seemed simply to be tired of their duty. But Hather Lambisson of Sudrafell, though, hero of too many years of conflict and deceit, sensed that something foul awaited his discovery.

Motioning Olaf to stay behind him he approached the vestibule. Apart from the two bodies, supported by sticks driven into the ground at one end and the bases of their skulls at the other, it was empty. The inner door stood firmly closed.

His face flushed with outrage, his eyes glittering slits in his weathered face, Hather lifted one body free of the sharpened stave and signed for Olaf to do likewise with the other. With slight grating, sucking sounds the staves came free.

Olaf, less used to the casual violence of the world outside Sudrafell, felt his gorge begin to rise at the grisly task. With a fine effort he fought it down, knowing full well that this was not the moment to show anything less than that strength he had inherited from his father.

They lowered the bodies to the floor and, armed with the sharpened sticks, stood before the inner door. Hather glanced at his scowling son, and moved his lips in a silent count.

One . . . two . . .

On *three* they raised their feet and kicked together at the catch, shattering the wooden frame about it and sending the door crashing inwards. The main hall before them appeared to be empty. Upon a trestle table, on the further side, their swords, and those of the dead guards, lay waiting with their hilts towards them.

With his free hand Hather gestured to either side of the door, implying that they should beware of assailants beyond their view. With another count they sprang into the hall, staves at the ready, and stood back to back, just inside the doorway, their eyes searching the shadowed interior for any sign of lurking danger.

There was nothing.

The far end of the hall was, as usual, partitioned off as bed-closets and servants' quarters. The partition door stood ajar, as it had been before they left for Aud's burial.

'Get our weapons,' Hather told Olaf. 'We'll make certain there's nothing hiding back there, then we'll go and see what Omund has to say about this.'

It was a mystery how the guards had been surprised, for they could only have been killed by someone, or something, from *inside* the longhouse.

Hather scowled. Besides, he had never left his sword lying across a table in his life. It was one of his personal quirks always to leave a weapon lying with the grain of the wood, not across it, as it was now.

As it was now.

Olaf was only a few feet from the table, already reaching for his sword. Suddenly Hather knew.

'Olaf!' he cried. 'Olaf, *wait*!'

Even as he shouted he launched himself across the hall towards his son. Something in the lie of the rushes was wrong. Olaf turned, one of his feet pressed down on the disturbed area, and went through it.

Olaf cried out as the floor of the longhouse gave way beneath him. Even as he began to fall Hather slammed into him and hurled them both clear. As they rolled away the floor before the table fell, revealing a dark pit in the floor, a pit aswarm with shadowy figures now covered in splintered wood, earth and rushes.

In an instant Hather was on his feet. Springing around the table he threw Olaf his sword and siezed his own. With a hefty kick he upset the trestles, sending the top of the table slamming down over the hole. A howl of pain echoed up from beneath and a hand, trapped beneath the table-top, dropped its weapon from clawing fingers. With a sweeping scythe of his blade Olaf chopped at the hand, severing two fingers before it was withdrawn with a scream.

'Come on!' Hather snapped.

They tore the trestle-boards away from the hole and launched themselves down into it. For an instant they glimpsed a dark opening in one of the walls of the pit, then a barrage of stones flew at them, forcing them to turn their heads to protect their eyes from flying debris. They spluttered and coughed through the shower of soil, and by the time it was done, the hole in the side of the pit was almost totally sealed.

Together they climbed back up into the hall. The two severed fingers still lay where they had fallen. Hather picked them up and examined them carefully, laying them upon the palm of one hand and turning them with the other. They were broad and strong, worn-down nails caked with dirt, the third and little fingers of a man's right hand.

'A big man,' Hather mused. 'And a fighter, by the looks of it. Only a fool would send an incompetent slave against me. So, there can be few men in the palace who would even try. And one of them's missing two fingers now.'

He looked up. 'We'll find him, Olaf,' he grinned. 'And when we do I believe we'll have Aud's murderer as well.'

Olaf said nothing. 'Come on, son,' Hather said. 'Out with it. What's bothering you?'

Olaf forced a smile. 'I'm wondering why they went to all this trouble,' he began. 'Why tunnel underneath the longhouse like that? And why try to kill you when it's perfectly obvious that they'd give themselves away if they failed? I don't understand it, father. The killers have given you a way to find them. They didn't *need* to kill you, so why take such a chance?'

It was Hather's turn to scowl. Olaf was right. The killer, or killers, didn't need Hather dead to protect themselves.

And that meant that the reason for the attack was something else, something beyond fear of discovery.

He wrapped the severed fingers in a shred of rag and put them into the pouch at his belt. 'Come on,' he said. 'First things first. And the first thing is to take a look at the floor of Aud's quarters.'

They left the hall, and crossed the compound to the queen's longhouse. The sentries, from Omund's personal guard, let them inside, and they began a careful search of the floor where Aud's body had been discovered. The dirt floor, now cleaned of blood and covered with fresh rushes, seemed entirely solid. In a raised wooden dais, however, Olaf was able to discern the outline of a cleverly concealed trap-door. Setting his sword to it he prised the trap open and peered down inside.

Hather stood beside him, staring at the pit beneath. Like the one in their own longhouse this one showed signs of being the sealed-off entrance to a tunnel.

'You were right,' Olaf told him. 'That's how the killer got in without anyone seeing him. All it needed was for the queen to have her back to him and he'd have been upon her without her realising a thing. You heard how silently I opened it?'

'Perhaps,' Hather answered. 'But when we found Aud, her seat had fallen over facing the dais. That means that she was sitting facing it. It also means that, unless she was asleep, she not only saw her killer come up out of the ground, but wasn't surprised to see him entering her quarters that way!'

And if I'm right, he added inwardly, there's only one man in the whole of Sweden who could have come through that trap-door. But I need more than this before I can accuse the High King of the murder of his queen!

'I'm getting old, Olaf,' Hather said sullenly. 'I'm forgetting the obvious. Now, this is what I want you to do. Alert the sentries on the gates that no one with an injured hand, no matter who they are, is to leave the palace without my personal order. Then find your sister. I want her here as soon as possible. After that fetch the rest of our men from the barracks, and see that they have digging tools with them. I want to know where these tunnels go. Try to find Omund's master-builder as well.'

He watched Olaf go, and could not help making a comparison between his two sons. The strong, blond, handsome youth Saeunna had borne him was destined to become a good, decent warrior-chief if he lived that long. Olaf was intelligent but inexperienced. He had a good brain, though he'd not been called upon to use it overmuch. Perhaps that's my fault, Hather reflected. I've been thinking for myself ever since I was fifteen, and it's hard for me to let even my son try to do it for me. It's not that I doubt his ability. No, not that. Rather I'm too certain of my own.

Now Svipdag, with his woman's beauty, his *mother's* beauty, and his love of dark things, is totally different. He's as different from Olaf as Astrid was different from Saeunna. Yet I loved both mothers, and I love both sons. I may have doubts about Svipdag, but I don't think he'd betray me, no matter what Omund might have promised him.

Yes, I'm right in that. I *have* to be. Before this is over I may well have staked my life upon that belief, and the rest of my family's lives as well.

8

A New High Queen for Sweden

Olaf returned with Gudrun a few minutes later. He was worried.

He said: 'The guards at the gate reported that a mercenary captain rode out of the palace with a bandaged hand a little while before I spoke to them, father.'

Hather nodded. 'I suspected as much. That's what made me realise how old I'm getting. I should have thought of that before we came here. We gave him time to get away. Did they tell you who it was?'

'They said his name was Thorgrim Ironfist.'

'Ironfist? That doesn't surprise me. He was always a brutal sort, ready to sell his sword for whatever butcher-work was required. Still, they'll have to call him Half-hand after this day's work.

'What about our men? Did you see them?'

'Yes,' Olaf replied. 'They're finding some tools.'

'And Omund's master-builder?'

'Him as well.'

'That's good. Now, Gudrun, I want you to cast your mind back to the day Aud died. There's something I need to know.'

Gudrun struggled to force a smile. 'You know I'll do anything I can to help you,' she said.

Hather felt his heart rise towards his throat as she spoke. How like Saeunna she was, so young and lovely, like the woman he'd first met at the crossing on the Dalalven whilst he was struggling to save Svipdag from the *vargr*. Golden-haired, green-eyed, her features even lovelier than her mother's.

'It's not easy for you, I know,' Hather told her. 'That chair. Which way round did the High Queen sit in it, can you remember? Was its back towards this dais or away from it? Did Aud sit facing this way, or that?'

Gudrun thought for a moment. 'Why, both ways,' she answered.

Hather's brows creased. 'What does that mean?'

'She liked to keep the sun behind her, father. In the morning, when it came through those windows, she sat that way. In the afternoon, when it shone through those over there, she turned her chair to keep it behind her.'

Hather and Olaf exchanged glances.

'That means that the seat was moved in the struggle,' Olaf ventured.

Hather first felt relief, then even greater disquiet. The back of the chair would have been towards the dais, preventing Aud seeing anyone who came up through the silently-opened trap-door. So it need not have been Omund; it could just as easily have been Thorgrim Ironfist.

Why Thorgrim? Because he was paid to, the answer came back. But who paid him, Hather Lambisson? Who paid the mercenary to kill the High Queen, and try to kill you as well?

Instinct told him that it had to be Omund. Omund had always wanted him dead, if for no other reason than because he had once shamed Omund by saving the High King's life.

'The . . . trap-door,' Gudrun began hesitantly, pointing towards where it still stood open, 'is that how the killer got in, father?'

'Probably,' Hather replied. 'For now, though, I can't say any more than that. I can't even be certain that Thorgrim killed Aud. And if I'm honest, I can't even be certain that Thorgrim was trying to kill me, or Olaf.'

'But the pit . . . the fingers . . .'

'Merely proof of an attempt to do *something*. That they

were armed is no indication of intent to kill. It's simply an indication of an intent to compel by force. And that's a different thing altogether. Now, I want you two to stay here and wait for the master-builder and my men. When they arrive I want to know from the master-builder whether those tunnels were a part of the original plan for the palace complex. If not, as I suspect, then I want our men to find out where they go, even if they have to dig through a mountain of back-fill down there.'

'And where will you be, father?' Olaf asked.

Hather grinned. 'I shall be talking to the High King. I want to see what he thinks of what I've discovered so far. It can be very informative to watch Omund's face, you know.'

With that he left them and made his way to Omund's quarters. The guards admitted him at once.

Omund was slumped in a chair with a goblet of wine in his hand. His expression was sullen and mournful, intended to express to any who saw it how truly upset he was by his wife's death. He looked up as Hather entered. Hather helped himself to some wine without waiting to be asked. Omund's eyes narrowed, but the High King did not protest.

'Do you have something to tell me, King Hather?' Omund asked him.

'I know how they got into the longhouse,' Hather answered.

Omund's slump disappeared. He sat up and regarded Hather intently. 'How?' he demanded.

'By tunnels,' came the reply.

'Tunnels?' Omund snorted. 'Impossible. There aren't any. I'd know if there were tunnels under here.'

'I'm afraid you're wrong,' Hather answered him. 'There are tunnels. My men are excavating one of them right now.'

'But . . . how did you learn about them?' Omund asked him.

'Oh, quite by accident. Or, rather, by a design which went wrong,' came the reply.

'I'm in no mood for riddles,' Omund said crossly.

'Nor am I. When I returned from the High Queen's burial I found two of my guards dead. In my longhouse there's a pit which I, or my son, or both of us were supposed to fall into. Whether Thorgrim wanted us dead or alive, I can't say . . .'

'Thorgrim?' the High King demanded. 'Thorgrim Ironfist?'

Hather grinned. 'Thorgrim Half-hand now,' he corrected. 'He left two fingers severed upon the floor. That's how I identified him.'

Omund's face clouded. 'But why would Thorgrim want you dead?'

'I don't know that he did,' Hather answered. 'All I know is that he was part of a plot to trap either my son or myself.'

'But why?'

Hather shrugged. 'Apart from the obvious answer, which is that he was paid to, I don't know. Not yet,' he added ominously.

He watched Omund's face as he spoke. The High King appeared obviously troubled. The question Hather continued to ask himself, without reaching a definite conclusion, was whether Omund's perplexity was because of the failure of some scheme, or because he felt threatened by the attack upon one of his vassal kings.

'And where is Thorgrim now?' Omund enquired.

'Fled. He left the palace shortly before we alerted the guards.'

Omund set his glass down with a thump that could well have broken it. 'I'll have the dog hunted down,' he growled. 'I'll bring him back here to answer with the blood-eagle for his crimes.'

'We can't be certain yet exactly what his crimes are,' Hather said blandly.

Omund scowled. 'He tried to kill you. And, from what you say, he murdered my beloved Aud. That's good enough for me!'

'But not for me, King Omund. Still, it's not going to

hurt to have Thorgrim found and brought back here. Will you give the order or shall I?'

'I'll do it, Hather,' Omund replied. 'There's another task I'd like to entrust to you.'

'What is it?'

'I'm expecting a guest. I'd like you to meet that guest for me.'

Hather felt his eyes narrow. Only a royal guest would prompt Omund to send one of his vassal kings out as an embassy of welcome. And it would not be a Swedish guest he was expecting, Hather reasoned. No native-born noble would warrent such a welcome.

'Might I ask who your guest is to be, King Omund?'

'I'm delighted to tell you. Her name is Hanni, and she is the daughter of King Ulf of the Dane-Lands. By now I expect her party will have reached your estates at Sudrafell. I've sent messengers to your wife requesting that Princess Hanni be received there. Would it not be a pleasant duty for you to return home and escort her to Uppsala for me?'

Somehow, Hather thought, this apparently innocent suggestion of Omund's stank like a rotting fish.

'It sounds a worthwhile venture to me, father,' said a voice behind him.

Hather turned, then sprang to his feet. Dressed in heavy furs, smiling from the doorway, extending his hand to clasp wrists and as well and fit as his father had ever seen him, was the King's Marshal, Svipdag Hathersson.

THE SECOND PART

OF DANES AND SORCERY

1

Answers to Some Questions

They greeted one another as if they had been separated for an eternity instead of a few short weeks. They clasped wrists and Svipdag fell into Hather's open arms and embraced his father warmly.

'It's good to see you back,' Hather told him. 'I wondered where you were when you went off like that without a word.'

'I have to obey the High King's orders, father,' came the reply. 'When I'm sent upon an errand for Omund, I go. Would Vermund have done any less?'

Hather masked his scowl as best he could. 'You know Vermund is dead?' he enquired.

Svipdag nodded. 'The men at the gate told me,' he replied. 'I'm so sorry. I loved the old man, you know.'

'As did we all,' Hather answered gently. 'And you know that Aud's dead as well?'

'Yes. That was sad news.'

'I thank you for your words, Svipdag Hathersson,' Omund responded. 'I feel her death very keenly. I believe I shall for some time.'

Hather in turn bowed to the High King. 'Matters of state must take precedence over family affairs,' he began. 'I shall withdraw, with your permission, and leave my son to report to you.'

Svipdag clapped his father upon the shoulder. 'You make it sound like a little boy getting into mischief, father. In reality the one thing I can say is that it was very, very cold. But you know, of course, that I travelled north to Finnmark?'

'The High King has said nothing to me of your mission,' Hather replied, weighing his own words as carefully as he weighed his son's. No, Omund hadn't told him. But old Skeggja had. Hather wondered whether Svipdag had been to talk to the old lappish witch before coming to report to the King.

Dear Odin! he thought. Must I always think like this? Is it my fate even to suspect my own son of treachery? Will I never be able to live at peace even with my own family?

But you have lived at peace with your family, Hather Lambisson, came the unfamiliar and unrecognised prompting of Mother Skuld. That's what you're paying for now. Should you be left in peace though the rest of the world is tormented? Is that truly what you would wish? Of course it isn't. You're too fine a hero for that, Hather Lambisson.

He wanted to shout down the mocking voice inside his head, render it impotent. Instead he simply said: 'With your permission I shall see my son later, sir.'

Then he withdrew.

Oh, he'd meet this Hanni of the Dane-Lands. It wouldn't keep him away from the court for too long. But that night he'd see Svipdag; he'd feast his son's return before he left. And he'd get the answers to some questions that had remained unasked for too long.

All this he thought as he returned to Aud's longhouse, where his men were digging beneath the trap-door. Olaf told him that the master-builder had been and gone, that he had stared down the open trap with such an expression as to assure even the most doubting of watchers that he knew nothing, as Omund had said, of any tunnels beneath the palace compound.

That worried Hather more than anything except the possibility of Svipdag's involvement with sorcery. If the tunnels were new, if they had been craftily and stealthily excavated without anyone above ground noticing, then they could be anywhere. Every step upon apparently solid ground was now fraught with danger. And if a man could not trust the very earth he walked upon, then how could he trust the Norns and gods above him?

There was a subtle torment in all this that made Hather pleased to take his younger son and daughter with him back to Sudrafell. If the tunnels were spread as widely as he believed, then no one was safe any more. And the absence of Thorgrim was no indication of safety, either. He was simply the one they knew about; he had not acted alone.

That night Hather drew upon servants from Svipdag's own household to organise a feast to celebrate his elder son's return to Uppsala. He kept his doubts to himself, shielding both Olaf and Gudrun from them, until most of the food had been eaten and an inordinate quantity of wine appeared to have been consumed by Svipdag and himself. In fact a careful observer might have noticed that the floor about Hather's seat was sodden with wasted drink, though that same observer would have watched the King of Ostragotland drink enough to render a lesser man totally incapable.

'So tell me, son of mine?' Hather began, his speech slurred and his eyes rolling disturbingly out of control. 'What was this mushing . . . missing . . . mushion . . . that Omummmd sent you on, eh?'

Svipdag tapped his nose with a food-grimed finger. 'North,' he said, trying hard not to roll the R too much.

'Norrth, eh? Norrrth. 'S'a good as anywhere. Norrrrth.'

Svipdag nodded sagely, then wished he hadn't. Hather forced a belch.

'Finnnnmarrrk,' Svipdag confided in a hoarse whisper. '*That* farrr norrrth.'

'And what did you have to do there?' Hather enquired, carelessly slipping his guard for a moment in his eagerness.

Svipdag leaned closer. 'Things,' he confided, tapping his nose again. 'Things, at the burrning stonesss.'

The burning stones. Hather had heard those words before. He shook his head, trying to clear it of drink. The burning stones. That meant something to him. If only he could remember what.

'And what did you do at the burrrning stones?' he asked.

Svipdag grinned. 'I saw himmm.'

'Him?'

'The sorcerer. Vult . . . Vultik . . . Vultikamian!'

'Vultikamian?'

'The one Omund sent me norrrth to seee.'

Hather forced a grin. 'Ah, him,' he said aloud.

'Thasss the one.'

'And you saw him?'

Svipdag waved his head in a conspiratorial agreement. 'That I did,' he answered.

'All of him?' Hather asked.

'Not a bit. Only the robes and the hood.'

'But enough?'

Svipdag nodded. 'Enough. And he told me . . . what I wanted to know. He did, you know.'

'I know,' Hather agreed. 'He would. He's like that. What did he say?'

'What Omunnnd . . . wanted him to.'

'Which was?'

'That he'd help to keel . . . to kleep . . . to keep the old fart frrruitfulll.'

'So thass why he wants another wife?'

'Thasssitt. More children. He's worried about what ol' Skeggi said at my feast. He wansss more childersss. More'n he's got nowww. An' that means a younger wiyfeee . . .'

Hather felt the barb of Svipdag's words strike home. So Omund had been seeking a new bride even before Aud's death. How, then, could the High King not be implicated in her murder?

'And this Vulp . . . Vluth . . .'

'Vultikamiannn.'

'This Vultikamian . . . he's a wizard?'

Svipdag unwisely shook his head. The hall began to reel around him. He fought it to a standstill, then said: 'He's *the* wizard. The greatest sorcerer in the whole of Finnmark. Thasss who he is.'

Hather felt his skin grow cold. He'd fought mad kings and *vargrs*. He'd faced dwarfs, both in and out of Trollheim. He'd stood before the Allfather himself. He'd known wizards, yes – old Tisti, his nurse, had been a Lappish witch in her own way – Kulubak Magri, the dwarfish sorcerer who had attempted to conspire with Odin for his own ends at Skroggrmagi, had been more powerful than any of the lesser wizards he'd encountered. But this Vultikamian . . .

Hather didn't like sorcery. He knew enough about it, and what it could do, to leave it strictly alone. Show him an enemy with a sword, or spear, or beard-axe, and he knew how to fight him, how to survive. Yet in the face of sorcery there was little enough that he could do. A strong sword might shear a mortal in two, but that same sword, confronted with magic, might create two enemies where there had only been one before.

And Vultikamian was the greatest wizard in the whole of Finnmark, the most powerful of a race of powerful magicians. In that moment Hather knew that it was Vultikamian who had stood before him, having taken old Vermund's body for the purpose, in the mist. He also knew that it was that same Vultikamian who had spoken to Omund and himself through Skeggja at Svipdag's feast.

So, at last, he knew his enemy. And he was afraid.

Very well, he told himself. Be afraid. Fear has saved your life, and the Yngling line, before now, Hather Lambisson. It may well do so again. So, keep your fear. Hold to it as a drowning man may hold to a spar from the wreckage of his ship. It can be your salvation when even your sword has failed you.

Though is my own salvation really so important? he asked himself. I've lived well enough. I've loved; I've fathered children of my blood to succeed me. Perhaps that voice I heard earlier today was right. Perhaps I've had my happiness, and the time has come now for me to settle the account, with my life if necessary. Very well. I'll do what I have to. Harbard, Odin, Allfather, whatever his name is, will see that I do what's required of me.

'The greatest wizard in the whole of Finnmark to keep Omund's prick straight? And him with delicious young flesh on the way from the Dane-Lands?'

'Thassit.'

So Svipdag knew about Princess Hanni. But had he known before he left for Finnmark?

'Pretty, is she?'

'Ver' pretty.'

'When'd he send for her?'

Svipdag shrugged. 'Some time back.'

Before Aud's death? From his reply, it sounded as if Svipdag *had* known.

Yet it still wasn't proof.

Hather attempted to sort out what he knew. He knew that Omund had invited Hanni of the Dane-Lands to the court at Uppsala. He also knew that Omund had issued the invitation before Aud's death, and with the intention of making Hanni his wife. Such an alliance was dynastically sound because it would achieve for Omund what his plan of conquest, originated for him by the *vargr*, had failed to do. It would link Sweden and the Dane-Lands and ultimately provide Omund with an enlarged empire which could virtually control the north.

Hather also knew that Omund was worried about his potency, as any man of fifty-odd who had not fathered a child for more than ten years would be. Yet to seek the help of a wizard, and not just any wizard, but the most powerful of an entire race of sorcerers, to ensure his potency, struck Hather as rather excessive, especially as he was now sure that he'd seen Vultikamian's power for himself, and was mortally afraid of it.

The most important question had yet to be asked. He needed to know to what extent Svipdag was either a dupe of Omund's or a willing participant in the High King's schemes, and he had to know for certain to what extent his son, though a man of over thirty, was a tool of the sorcerer Vultikamian.

He clapped Svipdag upon the shoulder. Svipdag grinned broadly.

'Who controls our destinies?' Hather asked, under cover of the wine he appeared to have consumed.

Then Svipdag offered an answer which sent chill shivers down his father's spine.

'Why, Vultikamian does,' he answered, smiling.

2

Hanni of the Dane-Lands

Svipdag's answer was still ringing in Hather's ears as he rode, with Olaf and Gudrun and the sad remnants of his retinue, for Sudrafell the following morning.

Despite their labours the guards had been unable to dig back through the tunnels to find their source. It was as if the cavities had been filled in with more than human skill, baffling their efforts and maintaining the secret of the underground corridors intact.

Hather could have ordered them to continue indefinately, of course. Yet it would have been a waste of time to do so, and he knew that such would be the case. Whoever and whatever had filled in the tunnels was too careful, too crafty, to betray their origin.

The game was set, and Hather knew himself to be simply a gaming-piece upon the board which the gods and the Norns and possibly Vultikamian as well, had set up. All that he did, he might believe to be of his own free will. Yet it would not be so. He would move in a fashion as pre-determined as that of any piece the *tafl*-player chose and moved upon the eleven square board.

And so it was that Hather Lambisson, accompanied by his daughter and younger son, rode back to Sudrafell at Omund's request to greet Hanni of the Dane-Lands, the woman Omund had decided should be the new High Queen of Sweden. He rode with a heavy heart, fearful of what treachery, what threat to his son Svipdag, might remain behind him at Uppsala.

It was the better part of a week's hard ride from

Omund's capital to Sudrafell, and Hather was riding his company hard. The sooner they arrived the sooner they could start back towards Uppsala. There was always at the back of Hather's mind the memory of what had happened the last time Omund had persuaded him to undertake a mission, simply to get him out of the way while the High King pursued his own schemes. That time Omund had been allied with a *vargr*. This time he had leagued himself with a sorcerer, and one more powerful than the north had ever seen.

As they rode down out of the hills towards Sudrafell Hather felt immediate relief at the sight of his distant domain, intact, standing proud and prosperous and peaceful upon the Baltic coast. He sent messengers ahead, and they in turn were met by others riding out from the city. Lurs began to sound distantly and crowds gathered in the streets to see their king return. They rode on towards the open gates of the palace, smiling and waving, accepting greetings from the people, yet Hather's dark suspicions made him want to hurry his horse towards the sanctuary of his home.

Once through the gates they dismounted. Servants came running to take their horses and Hather and Olaf, slapping the dust from their clothing as they went, strode towards the main audience hall.

Inside, Saeunna was waiting with a gathering of Hather's stewards and captains. Preparations for a welcoming feast were going on about them, and servant-girls were tending the roasting carcasses on spits above the long fire at the centre of the hall. It smelled warm and comforting to the travel-weary king, but the most welcoming thing of all was his wife, waiting with open arms to embrace her husband and her son.

The greetings over, the partition-door at the back of the hall opened, admitting a slender figure surrounded by maids and armed attendants. Olaf's eyes widened and he could hardly close his mouth sufficiently to form a welcoming smile. His surprise was understandable, Hather thought to himself, for Hanni of the Dane-Lands was one of the loveliest young women he had ever seen.

Her long, plaited hair, was the white-gold of afternoon snow. Her figure, beneath a dress of embroidered Byzantine silk, held the promise of a real woman, a promise emphasised by the slight swing of her hips as she walked. Her hands were small, her bare arms bright with bracelets, her graceful neck adorned with a heavy necklace of glittering gold and carnelian. Her face was pretty, with a small nose and full lips, and her eyes were dove-grey with long, fair lashes and mingled invitation with innocence.

'Welcome to Sudrafell, Princess Hanni,' Hather began, stepping towards her. The attendants parted and Hather took Hanni's long, slender fingers in his grasp, bending to kiss them. 'You are welcome in my home, Princess,' Hather told her. 'May I present my younger son, Olaf.'

Olaf bowed, a shade awkwardly he thought. Hanni smiled. Their eyes met and began to explore one another's depths. Clearly Olaf shared his father's opinion that the Danish princess was a very pretty girl indeed.

'And now,' Hather continued, 'if you will excuse us, Princess, we are dirty after our journey. We shall meet again this evening, when we dine.'

He bowed. Reluctantly Olaf did the same. Saeunna slipped her arm through Hather's and sniffed at his travel-stained clothing. 'Come along, King Hather,' she whispered. 'I'll wash your back for you.'

Servants prepared a steaming tub, then left Saeunna to help the rapidly-stiffening Hather out of his dust-caked clothes. 'You know, my love,' he groaned, alone with his wife in the privacy of their quarters, pressing his hands to the nagging pain in the small of his back, 'I'm getting older.'

She helped him into the bath and began to scrub his shoulders with lye soap. 'You've thickened a little around the middle,' she replied. 'And there are a few more scars than when we met – in there as well,' she added, lightly tapping the side of his head. 'And you certainly don't bathe as often,' she chided. 'But you're still Hather of

Sudrafell, King of Ostragotland, and I still have to share your love with the people you rule. I just hope we will have many more years together.'

He took her wrist in his hand to stop her scrubbing and stared up into her worried green eyes. 'What is it, Saeunna?' he asked her. 'Why are you talking like this?'

She stroked his forehead, pushing the caked strands of yellow-grey hair aside. 'I've started to dream again,' she answered simply.

Hather released her wrist. He knew better than to dismiss Saeunna's dreams as bad digestion or feeble-mindedness. They had helped and warned him before, sometimes even carrying messages from Odin to help him in times of peril, and Hather knew that he would need such help again, especially now.

'Will you tell me about it?' he asked.

'Later,' she answered. 'For now, let's get you clean and back to your guests. From the look our son gave Hanni I think he'll be out there ahead of you. Oh, and there's one more thing.'

'What's that?'

Lathering his hair, Saeunna dropped the soap into the bath and left Hather sitting there with suds in his eyes. Whilst he struggled to wash them clear she crossed to the door, opened it, and handed a pail of fresh water to the man who now stepped into the room, grinning and showing slightly-discoloured teeth in a dark, tanned face. Grey eyes glinted mischievously and, for a large man of well over sixty, he used remarkable stealth in approaching the temporarily-blinded Hather.

With a slow, deliberate movement the newcomer raised the pail and slowly poured the icy water over Hather's head, ignoring the howls of outrage which issued from the tub. Hather shook the water from his eyes and raised himself in a defensive crouch as he began to focus on the battered Lappish coat of whalebone plates between layers of leather that the newcomer wore.

Then he saw the face. The laugh-lines around the nose and mouth had deepened, but the eyes were still clear and the nose still jutted like an eagle's neb. A deep scar ran down beside the right eye, pulling slightly at the outer corner. The features were framed with white hair and a white beard, though the Dane wore no moustache.

Atyl Skin threw the pail away and extended his hand. 'Greetings, Hather of Ostragotland,' he grinned.

Hather stood up and they clasped wrists. As he stepped out of the tub he twisted violently to the side, catching Atyl Skin off balance and hurling him, with an almighty splash, into the water. As the Dane spluttered in outrage it was Hather's turn to laugh.

'Greetings, Atyl Skin,' Hather smiled down at him. 'You did want a bath, didn't you?'

'Of course I did,' came the reply. 'Thor knows I've come far enough to take one, you old rogue.'

They dried off, Saeunna staying out of the way in case the two old friends decided that she needed a bath as well. Hather supplied the Dane with fresh clothing from his own wardrobe and that night, at the feast, they sat together drinking and reliving memories of the good and bad old days. Together they had fought the *vargr* and foiled Omund's scheme to conquer the Dane-Lands. Together they had found a way to permit the scheming monarch to maintain his position whilst effectively losing his power. Since then they had met only seldom, but each had saved the other's life and the bond of friendship between them was deeper than Hather could recall with any man still living.

Saeunna sat with Olaf and Hanni, deeming it wisest to keep an eye on the attraction they were obviously beginning to feel for one another. From her behaviour and conversation Saeunna found her an accomplished and surprisingly well-educated young lady. Her father, Ulf of the Dane-Lands, had entertained Christian missionaries at the court at Jelling, and Hanni knew more than a smattering of that mysterious script they called the monkalpha, the Latin alphabet. Hanni's birth, education and beauty combined to make her a magnificent catch for any man, and the little Hather had said regarding his suspicions of Omund's intentions caused Saeunna grave misgiving. Hanni was young enough to be broken by the wrong man, and Omund could only be described as the wrong man.

Later, when the old memories had been relived, when the guests were in their quarters and Hather and Saeunna had retired to the privacy of their bed-closet, Saeunna told her husband about her dreams.

'I saw images, one after another,' she began, trying to explain.

Hather held her in his arms, her face against his chest. 'What did you see?' he asked her.

'Oh, grim things. Dreadful things. I saw a tiny child upon a rough stone altar, and something towering over it to take its life. I saw a trail of Yngling dead, Omund's children and their children, stretched out upon the blood-stained snow. I saw your Svipdag, with his hand raised against you . . .'

She fell silent, but Hather knew her too well. 'You saw something else, Saeunna, didn't you?'

She shook her head, a little too quickly, Hather thought. Then he felt the salt rain of her tears upon his chest.

'You must tell me, my love,' he urged. 'I know you don't want to, so I suppose it bodes no good for us. We've had a good run, though, you and I. We've had our time of peace, our time to love and be loved. Sooner or later everything must come to an end. You know what they say: the only certain thing in life is its ending. Is that what you saw, Saeunna? Our ending?'

She raised her tear-misted eyes to look at him. He was so strong, so fine. He'd do whatever he had to, whatever Allfather might ask of him, to preserve the Yngling dynasty, though Saeunna wondered exactly what there was about the Ynglings which made those demented, weak, treacherous kings so worthy of preservation.

'I saw . . . your ending, Hather,' she told him, reluctantly.

He forced a smile. 'I hope I made a good end,' he whispered.

'It was a fighting end,' she said.

'And who was I fighting?' Hather asked. 'Was it this sorcerer, this Vultikamian Svipdag travelled north to see for Omund?'

'No,' Saeunna sighed. 'I saw nothing of him.'

'Then who was it? Can you tell me?'

She brushed the tears from her eyes. Then she said: 'You were fighting an old enemy upon the surface of a frozen lake . . .'

'That's a hard thing to do without bruising your arse.'

'You were both on skates. Oh, you might have been dancing in some dreadful dance of death, Hather. I suppose you were. The vision wasn't very clear, but I saw you both, I watched you both. And . . . I saw him thrust his sword into you . . . through you, my love . . .'

'You've not yet told me who I was fighting, Saeunna. If there's a chance of proving you wrong, I have to know that.'

She nodded, gazing at him through sad, loving eyes.

'You were fighting Omund,' she told him simply.

3

The Contents of Another Mound

While Hather was resting after his return to Sudrafell, his elder son had assumed his father's responsibility for finding the killer of Queen Aud. Svipdag had questioned Hather for some time regarding the tunnels and Thorgrim Ironfist, and no doubt remained in his mind concerning the missing mercenary's guilt.

Although nearly twenty years younger than Hather, Svipdag knew a great deal about both court life and the treacherous politics of the times. He reasoned that, whilst Thorgrim might well be the actual killer, he also required some kind of motive. If that motive was the usual one for a mercenary a further question must be asked: Who was paying him?

That Omund was contemplating remarriage, and had been considering the possibility even before Aud's death, was evident from Hanni's visit to Sweden. But surely it was inconceivable that he would have given the order for Aud's death himself. Omund and Aud had been married for nearly thirty years. She had given him three fine sons to continue the Yngling line . . .

Svipdag began to wonder, as he stared down through the trap in the dais at the partly-excavated tunnel beneath his feet, about the prophecy which had been spoken at the feast. At the time he had taken symbolically the pronouncement that Omund would outlive his progeny, believing it to be merely a way of foretelling of great fame to come for the High King, destined to be the longest-lived of all the Ynglings. Yet since that time he had travelled north into the wastes of Finnmark, to the circle of the burning stones where Vultikamian held a very different kind of court. Whilst the sorcerer had worked no magic to impress his visitor, regarding even the King's Marshal as unworthy of the kind of wizardry he had shown to Mother Skuld, his very appearance, not to mention the burning stones themselves, was enough to make Svipdag aware that he stood between two worlds, in some shadowed middle ground between the realms of man and those of the gods and the Norns.

Only after his interview with the strange, gaunt, robed figure, its face and limbs concealed by shapeless coverings of dirty white, only after he had learned to shudder at the insidious evil in that whispering voice, did he realise that his mission, as explained to him by Omund and Skeggja, was in many ways ridiculous.

Go north, Svipdag Hathersson, Omund had said. Find the legendary sorcerer Vultikamian. Ask of him how I may ensure the potency of this aging flesh to preserve my royal line.

He took the order apart, word by word.

Well, he had gone north. He had found the legendary Vultikamian. But why should Omund call him legendary? In all the time Svipdag had spent with old Skeggi learning some lesser magics, in all the hours he had sat before her, man and boy, listening to her tales of other lands and other gods, he had never once heard mention of Vultikamian by name.

True, he reflected, his colour-changed eyes glittering at the thought, he now had reason to connect Vultikamian with the one whom the old witch described as her master, but was Omund to know that? And the so-called preservation of the royal line: why was Omund suddenly so worried about that? He had been told that the dynasty would end with him, that he was to be the last and greatest and longest-lived of all the Ynglings, so why should he require advice about his potency? It had never been called into doubt before, not with three fine sons and . . . how many grandchildren?

No, something told the King's Marshal that his errand had been for some other reason than the one given to him. Yet what its purpose was remained a mystery, and how it was to fit in with his own ambitions was completely beyond him.

For Svipdag Hathersson had ambitions. Sooner or later, he believed, the High King would lose what little respect the people still retained for him. When that time came, and old Skeggi had already promised Svipdag that it would, the King's Marshal, the man who commanded the forces of the kingdom, would command the kingdom itself.

He sighed and turned away from the tunnel. Doubtless the old witch and her master had their reasons for this mysterious alliance with Omund, for all that Svipdag couldn't find the head or the tail of this particular fish.

Svipdag turned to the captain behind him. 'Have your men continue where my father's left off,' he ordered. 'I want to know where that tunnel came from. Do you understand? I don't care how long it takes, but I need to know. Draw whatever tools and timber for shoring you need from the palace stores. And lamps. I want the work to continue day and night.'

As the captain saluted, Svipdag, his dark hair flying out behind him, strode out of the High Queen's quarters.

As he walked across the palace compound, drawing his hood over his head against the unseasonably-biting wind, Svipdag smiled bitterly to himself. He knew that when at last he became High King despite the public prophecy made to Omund, or possibly even because of it, he would not be either loved or trusted. That was why he had become King's Marshal. No, the people would never love or trust any man whose mother had become *vargr*. That was one of the reasons that they stared at him so. The other was the knowledge that here was a man who had vanished for two days into the magic and sorcery-laden wastes of the north. He had left his men with blue eyes, his father's eyes. Upon his return, though, their colour had changed to the deep, purplish-brown of nightshade berries. A man's eyes didn't do that, not the eyes of a normal man.

And so they watched him, seeking reasons, explanations, which neither he nor they could find. No one, not even his famous father, could say with certainty why the lovely Astrid had become so twisted as to seek revenge upon even her husband and child for the slaying of her father by mad king Oli the Great. Svipdag had long since come to realise that. It was now simply part of him, something to be accepted rather than questioned.

The other thing, though, those missing two days, was an even greater puzzle. Time and again he tried to remember what had happened, always to be defeated by a total absence of memory. Occasionally he wondered if he had caught a glimpse, through confusing, snow-white mist, of a Lappish yurt surrounded by standing totems. Sometimes an ancient, seamed, stubble-crusted face with dying eyes had appeared to gaze into his own. But he could not be certain. Whatever he thought he remembered, there was always a curtain of doubt which he could not draw or tear aside.

He stood alone, whipped by the wind. At that moment, as at so many moments in his life, Svipdag Hathersson felt terribly alone. His wife, now heavy with a third child, and two sons, were at his estate, a day's ride to the north. While he knew most of the court he had few friends there, either his position or his history having precluded easy friendships. He'd struggled for so long to be his own man, instead of simply the son of a famous father, that he had even come to prefer his own company most of the time.

A human voice, a kindly face, a hand clasped in friendship or offering a cup of wine, was all that he needed at that moment. For that moment not even the schemes or the answers, or the sorcery which would speed him to his ends, mattered even slightly.

The wind bit at his eyes, making them water. He brushed the tears away on the back of his glove, then he felt the first lash of slanting rain shaft down upon his face.

The skies had long been threatening a storm, and now at last it was beginning to break.

The guard came running up behind him, halted and saluted. The man was dressed in the uniform of the High King's personal guard, tall and strong, but his eyes showed traces of fear before the King's Marshal's scrutiny.

'You have something to tell me?' Svipdag demanded wearily.

'The High King is asking for you, sir,' came the reply. 'Will you come with me?'

Svipdag sighed. He wanted to rest in his wife's arms, to lay his head upon her swelling belly and listen for the sounds of the new life growing within. He didn't want to be bothered with Omund and his whims and fantasies, not just then. But he nodded, and followed, and his mood began to change when he realised that the soldier was taking him, not to Omund's quarters, but to those of his eldest son, Egil Omundsson. As they approached he saw that Omund's guards were pushing back a crowd which had gathered in and around the vestibule.

The soldiers cleared a path for him and he strode through and into the main hall. The scene which met him must have been very similar, he thought, to that which had greeted his father upon entering Aud's quarters.

Except that there were more bodies.

Guards stood about the hall, their weapons drawn, their faces ashen. Omund stood amongst them, shaking, his face livid with grief and fury, his hands clenching and unclenching impotently at his sides.

Egil Omundsson sat upon his high seat, slumped amidst the slimy, reddened tangle of his own entrails, a look of surprised horror frozen onto his stiffening features. Beside him, the remains of his wife and two of their three children stared sightlessly up from a widening pool of blood, their bodies mutilated almost beyond recognition. A little way away, spreadeagled upon the rush floor, the grey-pink smear of his brains upon the nearby wall, the

High King's eldest grandson had entered Valhalla after only nine years of childhood.

Svipdag was stunned by the grisly horror of the scene, and when Omund came up to him, thrusting his contorted face almost into Svipdag's, it took a moment for him to hear what he was saying.

'Find them, Svipdag,' the High King hissed. 'Find them and bring them to me.' His voice began to rise, flecks of spittle from his fury dashing into Svipdag's face. 'Find them all, no matter how many men or how much money it takes. I want them here. I want them to suffer everything that I have suffered at their hands. But slowly. Oh, so slowly, Svipdag. They thought my father was a master of the blood-eagle, but they were wrong. The skalds shall sing of my vengeance. They shall sing of me as Omund Blood-Letter! So find them!'

Svipdag nodded. 'I'm truly sorry . . .' he began, but Omund interrupted.

'Don't be sorry! There's time for that later. Find the butcher who gutted my son!'

For the first time since his installation as King's Marshal, Svipdag came to attention before the High King. Then he stepped back, beckoned to the guards, and began to give orders.

'You there, arrange for the bodies to be taken away. You, have the palace sealed. You, assemble the court. I want to see everyone. Everyone! And you, start searching for the tunnels. Even if you have to dig up the whole place I want a tunnel found in here.

'I want the entire guard turned out,' he continued. 'Every man is to examine the man next to him for blood on his weapons or clothes. Anyone who has it will be suspect, and will be confined. The same goes for the court. This blood has only just been shed. Anyone found washing clothing or person is also suspect. *Anyone*: maids, slaves, washerwomen, all of them. Company commanders are to report to me personally. Is that quite clear?'

The men hurried off about their assignments. Svipdag

turned to the High King. 'You shall have them, sir,' he asssured him.

Omund lowered his head, shaking it sadly. The tears still ran from his eyes and dropped from the point of his nose. 'I don't understand it,' he whispered. 'First . . . Aud. And now . . .'

His voice broke with a sob. Svipdag clasped his wrist firmly and led him over to a bench; together they sat down. A grim-faced servant handed them goblets of strong wine. Omund simply held his in both hands. Svipdag drained his, then held it out for more.

Svipdag felt his thoughts returning to the prophecy old Skeggi had spoken, or which the sorcerer Vultikamian had spoken through her. Well, Omund had certainly outlived his eldest son and his family. The question now was whether his other sons were safe.

Or even guilty?

It wouldn't be the first time that an Yngling prince had murdered his way to the throne. Possibly one of them was attempting to use the prophecy as a cover for some grim design of his own. The important thing, he decided, was Omund's safety. If the second son, Harek, was responsible, then the High King would be next to die. His younger brother Flosi could be dealt with once Harek had the throne. Yet if Flosi was the killer, Harek would be next, clearing Flosi's path once Omund was out of the way. Either way, it was Omund who required protecting, at least until the culprits were found.

Svipdag drained his wine and set the goblet down on the bench. A third possible solution to the mystery had just occurred to him, but one which he immediately dismissed. Omund's grief was too deep, too real, for the High King himself to be using the prophecy to his own ends. It was quite unthinkable for Omund to have organised the murders of his wife and son.

The High King's body servants came to lead him back to his own apartments. Svipdag stayed in Egil Omundsson's blood-spattered hall, watching as the guards cleared away the rushes and began a careful examination of the packed-earth floor.

Would the killers, who must have known that their tunnels had been discovered, have used another one here, Svipdag asked himself? Possibly. It was a certain way of entering the hall unobserved, and no one had suspected at the time that Egil and his family would be next. Well, at least he could make certain that there were no tunnels under Harek's or Flosi's quarters. Or under Omund's. And he'd have them all well-guarded.

The search of the main floor completed, the men turned their attention to the raised wooden dais, dismantling it to search for concealed trap-doors. They found nothing.

Svipdag then ordered trestles set up in the main hall on which to lay the bodies. Somewhere, he knew, there was a tunnel, and he intended to find it, even if it meant taking the whole longhouse apart.

He left his post only when he was told that the court had been assembled under guard. Before going to the audience-hall, he checked with the commanders regarding their own men and was told that they had failed to find any with blood-stained clothing or weapons. He ordered that the entire palace be searched, then made his way to the audience-hall to supervise the examination of the waiting courtiers. This was almost completed, as was the search of the guest-quarters, when a messenger arrived from Egil's longhouse and whispered to him.

Svipdag's dark eyes grew bright. Delegating the last stage of the fruitless examination he returned to the scene of the carnage and passed through the partition-door to the bed-closets beyond. Here, in the floor of Egil Omundsson's own bed-closet, gaped the entrance to a tunnel. Men were already working inside it, excavating the back-filled pit.

Svipdag settled down to wait. The search for other tunnels in the palace compound was already under way, and before long reports reached him that three more had been found, and that not one of them had yet been filled in.

One was under Harek's longhouse, coming up beneath the dais. One was in Flosi's, in the children's bed-closet. The third, however, was in the High King's own quarters, and it penetrated the floor of the main hall close by the piled stone surround of the long fire at its centre, where anyone in the hall would be certain to notice it.

Whilst the reports were welcome, they did little to enlighten him as to the identity of the killers.

Instead of solving the mystery, Svipdag felt himself confronted by a further one. Egil's, Harek's and Flosi's tunnels all had entrances which were perfectly concealed, as had Aud's. Omund's had not. And the only reason that anyone had found the tunnels in the first place was the abortive attempt to kill or capture Hather, for which no reason had yet been found. Doubtless, Svipdag reasoned, if the attempt had been successful the tunnel would have been concealed and no one would ever have suspected its existence.

Svipdag went to Flosi's longhouse and, with guards before and behind bearing lights and weapons, lowered himself into the tunnel. The weapons, he soon realised, would be next to useless if needed, for the tunnel was so low that he and his men were forced to crawl on hands and knees.

They made their slow way along to a fork in the tunnel, where Svipdag ordered one of the men to go back and send parties down the other two tunnels to link up with them. Meanwhile he waited in the confined space, in the flickering, smoky light of the lamps, rapidly growing stiffer. After what seemed an eternity the front man challenged an approaching light, to learn that it had come from Harek's longhouse. A little later this second party discovered a third behind it. Svipdag questioned the men as best he could, learning that the third party had originally been six in number, but that two divisions in the underground network had been discovered, and two men detailed off along each one. A third division had obviously led back to Harek's longhouse, so they had not pursued it, and there was evidence of a fourth which had been filled in.

They returned to the surface and assembled again in Egil's longhouse. From the information the men gave, Svipdag drew a map of the tunnel system with the point of his sword on the earthen floor. Two of the men had still not returned when he had sent for a scribe to copy the diagram on to parchment.

'Should we search for them?' a captain asked.

Svipdag shook his head. 'We'll wait a little longer.'

The size of the tunnels was beginning to worry him. They had been carefully constructed and, whilst they might fork and divide along their lengths, had been meticulously planned with no false starts or twists. Whoever had dug them had taken time and care, and had worked slowly and silently to avoid alerting those above ground. But why make them so small? It made them difficult to use which, as their purpose was to provide cover for some murderous subterfuge, was ridiculous. If the tunnels had been larger perhaps Thorgrim Ironfist would have saved his fingers. Obviously the builders had had time in plenty, otherwise less care would have been taken.

So, why make them so small?

The two missing men returned, saluting formally as they stood before the King's Marshal.

'We've had a fair distance to come, sir,' one of them explained. 'It's a long tunnel. It comes out beyond the palace, in a hut on the very edge of the city.'

'Whose hut?' Svipdag demanded.

'Nobody seems to know, sir. We asked about but nobody could tell us. They did say that the place has an evil reputation, though, that strange people go in and never seem to come out, or come out when they've not been seen to go in. I expect that's because they go into the tunnels.'

'Strange people? What kind of strange people?'

'That's just it. They don't know. All they really see are shapes after dark. Some think they're some kind of ghost, sort of small and humpish, with eyes that look odd in the torchlight.'

Svipdag's mouth tightened. 'Very well,' he muttered. 'You're dismissed. All of you.'

So one more question had arisen to beg an answer. Why had Thorgrim Ironfist, with an underground escape route which would have taken him clear of the palace, chosen to ride out through the gates?

The so-called ghosts worried him as well. Somehow, that description of small, humped shapes with unnatural eyes, shapes that could move swiftly along tunnels too small for normal men, was beginning to sound familiar.

And then Svipdag Hathersson knew, and the blood in his veins turned to frozen winter river-water. Of course the description sounded familiar. In the moments of his greatest fear, in the darkness of the death-laden night, as a ten-year-old boy waiting to die at the hand of his *vargr* mother, *he had seen them*.

They were not ghosts. Now hardly ever glimpsed by men and almost forgotten, banished into the misted realms of myth, the dwarfs had once been mighty upon the earth, knowing skills of metalworking and building which men had still to learn. And what skills they had been. Why, they had even created that terrible masterpiece, the towering citadel which, bridge-like, had spanned the gorge beneath the frozen waterfall at Skroggrmagi.

4

The Tunnels of Trollheim

The day following Hather's return to Sudrafell was spent in preparation for the return to Uppsala. Whilst Saeunna's dream had done little to reassure him of the successful outcome to his mission, it had at least served to alert Hather to the possible perils which lay ahead. Also he took heart from the presence of the ageing, but still robust and active, Atyl Skin.

Saeunna chose also to return to Omund's capital and rode with the party. Olaf, by this time, had appointed himself Hanni's personal guardian and companion, a role to which neither Hanni nor Atyl Skin, who travelled as her advisor, appeared to have any objection.

The journey from Sudrafell to Uppsala was one that Hather had made many times. He had come this way, some forty years before, as a mere youth bearing an accursed sword, to avenge the death of his grandfather. On the Uppsala side of the mountains, at the meeting of two streams, he and Starkadder had met and fought. Starkadder had shown him the fearsome power of the sword Tyrfing, and together they had travelled to the gates of Trollheim which Harbard had opened for them, to a meeting with the dwarf-king Dvalin in his castle at the centre of the burning lake.

A great deal had happened since then, Hather reflected. Dvalin was dead, turned to stone upon his high tower. His successor Alvis was also dead, buried in the rubble of Skroggrmagi. Since then he had known little of affairs amongst the dwarfs, who appeared to have sealed

Trollheim against contact with ordinary humans. He suspected, though, that without a ruler the dwarfish kingdom had degenerated into petty squabbles.

The sword Tyrfing, the symbol of dwarfish sovereignty, had vanished from the realms of man, taken by Starkadder whom Odin had released from Valhalla to retrieve it. Hather knew that he would never again see either that vicious blade or the old warrior who had become a father to him this side of the grave.

He smiled wryly to himself. If Saeunna was right, if even the stiffening in his joints and bones was right, it wouldn't be so long to wait for that reunion.

They rode on, Saeunna's smile brightening her husband's journey, helping to lift the grim dread which clawed at both their hearts.

A little over a day's ride from Uppsala, a rider was sent across the plain to alert Omund to arrange an appropriate welcome for his royal guest. That Atyl Skin's presence in the party would be a cause of aggravation to Omund Hather didn't doubt for a moment. Atyl had played too great a part in defeating the High King's plans. Yet that had all been well over twenty years ago, and Omund had a new pleasure in store, the Princess Hanni, which would more than compensate for his scratch at an old wound.

Hather sighed to himself as they set off to cross the plain. Life had been so good, so peaceful, in the intervening years. Whatever bargain Odin and Mother Skuld had struck to give him that peace, and the chance to see his family grow up in safety at Sudrafell, had been a good one. That it had now expired he felt certain. The old apprehensions had stolen back with the stealth of an approaching winter. Though he could not say how, he *knew* that some dreadful conflict lay ahead, and Saeunna's dream, of his body struck through with Omund's sword, did nothing to quiet his fears.

As befitted a true worshipper of the warrior god Odin, the Allfather, Hather felt no fear of death. For him it would be a reunion with so many old friends who had gone ahead: Thorvald Brotamad, killed at the crossing of the Dalalven; Horsetail and Leif Half-Foot, killed at Skroggrmagi; dear old Vermund Bjarnisson; and his father Lambi Nef. And with Starkadder, that grim, accursed warrior who had turned an untried boy into a champion. They would all be waiting for him, keeping his seat close by their own in Odin's hall. But he couldn't die yet. He had to survive a little while longer, see the Yngling dynasty safe for as long as Odin needed it. He knew now that such was his part in the game that the gods and Norns played with his life, and with the precious lives of those he loved.

And then Hanni disappeared into the earth.

Without a cry, without any sound other than the crashing of horse and rider, Hanni of the Dane-Lands plunged through the pit which had opened beneath her and vanished.

Olaf shouted frantically and flung himself off his horse. The column behind them halted and men began to swarm about the opening in the earth. Hather turned his mount and galloped back, eyes blazing, his sword drawn in his hand. He leapt from his horse and pushed his way to the pit. It was black, silent and empty. Atyl Skin was leaning head first into the darkness, calling down: 'Hanni! Princess! Can you hear me?'

No answer came back.

'Get your mother to Uppsala,' Hather ordered Olaf. 'Take an escort with you. Tell Omund what's happened. The rest of you, start searching for concealed openings.'

'And yourself?' Atyl Skin asked him.

'I'm going down to see what's happened. Alone,' Hather added firmly.

Atyl Skin smiled slightly. 'You're the leader,' he replied.

Hather lowered himself into the opening and dropped, legs bent to lessen the impact of his landing, to the earthen floor. Gaining his feet he stumbled against the carcass of Hanni's mount. As his eyes grew accustomed to the dim light he saw a gaping wound where the animal had been pole-axed.

'Hanni!' he called. 'Hanni, where are you?'

Still no answer. Ahead of him stretched a tunnel, somewhat larger than the ones he had discovered at Uppsala. Behind him there was only a wall of earth and stones which showed no signs of being a back-fill. With his sword at the ready, his eyes straining at the darkness, Hather clambered over the dead horse and began a wary progress down the tunnel. In the distance, far enough away to seem a mere pinprick of light, appeared the yellow flaming of a torch.

The tunnel was undoubtedly of dwarfish construction. Certainly it was better made than any similar work of man would have been. But dwarfs didn't need torchlight to see by. His heart hammering, Hather approached the light, until he came to a large chamber hollowed from the earth, a chamber where several tunnels appeared to meet.

Hanni, milk-pale and shaking, stood in the middle of the chamber, alone.

Hather felt the ground give very slightly beneath his feet as he entered the chamber and ran to the frightened princess.

'Hanni, are you all right?' he asked, his eyes darting about the deep black entrances to the other tunnels.

'She is for now, King Hather,' said a deep voice behind him.

Hather turned, sword ready for combat, to see a tall figure standing at the entrance of the tunnel he had just left. Behind, a rabble of dwarfs came scrambling up through the trap-door his feet had almost pushed through, and gathered at the entrances to the other tunnels.

'Who are you?' Hather demanded.

In reply the tall figure stepped forward into the torchlight, holding up a bandaged right hand. 'Someone you owe some fingers to,' came Thorgrim Ironfist's reply.

'Working for dwarfs? Are you that short of money, mercenary?'

'Not working *for* dwarfs, Hather Lambisson,' came a whispering voice from somewhere below his right shoulder. 'Our friend Thorgrim is working *with* us.'

Hather lowered his gaze to discern a small, amber-eyed figure with earth-stained robes. 'And who might you be?' he growled.

'I am the one who has you prisoner, King Hather. I too am a king, or I shall be very shortly. My name is Bombor, and I am the legitimate successor to King Alvis. That is why you and this pretty princess are here, my friend, to assist my claim.'

'I have no part in dwarfish politics, Bombor.'

'Oh, but you do, Hather, you do. And you may as well put up your sword,' Bombor added. 'It would be foolish in the extreme to attempt to fight your way out of here.'

Bombor had seamed, sparse features, clean-shaven and sharp-nosed. His mouth was cruel, his smile unpleasant. It was a smile Hather had seen before, when Dvalin promised to remove the curse on Tyrfing.

Yes, he thought, this creature's claim to the throne could well be legitimate. There's enough of Dvalin in his features to make it so. With a shrug he sheathed his sword. A handful of soil fell onto his face from the roof, and he looked up to where beams had been set across it to support the earth above.

Thorgrim, dark-bearded and hate-eyed, followed Hather's gaze. 'There's someone moving about up there,' he growled, his wickedly-sharp beard-axe held in his good hand.

'Keep your voice down,' Bombor hissed. 'And now, Hather, you and this pretty lady will come with us.'

Hather stood his ground, stalling for time, hoping for a chance to thwart whatever this unholy alliance of dwarf and human was plotting. 'You haven't told us why you have taken such trouble to make us your prisoners,' he began. 'We won't move from here unless you do.'

'If you don't move we'll gut you,' Thorgrim snarled. 'And you know how fond dwarfs are of our women, so you can guess what'll happen to this one,' he added, gesturing with the axe towards the terrified Hanni.

Hather knew. Dwarf-women were hideously ugly, even to the dwarfs themselves. Human women falling into dwarfish clutches would be unlucky to survive the services which their captors required of them. The fortunate ones went mad within the first few hours. Yet he met bluff with bluff: 'If you wanted us dead you'd not have gone to this trouble to capture us alive,' he growled.

Bombor grinned disturbingly. 'You seem very certain of that. But then again,' he sighed, 'you have had dealings with my subjects before, so I cannot expect to fool you easily.

'Very well, Hather. You are here because you are Champion of the Ynglings. This is more than simply a courtesy title, as even the briefest examination of your life would show. You are, for some strange reason, beloved of Odin.'

Another handful of earth fell. Hather showed no sign of noticing it. 'And you want to strike an alliance with Odin, using me to force the Allfather to agree?' he demanded mockingly.

'That is correct.'

'And Princess Hanni? You can't want her for anything now you have me. Let her go, Bombor.'

'I regret that would be impossible,' came the reply. 'This lovely young lady is required for a, shall we say, secondary stratagem?'

'My men will be down here after me in a moment,' Hather warned the dwarf.

Thorgrim began to chuckle. 'Not with the amount of backfilling that's been going on behind me,' he laughed unpleasantly. 'You're on your own, finger-thief. And when Bombor's finished with you, you're mine!'

The timbers of the chamber-roof began to creak. Suddenly earth was falling like a shower of rain. A shaft of sunlight struck the earthern floor at Hather's feet.

'The light!' Bombor screamed. 'The light! Into the tunnels, quickly!'

As the opening above grew wider, the dwarfs scurried into the dark shelter of their tunnels. One attempted to grab Hanni but Hather tore him loose and thrust him into the sunlight. With a cracked howl the creature stiffened as the first terrible hardening of his flesh began. Thorgrim screamed with rage and lifted the beard-axe to strike, but Hather dodged the blow and drew his sword, thrusting past the mercenary's guard as Olaf and Atyl Skin leaped down through the opening in the roof. Thorgrim staggered to a halt and the axe slipped from his grasp. For a moment he stared down at the blade which had transfixed him with blank disbelief. Then his eyes glazed and he slid back along its length, pulling free and slumping to the ground.

Hather wiped his blade clean on the dead mercenary's cloak and sheathed it, shaking his head. 'I could have done with that one alive,' he told Atyl Skin. 'The dwarfs said he was working with them, but I don't know why. Whatever the reason, I doubt that it would have been his own idea.'

'Aren't you going to thank us?' the Dane demanded.

Hather grinned. 'Of course I am,' he replied. 'Though I'd like to know why it took you so long. You must have had twenty men up there with their ears pressed to the ground. And you,' he snapped at Olaf. 'I thought I told you to go to Uppsala with your mother?'

'You know mother,' Olaf replied, smiling. 'She flatly refused to go until we'd found you, or at least failed to.'

Hather tousled his son's fair hair affectionately, then turned to Hanni. 'My apologies, princess,' he began. 'Your visit appears to have started some kind of bid for the throne of Trollheim. I regret that you have been subjected to such discomfort and danger whilst under my protection.'

Hanni managed a smile as Olaf put his arm about her shoulders. Above them men were lowering ropes to pull them free of the underground chamber. Once back on solid ground, amidst his cheering men with Saeunna's kiss fresh upon his lips, Hather nudged Atyl Skin and pointed to where Olaf was helping Hanni to mount.

'I know. She looks so much happier with him than she ever will with Omund,' the Dane replied broodingly. 'Hather, what was that all about?'

'I'll tell you as we ride,' Hather answered. 'There's grim work afoot, my friend, and there's an old, familiar nagging in my bones which tells me our old friend Omund has a hand, if not a whole arm, in it.'

'But why the dwarfs? And a human working with them?'

'It's always been like this,' came Hather's reply. 'Twice before I've known dwarfs, men, gods and Norns work together. This time, though, there's a sorcerer as well, and a powerful one at that. Powerful enough to kill Vermund and threaten the Ynglings at any rate.'

'I liked Vermund,' the Dane responded. 'He was a good friend. I've no love for the Ynglings, though. You should have deposed Omund and taken the throne yourself, after Skroggrmagi. You'd have made a better king than that spineless worm.'

Hather sighed. 'I'm sworn to protect the Ynglings, my friend. It's not simply a matter of choice. Their fate is interwoven with my own, whilst I live. Omund wants me to help them even less than I do myself, but I have to, come dwarfs or sorcerers.'

Atyl Skin nodded. 'Well,' he said, 'at least you won't do it alone. Not if you're willing to have me by your side, that is.'

'Old friends are best,' Hather replied as they clasped wrists. 'They understand each other. I thank you for that, Atyl Skin.'

'Don't thank me,' said Atyl Skin. 'Thank King Ulf of the Dane-Lands. That's why he sent me. He's not forgotten the service you did him all those years ago. Yes, he'd have beaten Omund, but it would have cost him a great many good lives and a mountain of money. He knows he's got a madman for a neighbour. He doesn't like sending Princess Hanni to Uppsala any more than you and I like taking her there. But he is scarcely in a position to refuse. He trusts you, with my help, to look after his interests and his daughter. So whatever you decide, Hather Lambisson, I'm with you. And through me you will have the support of the Dane-Lands as well.'

'Then I hope I can live up to your faith in me, and King Ulf's. I have to admit, though, at this particular moment, I have no very firm idea as to what's going on.'

'You're too modest, Hather.'

'No, I'm not being modest. I'm being honest with myself, Atyl. A man has to be honest with himself before he can be honest with others. Every time I think I know what's happening something new comes along. And I think I ought to tell you that Saeunna's had another of her dreams. She saw me fighting Omund upon the surface of a frozen lake. And she saw Omund kill me.'

Atyl Skin forced a derisory laugh. 'Well, there are no frozen lakes around Uppsala.'

'Not at this time of year, no,' came Hather's reply. 'But how far into the future was she seeing?'

5

Confrontation with a God

The two watchers upon Aud's grave-mound were so intent upon straining their eyes southward for the distant approach of Hather's company that they failed, for some moments, to notice one another. The two ravens, circling above them, had been mute for some time, but at last one of them cried out as the distant figures appeared like ants upon the skyline.

Mother Skuld heard, and peered skywards through her veil of wadmal. Close by, Allfather also looked up; Hugin and Munin, thought and memory, were flapping their tattered, midnight pinions amongst the clouds.

'What? Are you here, One-Eye?' Mother Skuld demanded.

'Where else should I be, Mother?' Odin asked her, sounding slightly hurt at her greeting.

'Only you can answer that,' came the reply.

The one-eyed god sighed wearily. 'You're cheating, you know,' he told her.

'Cheating? I like that. How am I cheating the Allfather by standing here?'

'By standing here? Why, not at all. You could never cheat by standing beside me, Norn. But you could cheat by standing somewhere else.'

'And where would that be, O Omniscient One?'

'In the circle of burning stones, perhaps.'

'The burning stones? I don't understand you, Odin. Is this some riddle of yours? If it is, you can save it for the dwarfs, for Grimnir, perhaps,' she added, alluding to a famous verbal duel Odin had conducted long ago.

'You understand me very well, little mother. You cheated when you made your bargain with Vultikamian. And don't try to tell me you don't know that Vultikamian is the most powerful wizard in Finnmark. You know I was watching you there.'

The Norn sighed. 'Perhaps you were. Even so, why should it not be in my power to begin the game? The pieces were set up upon the tafl-board.'

Odin said nothing.

'We made no bargain, you know,' Mother Skuld continued. 'You asked me to allow Hather Lambisson, your precious Champion of the Ynglings, time to enjoy some peace and bring up his family. Well, I've done that. He's had his peace. And so has your marvellous Yngling Omund.'

'There's nothing marvellous about Omund,' Odin countered.

'There's nothing marvellous about any Yngling yet born,' came the response. 'You tell me that you want to give mankind time, that that is why you need the Ynglings. You give me that as an explanation, but it's not a reason, Allfather. Why do they need time? What do they need this time for? Will you tell me the truth about that?'

'I have. Perhaps you weren't listening to me. You sometimes don't, you know. We're like an old married couple, you and I, in that respect.'

'Then let's behave like one. Tell me again.'

It was Odin's turn to sigh. Then he said: 'Very well, little Mother. But first I must ask you to tell me again what *you* want.'

'You know that already. I want to rest. I'm tired. My whole sisterhood is tired. We want to be free of the petty squabbles of men, free of having to see to their destinies. We want to rest, after so many thousands of years.'

'And you think that the gods are different?' Odin demanded. 'Why shouldn't it be the same for us? But we have our own fates, Mother Skuld. And they came to us with responsibilities attached. You're tired of sorting destinies. Don't you think I'm weary as well, after so many years of gathering warriors to stand beside me at the Ragnarok? I've had to betray so many of my followers to fill the benches in Valhalla. I've betrayed so many, it's a wonder I've any worshippers left, let alone good men like Hather Lambisson of Ostragotland. And that is why I need the time that the Yngling line, running its full length, will afford me. Will afford us,' he added.

'We exist to help the mortals,' Mother Skuld sneered in reply. 'Yet now you are hinting that the mortals can help us? Has the Allfather finally taken leave of what few senses he had?'

'Not at all. You're weary. I'm weary. All the gods and all the Norns are weary. But what do you think will happen to mankind if we leave them without the comfort they derive from worshipping us?'

'Worshipping you, you mean,' the Norn interrupted him.

'Very well, but they know of the Norns, your sisterhood, and they have regard to them, even though they may not sacrifice to them. Without us they would fall back into a greater barbarism than they know already. Without us the north would become godless and bloody. It would destroy itself as surely as if you intended to keep your bargain with Vultikamian. And that's why I need the Ynglings. Their span of time will afford an opportunity for the White Christ to complete his advance. With his coming there will be the time we crave, the years, the centuries of rest we have wanted for so long. But it will take the full span of the Yngling dynasty. Only when the last, yet unborn, Yngling dies, will the north be ready to admit the *Hvitakrist*.

'Look over there,' he continued. 'The grave-mound of Vermund Bjarnisson. That death was Vultikamian's doing, because of your pact with him. And here, where we stand now, is the grave-mound of the High Queen Aud. Her death was Vultikamian's work. Oh, not directly, I admit, but his work none the less. And there,' he pointed, 'that new mound over there. That's for Egil Omundsson, the High King's eldest son, and his family. Children of three, seven and nine butchered because of your precious Lappish sorcerer. And just there, there will be another mound in a few days . . .'

'You've been sitting upon your high seat and looking out over time again,' Mother Skuld teased defensively.

'And should I do otherwise?' the god demanded. 'These are people. These are lives. Oh, they are not the same as our lives, I grant you, but they are living things. And without us they will be even less than they are, unless they have something in our place. That is why I need the Ynglings, Mother Skuld. That is why I want Hather to live, to work for the preservation of the dynasty, against such as Vultikamian, and yourself. That is why I accuse you of cheating in our game of life, our game of lives.'

'Yet you yourself have cheated,' the Norn retorted. 'You stood over there, on Vermund's mound, and drew Hather to you for a warning. You're not the only one who can watch others, you know.'

'Would I need to if we had set rules, if I had known that the game was begun? You see? It comes back to your own cheating, which is what threatens the Ynglings. It even threatens the value of the game itself. And to ally yourself to Vultikamian, who has usurped one of my own titles . . .'

'Not usurped, Odin! He has adapted your title, not usurped it. You gained it by blinding your favourites in battle so that your daughters could gather them to Valhalla. Vultikamian uses it to signify mastery of life itself, the triumph over death he has created by his sorcery. His offer to Omund of immortality, or comparative immortality, is not simply a false boast. It is a fact, though the path to it is long and bloody and treacherous.'

'And there you speak a truth. Long and bloody and treacherous it is. But the treachery is not all his own, Mother Skuld. Much of it is yours.'

'And what if it is? Are you not also a betrayer? Didn't you tell me so just a few mortal moments ago?'

'*Mortal* moments is it, now? You twist the meanings of words to suit yourself, Mother. You are playing this game without rules, I think.'

'And if I am, Allfather?'

'Then you will discover that two of us can play that way.'

'So? Do it. Do your worst, Odin. Let's see if you can keep your precious Ynglings in such a game.'

The god smiled to himself, his single eye glittering evilly as he asked: 'Is that a challenge, Mother Skuld?'

'You may consider it one, if you wish.'

'A game without any rules at all?'

'So be it. No rules. Except one.'

'And what, might I ask, is that to be?'

'You may not appear to Hather Lambisson again in his lifetime, or the duration of our play.'

'Then I bind you likewise. You may not aid or counsel Vultikamian at all. Is that fair?'

The Norn shivered beneath her veil. It was fair enough. She had no desire to make herself known to Vultikamian again. Though she would not have admitted as much, she already regretted her pact with the Lappish sorcerer. Something in the way that he had requested the north for his *plaything* had disturbed her in a way that she could never have told Odin. So, she answered: 'That's fair. I accept.'

For Allfather it was enough. Each was bound to accept that they might not appear to their principal tafl-pieces. Odin knew that the Ynglings, at last, had a chance, though he could not be certain that the same could be said for Hather Lambisson.

On the horizon the approaching company drew closer. Soon Hather would reach Uppsala. There he would face one of the greatest decisions of his life. And Allfather would not be there to help him.

This was perhaps the ultimate test for the Champion of the Ynglings. If Hather could survive this, then there was hope. And if there was hope, then not even Vultikamian would be able to thwart Odin's plan for the future of mankind.

Or could he? The god found himself wondering.

6

Discoveries at Uppsala

Their journey, with its attendant mysteries and hazards, was almost over, and a thrill ran through the group of riders as Hather and his companions beheld Omund's capital basking in the afternoon sunlight. Hather felt the lift of spirits and glanced at Atyl Skin. The Dane smiled grimly.

'They think they'll be safe once they reach Uppsala,' he muttered.

His own memories of Uppsala were far from welcoming. Upon his first visit Omund had accused Atyl Skin of spying and cast him into an underground prison. The second time he'd set foot in Omund's city it had been to kill the High King, though in fact he'd saved Hather's life with the arrow which he'd intended for Omund. No, there would be little welcome or safety there for the Dane.

As they drew closer it was impossible for them not to notice the fresh burial-mound beyond the city. The earth heaped above it stood out stark red in the afternoon sun. It was too recent for the grass and weeds to grow which would eventually cover it, as they had those of Queen Aud and Vermund Bjarnisson.

As they drew closer to the town a company of Omund's guards rode out to escort them to the palace. Hather was delighted to see his eldest son, the King's Marshal, leading them, and he dismissed his doubts long enough to take pleasure in presenting Svipdag to his old friend and to the lovely Princess Hanni. Svipdag's dark eyes brightened at the sight of her, then he winked at his half-brother, immediately understanding how things stood.

Once inside the palace Hather and his family resumed their former guest-quarters, and Gudrun joined them there. Hanni and her escort were quartered separately to refresh themselves and to prepare for their coming audience with the High King. At Atyl Skin's suggestion, made to Hather and confirmed by Omund, Gudrun became lady-in-waiting to Hanni for the duration of her stay.

'She may need someone she can trust,' Hather explained to his daughter. 'And I'll feel happier with you there to keep me informed.'

That night Omund held a feast of welcome for his guest and her escorts. He was polite and formal in his greeting of Atyl Skin, showing the courtesy due to an ambassador from the Dane-Lands, though with a restraint which those aware of the Dane's past history easily understood. With Hanni, though, he was almost sickeningly courteous and attentive for one who had lost his wife, the mother of his children, such a little time before.

Above the palace heavy clouds began to gather, threatening a storm later. The sentries huddled into their cloaks and made silent prayers for the rain to hold off until the watch changed.

Hather sat with Svipdag, his brows heavy as he learned of the deaths of Egil Omundsson and his family. Svipdag confided his suspicions to his father, and Hather struggled to combine these with his own to draw some reason out of the bloody chaos which threatened to engulf them. He sat back, his drinking-horn untouched in his hand, and surveyed the feast-guests assembled in Omund's hall. The last time he'd sat here old Skeggja had prophesied Omund's greatness and immortality. Well, she wasn't here this particular evening, though Hather fancied that he felt her ancient eyes watching through her sorcery from afar. And if she wasn't here, he reflected, there was a reason for it.

And the name of that reason, the name of *all* her reasons, was Vultikamian.

Dwarfs and gods and sorcerers, beings he was probably powerless to fight, were combining against the Ynglings for some hidden purpose of their own. And he was Champion of the Ynglings. He was the one who once again had to find the answers, as he had done before.

Hather shook his head. Omund was struggling to find the wit to amuse Hanni. Atyl Skin sat with his arms affectionately around Saeunna and Gudrun. Olaf was scowling over his mead-horn at the High King's wooing. Flosi, Omund's youngest son, appeared sullen, doubtless at his father's behaviour with Aud and Egil scarce cold in their grave-mounds, and was resisting the efforts of his wife Thurid to amuse him. His brother Harek and his wife . . .

Were not there!

'Where's Harek?' Hather asked his son.

'Why, he's . . .' Svipdag's voice tailed into silence as his eyes sought Harek amongst the guests. 'I think we ought to find out.'

They left the feast as quietly as they could, not wishing to alarm any who might be watching them. Once outside, though, Svipdag's manner changed as they encountered a sentry.

'I want a squad of men,' the King's Marshal ordered. 'At once. Two to check the guards on the hut at the edge of the city, then to report back to me, the others are to join me at Prince Harek's quarters. Jump to it!'

As the guard disappeared, Hather and Svipdag made their way towards Harek's longhouse, unsheathing their weapons as they went. Above them the sky began to rumble, and the first vicious flash of lightning briefly illuminated the darkness of the palace, throwing the outlines of longhouses and sentries into stark relief. Seconds later shafts of cold, miserable rain lanced down upon them, stinging their hands and faces and weighting their woollen cloaks.

No light shone from the vellum windows of Harek's quarters. The vestibule, too, was in darkness, but a flash briefly revealed the sprawled bodies of the sentinels inside it. Hather stooped, scowling grimly, and set a hand to a back-wound. It came away wet.

'Recent,' he muttered. 'And taken from behind.'

Svipdag shook his head. 'Impossible. I had the tunnel guarded.'

Hather turned with a snarl. 'If these guards can be killed, then so can the others! Let's not waste any more time. Harek may still be alive in there!'

Together they kicked open the door to the hall and sprang through it. A figure lurched towards them, eyes rolling, voice gurgling as it attempted to speak through twin red mouths. The lightning showed them Harek's distorted, dying face for a moment before the prince keeled over on the rush-strewn floor. Beyond him other bodies littered the hall.

Small shapes with wickedly-glittering weapons were ranging themselves against the intruders.

'There's no sun to save you this time, Hather Lambisson,' hissed a familiar voice from the darkness. 'Take him alive!'

Hather and Svipdag advanced together, their eyes straining to make out their adversaries, their vision aided only for brief, terrifying moments by the rumbling storm. Their weapons slashed ahead of them, cutting low, seeking a chance contact. Hather swore as the tip of a blade slashed his left forearm, twisting his own sword to scythe at the dim shape of his foe. A piercing shriek told him of his success, but there was no time for self congratulation. There were more of them, slowly becoming clearer and more menacing as his vision grew more accustomed to the darkness.

'Use your advantage,' Bombor screamed from somewhere behind the massed dwarfs. 'Kill the other one. Get Hather alive! Cut his legs!'

They swarmed about him, their swords flashing evilly, seeking to inflict a hundred small, disabling wounds. Hather backed against a wall to protect his rear and noticed Svipdag, pinned in a corner, grimly hacking at the throng about him. A blade pierced Svipdag's calf and, in slashing down to kill the aggressor he twisted just in time for another to miss his left side.

'Bombor, wait!' Hather called. 'Spare my son and I'll come with you!'

'Not whilst I'm alive,' Svipdag snarled, shearing through a startled dwarfish face.

'No bargains, Hather,' Bombor sneered. 'Not with you, anyway. You're what *we* need to bargain with!'

'Then you'll not take either of us alive,' Hather roared, spinning suddenly to catch one dwarf in the throat and another about the temple.

But the dwarfs pressed the attack, the lightning revealing that for every one that died another took his place from the open tunnel behind the partition wall. It also showed Hather the mutilated bodies of Harek's wife and two daughters, as well as those of the guards Svipdag had placed to guard the tunnel entrance, obviously pressed back into the hall by sheer weight of numbers.

Tiring badly, feeling his years more desperately than at any other time, Hather continued the unequal combat. A dozen small wounds stung and trickled blood, making his clothing wet and sticky. Svipdag, badly cut near the left hip, was struggling to parry the strokes of his adversaries who were now openly playing with him, taking their merciless time about delivering a death-wound. For the Champion of the Ynglings and his eldest son time was running out.

And then they heard the sound of feet running through the storm outside. Torchlight flooded the hall as the guards Svipdag had summoned rushed with drawn weapons into the longhouse and fell upon the dwarfs. As their persecutors turned away to meet this unexpected threat, Hather and Svipdag were granted the respite they had craved so desperately. With the light of the torches to aid them the soldiers drove the dwarfs back towards the partition wall, hacking and slashing mercilessly at the terrible creatures which had sought the lives of the King of Ostragotland and the King's Marshal. Svipdag slumped in his corner, one hand pressed to the wound in his calf, the other attempting to stanch the flow of blood from his injured hip. Whilst neither wound was serious they were both painful and disabling, and there was no doubt that the soldiers he had summoned had saved his life.

Hather was still on his feet, though his clothing was spattered with bloody rents. As Svipdag watched, Hather staggered forward and set the edge of his blade to the throat of an injured dwarf.

'Why?' he demanded simply, both his action and his tone demanding some response.

'Because . . . because Bombor ordered it,' the pitiful figure squeaked.

Beyond them the other dwarfs had retreated before the furious guards, the conflict continuing as they sought escape through the tunnel beyond the partition wall.

'And why did Bombor order it?' Hather growled, his wounds stretching his patience to the limit. 'And the murders. Why Omund's sons?'

'I . . . don't know.'

The edge of Hather's blade began to bite. 'You know what Omund will do to you if I let you live? Someone will tell him about slow exposure to sunlight.'

The dwarf's eyes widened in terror. Sunlight turned dwarfs to stone. When completely exposed they died quickly. But slow petrification, exposing just a small part of their body or limbs at any one time, was the most terrible death any dwarf could even think about. Only the exposed parts turned to stone, whilst the surrounding flesh suppurated and became incredibly painful. Inevitably the petrified parts would snap off, leaving the disabled, miserable creature helpless to avoid the continuing torment. Such a death could take weeks, even months, of hideous agony.

'If I knew I'd tell you!' came the terrified scream.

Hather nodded. It was true. With a decapitating stroke he offered the injured dwarf the only mercy possible.

He sheathed his sword and stumbled over to where Svipdag sat with his back to the wall.

'Is it bad?' he asked.

Svipdag grinned painfully. 'It's been worse,' he said. 'Sometime it'll be worse again.'

Hather looked the length of the hall. There could be no doubt that the other corpses, both dwarf and human, which littered it were dead. Each lay motionless and silent in its own soaked patch of blood.

The guards, their weapons bloody, staggered back into the hall from behind the partition. 'Did you take any prisoners?' Hather asked.

The captain shook his head. 'No, sir,' he answered. 'Not a one.'

Then Bombor's escaped, Hather thought. He's not amongst the dead. I know he holds the key to this part of the mystery. No dwarf would deliberately set about the murder of Omund's family without a good reason. No dwarf would ally himself with a human unless there was some advantage to be had from it. So why is he doing this? And what did he mean when he said that he wanted me as the prize in some kind of bargain? He can't want me for Omund. If Omund really wanted me dead he'd have found a way by now. Besides, Bombor wanted me alive . . .

He turned back to Svipdag, suddenly very tired and feeling his wounds, slight though they were.

'You'll want to report to Omund,' he said. Then he instructed the captain, 'Have your men assist my son to the High King's quarters. Send a messenger to draw Omund from his feast. He'll want to hear this news in private.'

The captain saluted. 'Very good, King Hather. Shall I tell the leech to attend you?'

Hather smiled wearily. 'I'll stay here,' he replied. 'No leech, captain. But I'd be grateful if the Dane, Atyl Skin, could join me here.'

'I'll see that he's informed, sir.'

'And no fuss. Not a word of this to anyone. You understand me?'

'Completely, sir.'

He slumped onto a bench, there amongst the dead, and

watched them go. And then a voice began to whisper to him. *Odin's voice.*

Take Flosi away, it whispered. *Save Flosi. Save Flosi's children. That way at least the dynasty will have a chance.*

He could not mistake that insidious voice. Amid all the mess and confusion it made the only sense that Hather could recognise. Whatever was happening, Hather knew that Omund, or at least Omund's influence, lay behind it. Saving Flosi and his children was the one practical contribution he could make. At least with Flosi safe the Yngling line would still exist.

And if I wait? he asked. If I wait for a solution to present itself?

Then it would doom you all, came the reply. *It would doom you all as certainly as if you were already dead.*

Hather shuddered. He knew that those words were true, that his remaining at Uppsala would mean the end of the Ynglings, that he would not know the answers in time to take the action which would be required of him.

'I hope I made a good end,' he whispered to himself, the pain of his wounds banished by the knowledge of the answer he would receive.

'*You were fighting Omund*,' Saeunna's voice came out of the past.

So, I shall die fighting Omund, he thought. Saeunna has been right too many times for me to doubt her now. I shall fight Omund. Then Omund must be a murderer. There can be no question of it.

So why don't I kill him now?

The answer came without surprising him. *Because he will kill you*, it said. *Because there's no frozen lake for you to fight upon near Uppsala. It must be somewhere else.*

All the more reason to kill him now.

No. To destroy Saeunna's dream would be to destroy the fate which the gods had prepared for him. And that would mean destroying the hope of a future which still remained for the line he was sworn to defend with his life if need be.

Hather was still pondering these questions when Atyl Skin came back into the longhouse, and began to tear strips from the clothing of the corpses to bind up his wounds. Hather said: 'I can do this, Atyl. There's other work for you.'

'What do you have in mind?' the Dane asked.

'My first task is to get Hanni back to the safety of Sudrafell. And my family. And Prince Flosi and his family.'

'You don't believe that all this was Flosi's idea?'

Hather gave a cynical bark of laughter. 'Flosi allied with dwarfs? It's as likely as Omund making an alliance with the dwarfs.'

'Then you don't think Omund's done that?'

'I think someone's done it for him.'

'Who?'

'The sorcerer Vultikamian, for instance,' Hather answered. 'I still don't know why old Skeggja wasn't at the feast. She should have been. So, what's she up to, my friend?'

Before Atyl Skin could reply, Hather went on: 'I want you to assemble my family, and Hanni, and Flosi. They're to be ready to leave for Sudrafell within the hour. Bombor and his creatures could come back through the tunnels at any time. And next time they'll be coming for Flosi, according to Skeggja's prophecy. Sudrafell's smaller. That means I can defend it better.'

The Dane agreed. 'Of course.'

'Then do as I ask, Atyl. My family, Flosi's, and Hanni. All ready to leave Uppsala within the hour. Can you do that?'

'I can. But what about Svipdag? He's still with Omund.'

'I don't think Svipdag's in any danger. Omund needs him. If he didn't, I don't believe that Svipdag would have been appointed to Vermund's position. Besides, it could be said that I'm setting myself up against Omund by this action. It could be useful to have my eldest son in the High King's camp, if it comes to negotiating in the future.'

And I still don't trust him completely, he thought to himself. If he were with me he could betray me. If I leave him here he's at least at a safe distance.

And, if I'm right, that could save all our lives.

7

The Shifting of the Stars

Within the hour, as planned, they passed through the gates of the palace on the way back to Sudrafell. Olaf and Atyl Skin overpowered Omund's guards, enabling them to effect their departure without alarms. Flosi, his wife Thurid and his two little sons travelled with them, as well as Hanni and Gudrun. Flosi had needed little persuading after being told of Harek's death. His grief alone had been enough to tell Hather that the prince knew nothing about the deaths of his mother and brothers.

Sudrafell, Hather knew, was the only possible refuge and protection against the terrible plot which encompassed them all. Only there, on his own ground, within a stockade constructed to his own specifications and capable of withstanding the might of the High King should it need to, was safety to be found.

The storm roared through the treetops, and lightning flashed stark as it crackled through the clouds.

From the high tower in the forest, staring into her polished obsidian mirror, old Skeggja watched them go. She was still nursing the wounds Hather had given her at their last meeting, but she forgot the pain as she drooled over the images in her scrying glass. She was still drooling when the sound of footfalls upon the ladder made her aware of Omund's approach. She turned from the black depths of the mirror in time to see his face appear above the level of the trap-door in the floor.

'He's cheating me,' the High King scowled. 'Hather Lambisson is cheating me . . . us. He's cheating your master, Skeggja. He's taking Flosi and his family to safety.'

The old witch cackled. 'Is he, little Omund?' she teased. 'Is he really? Do you believe that any could cheat Vultikamian with impunity?'

Omund swallowed hard and held his tongue. There was something in that question which came too close to his own intentions to be completely comfortable. Cheat Vultikamian? Such a thing would ordinarily be unthinkable. But Omund knew that twice before the gods themselves had taken a hand to save the Yngling line. Allfather would not let it fall now. That was the High King's great advantage over the wizard of Finnmark.

'Perhaps not,' he replied at length. 'But what are we to do about it, old woman?'

'Why, we are to follow,' came the reply.

'Follow Hather Lambisson back to Sudrafell? And then what?'

'You are making assumptions, great king,' the witch mocked. 'Why should Hather be going back to Sudrafell?'

'Because he knows he will be safe there,' Omund retorted. 'It will take my army months to breach his walls.'

'But what makes you think that he is going to Sudrafell at all? Is he even travelling in that direction?'

The storm howled more furiously. With an effort Omund hauled himself onto the covered platform and slammed the trap-door shut behind him. 'Where else would he be going?' he snarled.

'Why, to find my master, King Omund. Hather has gone to meet Vultikamian. Could he do otherwise?'

'Taking his family, and Flosi's, with him? He'd be mad to do such a thing.'

'Or bewitched.'

'Bewitched? What do you mean, Skeggja? What are you trying to tell me?'

The old crone pointed to a hinged section of the roof of the platform, its outer area covered with skins to keep it waterproof. 'Take the pole over there,' she directed.

'That one, with the forked end. That's it. Now, King Omund, push that part of the roof open and look for the three stars which make up the rod of Lady Frigg's Distaff.* Now, can you see them?'

Omund spat as the rain streamed down into his face. 'Through this storm I can't see anything!' he snapped. 'What with rain and clouds there's nothing to see out there.'

Old Skeggja smiled. Hitching up her garments she straddled an earthenware pot upon the floor, and pissed in it noisily. As she rose and shook down her skirts the storm suddenly cleared and the rain stopped.

'Now look,' she ordered.

Omund peered into the suddenly clear sky towards that quarter where he expected to find the stars of Frigg's Distaff. His face anxious, he turned back to the old witch.

'You see?' she grinned behind her moustache. 'It isn't there, it is? It's not where you expected it to be. Now, look again, in the opposite quarter, King Omund.'

He looked. And he saw. And then he realised.

The stars should have been in the east, close to Thjazi's Eyes†, but instead both constellations were on the opposite side of the heavens, as if some giant hand had picked up the forest tower and set it down again the other way around.

The High King understood. With a grin he took the pole away, allowing the hinged section of roof to close with a crash. 'So if Hather's following the stars . . .'

'Then he's travelling north,' came the witch's reply. 'Not south towards Sudrafell as he supposes. Yes, he's travelling north, King Omund, north towards my master Vultikamian. And he'll deliver those he hoped to save into my master's hands. Now, do you see how we are working for you? How we are placing your enemy within your grasp?'

Omund saw. It was all plain to him at last. He would

---

* Orion's Belt.
† The stars Castor and Pollux of the constellation Gemini

follow the plan they had made, follow it until the end came and the bloody ambitions of the mad sorcerer Vultikamian were overturned by the direct intervention of the gods themselves, which would leave him, Omund Olisson, master of the north, the only survivor, the last and greatest king of the age-old Yngling line.

'And Hather?' he asked.

'Obliterated by the blinking of my master's eye.'

'And his son Svipdag?'

Skeggja shrugged. 'Yours for as long as you may require his service,' she replied. 'But be wary of him, King Omund. He can just as easily be treacherous to you as he can to his father. He has ambitions of his own, that one.'

So she *doesn't* serve Svipdag, Omund thought. She serves her master, and him alone. Then very well, when the time comes, she can die in her master's service.

'For now, though,' the old witch lied, 'Svipdag Hathersson's ambitions are for you alone. He wants to serve you, High King. He wants to serve you and become strong with you. Go to him. Speak with him. Believe his words, King Omund, for they will be the truth.'

Skeggja's words faded away into the sudden stillness which the passing of the storm had left behind. This foul, ugly old creature couldn't know of his intentions, Omund thought. It was impossible for any to know exactly what his plans were, for he'd not confided them to anyone. Oh, one here knew something, but the one here wouldn't be able to tell the one there. And the one there had no love or liking for the other one elsewhere. No, the pieces were scattered abroad too widely. Only he, Omund, knew all the plan. Skeggja and Vultikamian knew the end purpose of their own part, but not all of it.

And that was why Omund Olisson still trusted those he conspired with. Because none of them knew enough to be able to stop him.

He nodded and bade the old witch a good evening, words which made her chuckle deeply and disturbingly. Descending to the forest floor he moved through the circle of mist and mounted his waiting horse. The beast whinnied as he turned its head towards Uppsala, as if it sensed that the sky it rode beneath was strange, that the path below was not the right one for the path above.

As he rode Omund felt a strangeness in the night about him. There was the stillness, yes. But there was more than that. He saw his path ahead of him as if through a deep ravine, as if walls of impenetrable blackness hemmed him in, a blackness which refused to yield if he attempted to turn his mount towards it, which held his course towards the palace beneath unfamiliar stars.

He regained his quarters and imperiously summoned Svipdag Hathersson to his presence. His Marshal limped painfully into the High King's presence and stood before him, leaning against a spear-shaft.

'Where's your father, Svipdag?' Omund demanded.

'He has begun the return journey to Sudrafell, King Omund,' came the reply.

'Without my permission to leave the court?'

Svipdag scowled. Something was seriously wrong. Why wasn't the High King grieving and ranting for the death of his second son. Here was a man who had been dealt a succession of cruel blows. In a few short weeks he had lost his wife and two sons and their children. Yet his only concern now was for the whereabouts of Hather Lambisson.

'With respect, sir, you were not present to give or withhold your permission.'

It was Omund's turn to scowl. He gestured to Svipdag to sit down and his Marshal gladly took the weight off his injured legs. The leech had bound and cleansed the wounds, and Svipdag had drunk deeply to deaden the nagging pain.

'Who travelled with your father?' Omund asked wearily.

'The other members of my family.'

'And? Remember your position, my friend. It is your duty to hold nothing back from me. Exactly, now. Tell me all of them.'

Svipdag sighed. 'Princess Hanni and her party. And your son Flosi and his family.'

'To Sudrafell, you say?'

Svipdag nodded. 'My father felt that they would be safer there until we had discovered the reasons for these mysterious deaths. His action was considered, and taken in your own interest, he believed.'

Omund snorted derisively. '*If* he has gone to Sudrafell I will believe that. But I must tell you frankly, Svipdag, that I do not believe he has. Will you send a rider along the road to Sudrafell to confirm that he is travelling in that direction?'

For a moment the King's Marshal studied Omund through dark eyes. Then he turned upon his seat and motioned to a guard standing beside the door. 'Do it,' he ordered. Turning to Omund once more he asked: 'What do you suspect?'

'For some time now I have believed your father to be in possession of a secret stronghold north of here. I think he has taken his party there.'

'But why should he?'

'Listen to me, Svipdag, very carefully. For many years now your father has been known quite wrongly as the Champion of the Ynglings. He has never liked me. When he found himself in a strong enough position he broke my power by imposing the vassal kingships upon me, and taking one of them for himself. And now, I believe, he has turned king-maker once more. He thinks it's time for me to be in my grave-mound, weighted down by some preposterous runestone. He wants a new, young Yngling on my throne, one who will be grateful to him for his help, who won't resent him for the meddling self-seeker he is. King Omund is dead. Long live King Flosi.'

Svipdag shook his head in bewilderment. 'Why Flosi?' he asked. 'Oh, I know that Flosi's the only one still alive . . .'

'Of course he is. Who do you think arranged for the murders of my wife and my other sons?'

'Not my father! I'd wager my life on it. It's not his way!'

'Isn't it?' Omund sneered, aware of the tiny seed of doubt he was planting in Svipdag's mind, a tiny seed that he could nourish and encourage to grow into a great, strangling weed. 'He's wanted me dead for years. You must have heard how his friend Starkadder tried to deny me the throne after he'd murdered my father!'

'But he killed Starkadder!'

'Only because he had to. Only because Starkadder's berserk fury continued after my father's murder and killed his own father, your grandfather Lambi Nef. He had to fight the blood-feud with Starkadder, and whilst he was doing that my position was strengthened for me by those truly loyal to the throne. And now, with my other sons dead, with Hather apparently the saviour of Flosi and the Yngling dynasty, this people's champion has a young, grateful princeling to supplant me with.'

Svipdag's brows furrowed. 'It's hard to believe,' he growled. 'The murders were done by dwarfs. I know that. My guards know it as well. And those same dwarfs wanted to take my father prisoner. So, how could he be in league with them?'

'Hasn't he had dealings with the dwarfs before? He and Starkadder compacted with them for my father's murder. Once a man has leagued himself with Trollheim he can do so again. But this is, I admit, only conjecture. I have no proof. Not yet.' Omund smiled at Svipdag.

'When your rider comes back and tells me that Hather's party is not on the road to Sudrafell, my friend, that will be proof.'

'And if they *are* travelling towards Sudrafell?'

Omund shrugged. 'Then I'm wrong, and we shall have to seek elsewhere for our solution to this mystery.'

'But if my father was in league with the dwarfs,' Svipdag began slowly, 'why did they want to take him prisoner?'

'They didn't. They were offering him an excuse in case you survived their attack.'

'But his wounds . . .'

'Nothing like as serious as your own. Simply another ploy. Who noticed Harek's absence from the feast? He did. He went to join his fellow conspirators, but you insisted on going with him. Well, he was prepared for that. Once inside Harek's longhouse he and his dwarfish allies acted out their plan to fool you in case they couldn't kill you. And it has fooled you, Svipdag. It's fooled you completely.'

Before Svipdag had managed to weigh Omund's argument a guard entered the High King's chambers and saluted. Omund looked up, his eyes questioning.

'King Hather's party is not upon the road to Sudrafell,' came the report.

Svipdag leapt to his feet. 'He has several hours' start,' he snapped. 'How can you be certain in the little time you've been gone?'

'With respect, sir, I didn't even need to leave the city. A party of Skanish merchants had just arrived in Uppsala. If King Hather had been upon the road to Sudrafell he would have passed them. They had encountered no one abroad in the night.'

Omund's smile broadened. 'You see?' he hissed smugly. 'Can you doubt me now?' Then, to the guard, 'Good. Leave us, now. Have fifty men ready to ride by dawn. And spare horses. Whatever speed Hather Lambisson is making must be matched and overtaken.'

The man saluted and withdrew. Svipdag slumped into his seat again, his stomach churning and his thoughts reeling. Eventually he asked: 'You . . . can't ask me to lead this party against my own father?'

Omund shook his head. 'I don't ask you to lead it, my friend. But I do ask you to ride with it, if your wounds will permit.'

Svipdag nodded. 'My wounds will stand it. Though if I don't lead the pursuit, who will?'

'Why, I shall, Marshal Svipdag,' came Omund's smug reply. 'I've waited most of my life to show your father up as the traitor he truly is, and nothing will stop me doing so now.'

And in the darkness of the night, as Omund prepared to execute his decision, two very different groups of travellers were progressing northwards in their separate ways. Hather's company rode at a steady but determined pace for the sanctuary they believed to lie ahead of them at Sudrafell. Behind them, travelling more slowly but with equal determination, Bombor's dwarfs were already in pursuit, ever aware of coming dawn, and the need for shelter which that dawn would bring for them.

Svipdag retired to his own quarters to take what rest he could before the journey which that dawn would mean for him. His thoughts were in turmoil after his audience with the High King. What Omund had told him could well be true. It had the ring of well-reasoned argument behind it. Yet in his heart Svipdag could not believe that his father, Hather Lambisson, King of Ostragotland, Champion of the Ynglings, would enter into the foul conspiracy of which Omund was accusing him. And the people of Sweden wouldn't believe it either . . .

Svipdag sat up suddenly, ignoring the pain from his injured hip. His colour-changed eyes were bright in the lamp-lit confines of his bed-closet, and the sheer import of his last thought was burning even more brightly within his brain.

It would take a great deal of persuasion for the people to believe that Hather had conspired against the throne he was sworn to defend. His reputation, that same reputation which had overshadowed Svipdag's own life and achievements, was far too strong to crumble with a mere word from King Omund. Hather's murder would cost Omund a great deal of the support he had traditionally enjoyed. It would weaken his standing as no other action could ever do. He had never known how to be truly popular, and the loss of what little popularity he had was exactly what Svipdag himself was seeking.

Whatever his old nurse Skeggi was up to was on his behalf. This was her work. It had to be. Oh, it might cost his father's life, but he'd be powerless to prevent that, and at least he could restore his father's reputation and standing after his death. And after Omund's death.

With both Hather and Omund gone, with Hather still a

national hero and Omund disgraced, the King's Marshal would control the kingdom. Flosi, the youngest son, was untrained and untried. If he survived he'd hold little more than the Yngling name for his own. The power, the *real* power, *would belong to Svipdag Hathersson alone!*

He smiled and snuffed the lamp, lying back upon his bed in the darkness. His thoughts might rob him of the sleep he needed, but they would provide him with another, greater strength that sleep alone could never have provided.

Nor was Svipdag the only one to pass that night without sleep. The High King was both awake and active whilst his Marshal's ambitions kept his eyes open. With a small party of his guards, their horses' hoofs muffled, together with a wagon which had also had its wheels wrapped with rags to deaden the sound, Omund returned to the tower in the forest. He dismounted in silence and walked through the mist to the ladder. As he ascended, beneath him the soldiers began to carry out their instructions.

Omund reached the top of the ladder and pushed open the trap-door in the floor.

Old Skeggja sat facing him, a huddled shape in the darkness. Yet her eyes were burning like twin fires, and her voice sent shivers down the High King's backbone.

'You've come to see me once again, King Omund?' she asked him, chuckling evilly. 'For the last time, perhaps, before you set out to meet my master at the burning stones?'

Omund faltered. How much did she know, this ancient crone with the power to shift the stars in the heavens, to still storms by simply pissing into a pot?

He forced himself to boldness. His sword slid from its scabbard. 'I seek your power to add strength to my blade,' he told her, advancing slowly, carefully holding the sword point-downwards to remove its naked threat.

'That is easily done, little king. You have only to thrust it into my body for my blood to add virtue to its temper.'

Omund's eyes widened. 'You don't believe me,

Skeggja? You think I've come here to kill you?' he bluffed.

'Should there be another reason? My work for you is done and your need for me has ended. Yet before you kill me, Omund Olisson, you must know that the work I have wrought for you, even the work I have wrought for my little Svipdag, has only been such as was permitted by my real master. Ah, but I forget. You have yet to meet my real master. You have yet to stand within the circle of the burning stones and face the most powerful creature in all the north. But you will, little Omund. You will. And in that moment you will understand why you were able to kill me so easily.

'You see,' she continued, whilst Omund stood fascinated like a shrew before a viper, 'I have worked my last service for Vultikamian as well. And I have served him best of all, you know. Ah, but I have served him the very best of all.'

'And . . . you knew that I would come for you. You knew that death was to be your reward, and still you worked for it? I don't understand you, old woman.'

'Do you not, my fine king? You call me old woman, and you are right. I am old. I was old when first I met my little Svipdag, more than twenty years ago. Yet I have aged only in years since then. I have not aged in my body, oh no. The power of Vultikamian prevented that. Tell me, King Omund. How old do you think I am? Am I not old enough for death to be the reward I long for? You seek immortality for yourself from my master. Oh, he can bestow that gift upon you. Do not doubt it. Look at me and know that I speak the truth.

'How old am I?' she taunted. 'Can you not guess? Eighty? Ninety? Perhaps even a hundred years old? Phah!' she spat. 'That is nothing. I tell you now, before you give me the death I crave for, the death which Vultikamian has promised for my payment. I am *a hundred and fifty-four years old!*'

He felt his breath catch in his throat at her words. It was true. She'd not aged an instant in all the time he'd known her, though that time was several years. So death was a mercy, was it? Very well, she should have it. But it would not be a merciful death.

He sheathed his sword and set his feet upon the ladder once again.

'A cruel death, then?' she called after him. 'Ah, my master chose you well, King Omund. What you lack in courage you make up for in guile and spite. Do you not even want to maim me so that I'm incapable of fleeing?'

He held his tongue as he descended to the ground. She wouldn't flee. She wanted to die too badly for that. Well, he'd give her what she wanted!

The wagon was unhitched and in position between the four trees which supported the platform. Its covering of hides had been removed to reveal its contents, bundles of brushwood and kindling packed around barrels of lamp-oil. A soldier stood beside it with a torch alight in his hand.

'Set it alight,' Omund ordered.

The soldier hesitated. 'I heard voices, sir,' he began. 'There's someone still up there . . .'

With a snarl Omund smashed the back of his hand against the guard's face and snatched the torch from his hand. He thrust the torch into the kindling on the wagon whilst his men watched in stunned silence.

'Now back to the palace,' Omund ordered, striding away from the flames, and mounting his horse.

'I shall see you again, little Omund,' old Skeggja's voice called after him. 'I shall see you again, High King. Oh, not in life, but I shall see you just the same . . .'

He rode from the forest, his men following as best they could. They felt the heat upon their backs as the lamp-oil ignited and whooshed up in a wicked rush of flame to sear the base of the platform. There was none to see it break through between the boards and clutch its fiery fingers to the old crone's clothing, none to see it lay its hold upon the thin hair which still covered her scalp. Only the heat and the glow behind them, and the fading, failing shrillness of her dying screams.

8

Into the Whiteness of the North

Even before the dawn came stealing across the landscape with its stealthy, roseate glow, hiding the treacherous stars behind its greater brightness, Hather realised that something was badly wrong. He looked across to Atyl Skin, riding beside him, his brows lowered and the eyes beneath them bright with anger and suspicion.

'This isn't the road to Sudrafell,' he growled.

The banks of darkness concealing the surrounding countryside were beginning to dissipate, revealing landmarks along their route.

Atyl Skin's scarred features crinkled in bewilderment. 'You're right,' he muttered. 'I've travelled to and from Sudrafell with you a few times. Certainly enough to know something of the way. And this isn't it. But how, Hather? It was dark, yes, but we had the stars to guide us. We shouldn't be this far out of our way.'

'Whatever this far means,' came the grim reply. 'Look there, to your right. That's the dawn in the distance. That means we're travelling north. If we were going south it would be to our left. We've gone badly wrong somehow.'

'Then we'd better turn back. Shall I give the order?'

Hather shook his head. 'If we do that we'll run straight into whoever Omund will have sent after us. You know my thoughts. I still think that some mad scheme of the High King's is behind this mystery. By now he'll have me branded as a traitor, and probably his son Flosi as well.'

'Then what do we do?' Atyl Skin asked, bewildered.

'What we're doing,' came Hather's reply.

I will help you as I have helped you before, the god had said, *but it must be in hints and riddles.*

This wasn't a hint, Hather reflected as he rode. But something, somehow, had turned their course about, even reversed the position of the stars in the heavens. And that was certainly a riddle.

The game is mine only to play. I do not make the rules.

'Hather?'

'Hm?' He turned to Atyl Skin, who clearly wanted to know Hather's thoughts.

'Listen to me, my friend,' he began. 'I told you once that I've faced this kind of puzzle before. I also said that my own fate is interwoven with that of the Ynglings. Now, we're riding in the wrong direction through no fault of our own. We're surrounded by a mystery that has brought gods and dwarfs and the Ynglings together within its toils. I'm prepared to have you disagree with me, and you'd have every right to do so, but I propose to continue in the direction we're travelling. And I'll tell you why.

'What Omund's up to I don't know. But he's up to something. What my son Svipdag is up to I don't know either, but he and that old Lappish witch are hatching some plot, and it involves a wizard in the north. We're travelling north because we've been misled into doing so. Why, I don't know. You see, there's not a great deal I do know,' he said with a forced grin.

'Even so,' Atyl Skin replied, 'I'm listening.'

'Let's look at it piece by piece. Firstly, let's see what the dwarfs are up to. They're killing off Omund's kin. They want me for some reason. They needed to take Hanni to get me, and probably to exercise some kind of hold over Omund as well. They have nothing to do with Svipdag because they tried to kill him in Harek's longhouse, but they probably have something to do with Omund. So much for the dwarfs.

'Now for the gods. I saw Allfather upon Vermund's grave-mound. He told me that this northern wizard, this Vultikamian, killed Vermund and is defying him. He said it was some kind of test for the House of Yngling. At least, that's my guess. And Odin thinks that the Norns are behind it. Now, as you know, my friend, the Norns control our fate. All our fates. Yours, mine, and the Ynglings'.

'That's the gods and the dwarfs. Now for the humans. Omund is too treacherous by nature to be entirely innocent of whatever's going on. He'd arranged for Hanni's visit before Aud's death. And that can only mean that he knew Aud was going to die. In turn, that implicates him in her death, strengthening the idea that he's in league with the dwarfs. What I don't know is why he's in league with the dwarfs. He'd like me out of the way, and the dwarfs want me alive. But why do they want me at all? What can I do for them?'

Atyl Skin's expression remained perplexed. 'You've still not said why you intend to keep travelling north,' he stated.

'Three reasons,' came Hather's reply. 'The most immediate is to avoid whoever Omund has sent to pursue us, and to keep both Hanni and Flosi safe for as long as possible. The second is to attempt to learn more about Vultikamian's role in all this, and we know that Vultikamian is in the north.'

'And the third?'

Hather shrugged. 'The simplest of the three,' he answered. 'Because we're going that way. We shouldn't be, but we are. And we are because we've been tricked into doing so. Someone, or something, wants us to travel in this direction, and wants it badly enough to make certain that we are. Understanding has little to do with it.

'Think about it this way, my friend. There are sixteen of us. You, me, Saeunna, Olaf, Gudrun, Hanni. That's six. Flosi and his wife and two children, ten. Two of Hanni's maids and four of your men make up the sixteen. Hanni's important to Omund: he wants to marry her. I'm important to Omund: he wants me out of the way. He's always wanted it, secretly. Well, we're out of his way and, whilst we are, Hanni's safe from him. If I put it that way, there's probably a fourth reason for continuing in this direction, though if we meet Vultikamian I've no idea what's likely to happen. What I have to ask you is: do you trust my judgement?'

Atyl Skin smiled grimly. 'It's always worked for me before,' he replied. 'I'm prepared to give it another chance.'

They leaned over to one another and clasped wrists. Then Hather said: 'Good. Will you leave me your men?'

'If that's what you want.'

'That's what I want. But not yet. There's a steading ahead where we should be able to purchase some supplies and a few spare horses. What we have won't last indefinitely and we may be travelling for some time. I'll tell you now, I don't know where we're going, or how long it will take to get there. The closest I can come is that we'll know it when we see it. The important thing is to keep Hanni and my family, not to mention the last few living Ynglings, as safe as possible. If we need to, if our pursuers draw too close, I'll fall back with your men and purchase some time. No argument, Atyl. Hanni will need you. So will Flosi and Saeunna.'

As he finished, the dawn began to brighten into morning. Olaf spurred his horse forward and voiced the suspicion they had already discovered for themselves, that they were travelling north instead of south. When they reached the steading, where a friendly farmer sold them the warm clothing and provisions they would need to continue their journey, Hather, suppported by Atyl Skin, explained his intentions. Hanni's maids showed some fear, but the others kept any misgivings they might have had to themselves.

They rested briefly at the steading, then pushed on again before noon, making what they could of their lead and the daylight hours to distance themselves from their pursuers. Despite the extra horses they had taken, Omund and his men did not catch up. In fact it was eight days later, with the Dalalven behind them and the beginnings of the snow-clad forests and mountains of the north in sight, that Olaf, riding last in the company, peered behind during the afternoon to see distant shapes a little below the horizon.

He reported to Hather, who nodded slowly. 'Fresh mounts at the Dalalven fortress,' he explained. 'We couldn't do that in case Omund had managed to get a message ahead of us.'

'Father,' Olaf asked, 'are we near Skroggrmagi?' The dwarfish citadel was little more than a legend to him; he hadn't been born at the time of Hather's hunt for the *vargr*.

'No. That's a few days west of here,' came the reply. 'It's completely destroyed, anyway. There's nothing to see. Now, I want you to ride up here with Atyl Skin. I have to drop back and talk to your mother.'

Olaf took his new place beside the Dane. Hather held his mount still as the column passed, smiling as Saeunna turned to keep him in sight for as long as possible. The four Danish soldiers also left the column and gathered about Hather.

The five riders had turned and begun to go back before Olaf fully realised what was going on. Before he could rein in his mount Atyl Skin's hand had reached across and clamped itself firmly on his wrist.

'When it's time,' the Dane began, 'we'll all do what we have to. It's your father's time now, young Olaf. It will be ours sometime soon. I know I don't need to tell you to be brave, but I will tell you to keep riding.'

Olaf watched as Hather and the soldiers began to diminish into the distance. He kept his expression set, determinedly fighting the tears which threatened to gather at the corners of his eyes. Yet his heart was pounding, and the question whirling in his brain was a natural one, even though it remained unvoiced.

Would he ever see his father alive again?

He wasn't alone in that. His mother and sister were silently asking the same thing, as was Atyl Skin. And the answer which came to all of them, as they rode on towards the frozen whiteness of the north, was that only the gods and Norns could decide the fate of the Champion of the Ynglings.

THE THIRD PART

THE WIZARD IN THE WASTES OF FINNMARK

1

The Shape-Shifter

Gudrun's face was a picture of worry as they continued northwards. She had always know of her father's reputation as a warrior, despite his considerable administrative skills, but she had never realised before just what risk and sacrifice could be involved. She looked at her mother, her eyes large and pleading.

Saeunna smiled gently. 'He'll do what he has to,' she told her. 'If he has to fight for our safety, then he'll fight like a berserker. Try not to worry about him too much, my dear. Your father has faced worse odds than this before. We both have.'

As she spoke the first chill flakes of snow began to fall from a luminous grey sky. The riders huddled into their furs, their hearts as heavy as the leaden skies above them, their eyes half-closed against the biting wind and the cold. Gudrun was not consoled by her mother's words. Hather was older now. His strength was slowly beginning to fail, though his mind was as quick as ever. The man who had faced the *vargr* at Skroggrmagi had been twenty years younger than the warrior who had taken their Danish guards to delay their pursuers.

The same thought had occurred to her brother, still riding with Atyl Skin at the head of the column. Olaf privately resolved that at the first opportunity which presented itself he would ride back to his father's aid. Another sword couldn't go amiss and, if the worst came to the worst, there was no man in Sweden at whose side Olaf Hathersson would rather die.

The light began to fade, and they decided not to make camp for the night just yet in view of the closeness of their pursuers. Suddenly Atyl Skin sighted a thin line of smoke drifting amongst the trees which topped a distant hill. Olaf followed the line of the Dane's pointing hand.

'This is a desolate place to live,' the younger man remarked. Atyl Skin shrugged. 'Some men like solitude. Still, as long as he's not hostile to visitors, it will be somewhere warm and dry for us to spend the night.'

He reined in and turned to look back down the column and point again towards the smoke. 'Shelter for the night,' he called, his words being greeted with sighs of relief from the women.

'This is going to get worse,' Atyl remarked, gesturing at the falling snow. 'It will cover our tracks and hide the smoke from the dwelling over there. Perhaps your father won't have to fight after all.'

The column turned towards the steading amongst the trees. Even as they did so the snowflakes increased in both size and denseness, obliterating the tracks they left behind them even before they were out of sight. Saeunna found herself reflecting that not only their pursuers, but Hather as well, would have a hard time finding them in such weather. She turned and glanced behind, smiling reassuringly at Flosi and his wife Thurid. Her mother's heart went out to the tiny children, swathed in furs and riding in their parents' arms, pale faced and whimpering with cold. Hanni and her maids, used to the slightly warmer climate of the Dane-Lands, also showed the discomfort that their flight was causing them. A warm fire, and some hot food eaten under a sheltering roof, would serve to restore them for whatever still lay ahead, Saeunna thought.

They drew closer to the steading, a low, long wooden structure sunk some feet into the ground and roofed with reindeer-hides over a strong frame. Close by stood a corral with reindeer penned inside, the beasts snorting steam into the snow and foraging for whatever food might lie upon the frozen ground beneath. The smell of the smoke issuing through the smoke-hole promised respite and comfort. Atyl Skin raised his hand and dismounted. With drawn sword he approached on foot, eying the dwelling with the caution of the professional soldier, wary of traps even in so isolated a place. Here, upon the fringes of the Finnmark forests, with Hather gone and Omund close behind, the last of the Ynglings now in his charge, the Dane was not about to scatter caution to the winds.

He paused before the depression in the snow which concealed the steps down to a low door of solid plank construction, set upon plaited leather hinges which made it difficult to open or close. That whoever lived there was inside was obvious from the lack of tracks to and from the door and the steady smoking of the fire. There was also a glimmer of lamp-light through a crack in the door, and no one who made his own lamp-fuel out of reindeer fat would go out and leave it to burn away for nothing.

Overhead the leaden grey of the sky had darkened to a heavy, starless blue-black, with only the whiteness of the snow reflecting light to see by. The snow was falling heavily in large flakes which would form banks and drifts amongst the trees if the wind strengthened during the night.

Atyl Skin raised his sword and struck the door with the pommel, listening to the blows echoing dully within the steading, listening for some sound which would betray movement and habitation. He lifted the hilt of his sword to strike another summons, only to find the heavy planks swinging slowly inwards upon their hinges.

Not too far, though. Only far enough to permit a narrow strip of light to splash out into the darkness, a strip broken at the upper end by the shape of part of a head peering out. The Dane could make out little of the features, staring into the light as he was, but he gained an impression of great age and wisps of thin white hair in the seamed and wrinkled features. And dark eyes which belied their years by the clarity and alertness of their gaze.

'You're lost,' a high, sharp voice snapped. 'Only lost

people come here.' The door opened a fraction wider as the old man peered past Atyl Skin to the snow-veiled shapes of the waiting company.

'More of you, eh? Who are you? What do you want?'

'A noble company requiring a night's shelter and something to eat,' the Dane replied.

'That doesn't tell me who you are.'

'I am Atyl Skin of Jelling in the Dane-Lands, but others greater than I are in need of your hospitality. Prince Flosi Omundsson, Princess Hanni of the Dane-Lands and Queen Saeunna of Ostragotland . . .'

'Saeunna wife of Hather Lambisson? Why didn't you say so sooner? Get them in, get them in. It's a foul night to be out there.'

The door swung wide and Atyl Skin, his sword still drawn, stepped inside. Only when he was certain that the old man was alone did he wave for the others to approach. As they dismounted, tethered their horses and filed into the warm interior the Dane looked at their ancient host properly for the first time. The old man's brown skin and berry-dark eyes proclaimed him unmistakably a Lapp. He was dressed in a suit of reindeer-hides, once embroidered with coloured threads and set with bone buttons, but now as shabby with wear and age as the body beneath it. Painfully thin, he was still alive and vital, his movements reminding Atyl Skin of a hungry sparrow's. It was impossible to tell his age with any accuracy, but he looked to be at least eighty and possibly much older, despite his sprightliness.

'Which is Saeunna?' the old man snapped. 'Which of you is Hather's wife?'

Saeunna pushed back the fur hood of her travelling cape and stepped towards him. 'I am Saeunna,' she said gently.

The ancient's eyes glittered for a moment, then misted as he took her hand in his own wrinkled claw and touched his lips to it. 'Hather's queen is ever welcome here,' he proclaimed. 'I have a great admiration for your husband. I met him once, you know. Ah, so many years ago. I was able to help him then, and I shall be proud if I may do so again before I die.'

There was a quality in his words, in the manner of their speaking, which immediately convinced Saeunna that he was speaking the truth. At some time in the distant past he *had* know Hather Lambisson.

'May I ask you your name?' Saeunna enquired, suddenly conscious that he had yet to release her hand.

'My name?' he queried. 'Ah, yes. My name. Forgive me, Queen Saeunna,' he continued, finally relinquishing his hold. 'I've been alone so long now that I have to think before I can remember it. My name, yes. My name is Bolli. Some have called me Reindeer Bolli, but that was almost fifty years ago, when I was a tracker in the service of King Oli the Great.'

He suddenly began to bustle about and behave like a willing host, settling his guests and preparing a meal of dry bread and hot reindeer-meat soup, seasoned with dried herbs which hung in bunches from the rafters and thickened with a soft cheese of reindeer-milk. While Bolli cooked and the women huddled about the fire, Olaf and Flosi and Atyl Skin erected a shelter of reindeer-hides on the far side of the steading and stabled their mounts beneath it. As they walked back around the end of the dwelling furthest from the corral Atyl Skin suddenly stiffened and stopped in his tracks, staring at the trees beyond the clearing.

'You and Flosi go inside,' the Dane ordered.

'What is it?' Flosi asked. 'What's the matter?'

'Probably nothing,' came the reply, 'but I'd rather be certain now than dead for my ignorance later.'

They unwillingly left him in the snow and returned to the warmth of the steading. Once certain of their safety he returned his gaze to the trees, peering at them through a curtain of steadily falling snow. Slowly, with drawn sword, he began to walk away from the dwelling, pulling the glove from his left hand with his teeth as he went.

Atyl Skin raised his bare hand and held it above his head for a few moments, turning it this way and that to feel for some trace of wind. There was none, so he wriggled his fingers back inside the glove before they began to chill.

The snowflakes were falling without disturbance, confirming the lack of wind. Yet the Dane was certain he had glimpsed a tall, white shape amongst the trees. It was impossible for it to have been a drift, and now, as he drew closer, he could see that it was no longer there. Nor were there any tracks upon the ground, which was sheltered from much of the snow by the laden branches above.

His eyes were getting old, but they had not yet got so bad that they played tricks upon him. Wary of his surroundings, still scouting for the vanished shape, he returned to the shelter of Bolli's dwelling, sheathing his sword only as he pushed open the door.

Inside, Bolli was scooping his thick soup into wooden bowls, the first of which he offered to Saeunna. The old man was not in the habit of receiving guests, and had only a few bowls, so some had to wait their turn. Saeunna handed her bowl, untasted, to Thurid, who fed the children first. Saeunna sat, searching her memory for some mention of Reindeer Bolli which might explain his kindness to her and his devotion to Hather. If he had been in the service of King Oli, then the Hather he had known would probably have been the youth who rode with Starkadder . . .

Hather had told her the story, at her request, shortly before their marriage. Since then Saeunna had fleshed out her husband's modest account of those days which had first written his name into legend with the accounts of others who had been there. Chief amongst these, and by far the most credible and dependable, was dear old Vermund Bjarnisson.

A tear crept into Saeunna's eyes, for Vermund now dead and in his grave-mound, and also for Hather, wherever he was. She checked herself before the others could see, reminding herself that she was still the woman who had fought beside Hather at Skroggrmagi for the life of his son. She mustn't give in to crying. She must stay outwardly calm, whatever turmoil of emotions might be raging within her, for the sake of the others, for her children, for Hanni and her maids, and for Flosi's children, the last heirs of the Yngling line, threatened by death and madness.

Yet even here, upon the edge of the Finnmark wastes, they had found an ally in the snow. It was impossible to doubt that Reindeer Bolli was a good friend, and all the better for having been encountered so unexpectedly.

Saeunna remembered. Bolli had been with the party led by Thorvald Brotamad, sent out by Oli to capture Starkadder. They had succeeded and were returning to Uppsala, where Starkadder would have been put to death by the blood-eagle. Hather was with them, still not certain whether Starkadder was friend or foe, when a strange mist had arisen. Bolli had seen that mist as a threat to the safety of all of them, and had freed Starkadder and sent him on his way with Hather to ensure their safety. The mist had taken Hather and Starkadder to the very gates of Trollheim, and the meeting with the dwarf-king Dvalin, which sealed mad Oli's doom at Starkadder's hands some days later.

Was that really forty years ago? Oh, how the years fled past. How desperately their days of love and life and happiness were fleeing. Could they ever be regained? she asked herself. Was Hather dead already, before he could ever know how the past itself had risen up to help them in the spindly, sparrow-like shape of this old tracker who took such pride in having played his part in Hather's legend?

Her turn came for a wiped-clean bowl. She ate her soup gladly, grateful, but with her thoughts somewhere else. There would come an end to all things. That was the only real certainty to follow birth. She herself had dreamed of Omund's sword skewering her husband's body, and she knew enough of her dreams to realise that the dreadful vision she had been vouchsafed could well come true. The consolation, the *only* consolation, was that they had yet to pass a frozen lake where that dreadful duel between the Yngling king and his acknowledged champion could take place.

When everyone had eaten, when Bolli had piled high the fire to warm them through the night, they settled down to sleep. There was no need for guards to be posted. The snow outside would have obliterated their tracks and, in continuing to fall, shielded the smoke of the fire from watching eyes. They were secure, for one night, and it was as well to make what use they could of their security before they were beset by the uncertainties which would be upon them with the dawn. Even Atyl Skin, the oldest and most experienced warrior of their party, slept without disturbance.

Bolli was awake long before dawn. He stretched and blinked and shook his head, forcing the cramps and stiffness of sleep out of his ancient limbs. Picking up his fur blanket he draped it about his shoulders and crossed to the door, pulling it open as quietly as he could to avoid disturbing his guests.

He was used to rising at this hour. Every morning when the snow was upon the ground he would go out to the storehouse by the corral to find fodder for his beasts. It was only after he had closed the door behind him and almost reached the storehouse that he saw, through the greyness of the distant day, that they had already been fed, that someone had opened the storehouse and distributed the feed before his rising.

The figure was waiting for him, standing beside the wooden fence of the corral. Just behind it lay the feed, scattered over the snow, but the reindeer were huddled away from it, on the futher side of the enclosure, as if they sensed some frightful evil, as Bolli did.

His eyes widened. He felt his feet, his legs, cease to move as if they had been bound with invisible fetters. His mouth hung open in amazement as he stared into the waiting figure's face.

And beheld his own.

The mouth creased slowly into a smile, then widened into a grin which displayed Bolli's own crumbling, discoloured teeth. The eyes, the nose, the stick-like limbs, the faded dress of reindeer-hides, all were his own. He stood before his other self, speechless with terror.

He worked his tongue to moisten the dryness of his mouth, to chase away the harsh taste of fear which furred his throat. With hardly any breath in his old lungs he croaked: 'Who . . . are you?'

'Don't you know?' his own voice replied. 'I'm Reindeer Bolli, Reindeer Bolli. I am you.'

'You . . . can't be me . . .'

'Can't I? But I am, you see. Now, you need to rest. Come with me, Bolli. Let me take you to your rest.'

He tried to turn, to run back to his home and rouse the others, to tell them about this new and terrible threat, but he couldn't turn, he couldn't run. He couldn't even cry out or speak any more. All he could do was watch the figure turn away and begin to walk towards the trees, then mutely follow.

They walked, one behind the other, in a grey, unhallowed snow-shrouded world of fear. Bolli was unable even to wonder why the figure left no footprints in the snow, simply passing between tree-trunks, as the shapeshifter led him to the place that was prepared, a place where four trees grew close together, a rope trailing from the trunk of each.

'Lie down,' the figure commanded. Unhesitating, completely helpless to resist, Reindeer Bolli lay down in the snow between the four trees and watched in silent terror as his tormentor tied first his wrists, then his ankles, to the ropes.

'You will be set free, my friend,' the figure sneered. 'As you are aware, there are wolves in these parts. After all, you've hunted them often enough. In time the wolves will come to free you, Bolli.'

He tried to cry out, but no voice came.

The false Bolli nodded sagely. 'It would be unfortunate if the others heard you call,' it said. 'It would spoil so many carefully laid plans, you understand. Yet if you still live after we have left here, after I have led your friends to where I want them, you shall have your voice back. It would be too unkind to let you die beneath the slavering jaws of your enemies without the comfort of a cry or two, and I have that much kindness in me.'

Bolli knew the words for the mockery they were, but he had no means of answering, bound and muted as he was. All he could do was twist his head to watch the figure leave him helpless and alone, and note that this time there were footprints in the snow to mark its passage.

And then he was alone. There were no flakes falling from the lightening sky, but the cold from the ground was biting into his spine and numbing his buttocks as his clothing became saturated by the snow melting beneath his body.

Bolli stared at the snow-clad branches overhead, peering through the gaps in their wintery canopy at the sky paling before the inexorable dawning of his final day. He thought back throughout his life to that time near the crossing of the streams, where he had freed Starkadder and played his part in the forging of a legend. Now, in his old age, when Hather's kin needed him as Hather had needed him then, he was powerless to do anything.

His eyes watered with both cold and tears as he realised that his dreadful double would betray the trust which Saeunna had placed in him. It would be, he knew, no ordinary betrayal.

Through the glaze of his grief, he saw the fur-clad muzzles approaching. There, beyond that tree he could see between his legs if he struggled to raise his head enough, two sets of amber eyes glittered hard and cold, watching him, appraising his helplessness, knowing that he had no voice with which to call against them.

Two wolves, jaws gaping, tongues lolling, their breath steaming, began their stealthy approach. They came slowly closer, closer, showing wicked teeth, panting rank carnivore breath at their helpless victim, until he could feel the warmth of their fur-covered bodies, a warmth that would have saved his life . . .

2

The Circles of History

Atyl Skin awoke suddenly, every fibre of his being aware that some thing was wrong, that there was a threat in the very air he breathed. He rose to his feet with surprising quietness for a man of his age, and loosened his sword in its scabbard, remembering his misgivings of the night before.

His eyes surveyed the dwelling, counting the sleeping forms, noting the absence of two of them. He scowled and sought to identify the missing sleepers. Their host, Reindeer Bolli, was one of them.

The other was Olaf Hathersson!

The Dane swore silently. The young fool had been so eager to return and help his father, even if it meant dying at Hather's side, that it was impossible for Atyl to doubt that Olaf had risen early, and ridden off to be with Hather. Probably old Bolli had heard him and tried to follow, which explained his own absence.

Atyl Skin stepped outside and drew his sword. The day smelled new and fresh; the snow had ceased falling and the trees cast long shadows. At least one set of footprints led from the steading to the corral, then out into the forest. Another set led around the back of the dwelling, obviously going towards the horses.

The familiar figure of Reindeer Bolli appeared out of the trees and stumped towards the Dane.

'Have you seen young Olaf?' Atyl called.

Bolli shook his head. 'I thought I heard something,' he explained in his high, squawking voice, 'so I got up and fed the reindeer. Then I thought I saw something amongst the trees.'

Atyl Skin nodded. 'I thought I saw something last night,' he replied.

'I went to have a look,' Bolli's shape continued, 'but I couldn't see anything. Now I'm back I can see more tracks going around to the horses. Is that young Olaf?'

The Dane nodded. 'I'm sure he's gone to find his father, though I've not followed the tracks yet.'

'Then we must find out if you're right,' the shape responded.

Together they walked around the end of the steading, following the prints in the snow. They were not surprised to find one of the horses missing and its hoofprints leading back the way they had come the day before.

'Young fool,' Atyl spat. 'He's likely to be more hindrance than help to Hather. Besides, he was told to stay with me.'

With Olaf gone, only Flosi and Atyl Skin were left to guard the women and children sleeping within the steading. It would have been impossible to leave them any more vulnerable.

Bolli's voice said: 'You must try to find him, Atyl Skin.' The Dane's eyes narrowed. 'That only leaves Flosi here to use a sword if need be,' he replied.

So, what a clever man you are. But you are not the only one, my poor fool.

'The others will be safe here,' the shape smiled. 'The snow has covered your tracks, and you left your route when you saw my smoke. If I do not relight the fire there is no chance of anyone finding this place. Besides', it added, 'you forget that I know this country, with or without a covering of snow. If you try to find Olaf and my old friend Hather I shall lead your friends south towards Sudrafell. I know a way that will take them out of the way of anyone who is following. Find Hather and the others and get them to follow me, or even return to Sudrafell by another route. You see, Atyl Skin, I can work your fate as surely as any Norn can.'

Bolli was making good sense. This flight into the north was hardly what they'd expected or been prepared for when they left Uppsala. The return to Sudrafell was both logical and, the way Bolli explained it, sensible. From there they would be in a position to hold off Omund's men, whereas here in the forests of the north they were vulnerable to any who chanced upon them.

Atyl Skin reflected, then decided. 'Very well,' he said. 'I'll see you on your way. Then I'll go after Olaf and Hather and try to take them south again. You're a good man, Bolli,' he added, extending his hand.

They clasped wrists, the shape's ancient talons digging into Atyl's sleeve. Within the hour the others were awake and prepared for travel. Saeunna, saddened by the disappearance of her son, kissed the Dane tenderly and charged him with Olaf's recovery. Atyl Skin waited to see Bolli lead them off towards the forest, and mounted his horse.

It was then that he heard the wolves howling in the distance.

Hather Lambisson reined in and eyed the distant riders. Whilst Saeunna and the others were approaching the shelter of Bolli's steading, Hather and his guards sought the shelter of a depression in the ground from which to observe their pursuers. As they watched, the sky began to shower them with flakes of snow, small at first but soon growing in intensity as the storm thickened.

Hather turned to the man beside him. 'This will hide all our tracks,' he grinned. 'If this keeps up they'll not see our trail or the others'.'

The soldier nodded. Hather was right. Besides, the afternoon was growing late. In a little while the pursuing force would have to stop for the night and search for shelter. That would buy all of them some time.

They dismounted and tethered the horses, weighting their reins with stones, and prepared to make a frugal meal of the dried rations they carried with them in their packs. Hather took the first watch, noting the preparations for camp being made by Omund's distant party.

Whilst he did so, however, a rebellion was being hatched by his reluctant companions.

'We don't belong here,' one of them hissed. 'We're Danes. We have no part in these Swedish politics. I say we kill this King Hather and join up with the others again. We'll stand some kind of a chance that way. Atyl Skin should never have put us under this man's command.'

Another growled: 'We don't need to kill him. We can simply desert. This weather's going to continue for some time, or I miss my guess. Sooner or later he's going to get lost and freeze to death. The others were bound in that direction,' he added, pointing. 'If we follow them in the night we'll soon catch up. It's a lot better than waiting here to die, anyway.'

The others agreed, and the plan was formed. All they waited was their chance, and that came soon enough.

One of the soldiers approached Hather, huddled in a fur cape. 'King Hather?' he asked.

There was no reply. The rigours of flight and command had wrapped the warrior in much-needed sleep.

The man signalled his companions, grinning.

They mounted up.

It was dawn before Hather, stiff with his vigil and numb with cold, his fur cape turned into a heavy white shroud with the snow which had fallen during the night, became conscious enough to realise that he must wake and rise or die where he was sitting. He hauled his almost frozen body to its feet and surveyed his surroundings.

A thin tendril of smoke from their dying fire still rose from Omund's distant camp. There was as yet no sign of activity there. And nor was there any sign of activity behind him. The Danish soldiers were gone, leaving him completely alone save for his horse. Stamping his feet to bring some life back to them, he walked to his horse and rubbed its legs vigorously to restore some warmth to both of them. Mounting the patient beast he turned it in the direction in which he knew Atyl Skin and the others had been travelling, finding his way by the line of the distant forest rather than anything else, for the snow during the night had obliterated any trail there might have been for him to follow.

The first thing he found, some minutes later, was the dead mount of one of his soldiers. Beyond it, frozen upright, his glazed face a mask of horror, its rider stood in the snowscape like a runestone.

As he went on he found the others, each one ice-bound in death. The last, the most dreadful, was still mounted, his dead horse frozen upright beneath him, his sword still clutched in death-frozen fingers, rime upon his beard and face and the sweat turned to ice glazing his armour to hold him in the grim monumental posture of death.

If they had frozen to death, Hather asked himself, then why hadn't he? And what could account for the frightful expression set in icy lines upon each of their dead faces?

Whatever had caused their deaths was beyond him, be it Allfather, Norn of sorcerer. Besides, there were more important things than a few Danish deserters. There was the fate of his family and Hanni to be considered. That he still lived whilst his men were dead was proof that he was reserved for another end.

But why? he asked himself. He had some idea why the dwarfs wanted him; Bombor had given that away by his words before they reached Uppsala. Bombor was a pretender to the throne of Trollheim. He needed some means of legitimising his claim, some means which only Hather could help him with. The symbol of the dwarfish kings was the sword which his mother Hervara had given him before he went to seek out Starkadder, the sword with which Starkadder had killed King Oli, and which his *vargr*-wife had sought to bargain with the dwarfish sorcerer Kulubak Magri for.

Tyrfing.

That was it. Bombor wanted him because he thought that, if he held Hather, he could get his hands upon Tyrfing.

But the sword Tyrfing had been taken by Starkadder's ghost at Skroggrmagi. It was no longer in the realms of men. And yet, Hather reflected, he was the champion of the Yngling dynasty, a dynasty which Odin wanted to preserve. If Bombor took him prisoner, preventing him from aiding the Ynglings, it might be possible to force Tyrfing from Allfather's clutches.

Oh, if he was right, the dwarfs would be following through their tunnels, making better progress now then Omund and his men across this frozen waste. And they had no love for men, no care whether the Ynglings perished or not, just as long as Tyrfing was delivered to Bombor, enabling him to ascend the throne of Trollheim. Hather could fail or succeed, depending upon Odin's surrender of the sword. It wouldn't matter to the dwarfs. King Dvalin had closed the gates of Trollheim against men, and closed they would remain, whether the Ynglings lived or died, so long as Bombor secured the means to the throne which Tyrfing represented.

The last of the smoke from Omund's camp had faded away, but it was reasonable to assume that the High King and his men would shortly be pursuing. If that was the case, they could soon be upon him, especially as the ending of the snowstorm had meant that he was leaving tracks which could easily be followed.

So Hather set off towards the forest. Somewhere ahead of him his family, and those he was sworn to defend, would be waiting, wondering if he was alive or dead.

He left the four frozen deserters stretched across the snowscape behind him. A chill wind had sprung up, biting at his face, whipping the powdery snow at his feet into tiny flurries as he led his horse towards the treees in the distance. He bowed his head to keep the stinging snow-crystals from his tired eyes, hoping for some sign which might restore his flagging spirits and so intent was he upon his progress that he was almost upon the figure with the drawn sword before he realised its presence.

He snatched at his scabbard, the fingers of his gloved hand wrapping themselves about the hilt of his weapon. The cold, red eyes of the two figures met, even as their sword-points touched, and then father and son knew each for the other and cast their weapons aside in a warm embrace.

Olaf felt the tears streaming down his face as he pressed it against his father's shoulder. 'I . . . thought you'd be dead by now,' he choked.

Hather patted his son's back. 'I would have been, if my companions had had their way,' he replied. 'I'm lucky that Atyl Skin isn't typical of the other Danes I've met. But what are you doing here?' Hather demanded, forcing his son to arm's length by grasping his shoulders.

'I thought you might need me,' came the reply.

'And the others? Your sister and mother?'

'They've found an old friend of yours, a Lapp called Reindeer Bolli.'

Hather began to laugh. 'Bolli?' he shouted, his voice incredulous. 'Is he still alive? The last I heard of him he was going home to Bjarmaland, and that was forty years ago.'

'He has a steading just by the edge of the forest,' Olaf answered. 'We spent the night there. He couldn't do enough to make mother welcome once he found out who she was.'

'Old friends are the best,' Hather said simply. 'And Bolli must be about the oldest friend I've got left. He'll take care of them, and do it well. I only met him once, and briefly, but he showed himself a true friend to Starkadder and me, even though he was betraying King Oli at the time.'

The snow-flurries about their feet strengthened and became small whirlwinds. Out of the dull sky above them more snow began to fall.

Olaf pointed. 'There, father,' he began. 'Riders, coming this way. And travelling fast.'

Hather followed his son's pointing finger. The riders were coming, all right, from the direction of Omund's camp. Hather was suddenly aware that he and Olaf must be standing out against the snow like coals at the bottom of a bowl of water. He glanced up. The storm of the night before was renewing itself, but this time there was a wind with it that would cover tracks and confuse both pursuers and pursued. 'We'll make for the forest,' he grunted. 'It's time I saw old Bolli again, not to mention Gudrun and your mother.'

They set off, leading their horses through the steadily worsening weather. Such storms, Hather felt, were unseasonable, and he began to wonder whether this was more than simply a natural meeting of clouds and conditions. Shielding his eyes with a gloved hand he glanced behind; the snow-flurries were rising to obscure their progress from Omund's men. Together with the memories of Reindeer Bolli which Olaf had reawakened with his news, that was enough to set Hather Lambisson remembering another time.

Forty years before, when Odin had wanted to lead Starkadder and himself towards the gates of Trollheim, a mist had arisen to mislead any who would thwart them in their progress. Now the very snow which had fallen was rising from the ground to do the same thing.

Things come, things go, Hather thought. With the coming of the mist we stood before King Dvalin in the circular tower which rose above the burning lake. This time, with the clearing of the snow, what shall we see?

Shall we stand before the sorcerer Vultikamian? Shall we know our fates, once and for ever, as we stand within the circle of the buring stones?

Allfather, I wish you could find a way to tell me. Is that what is to be? Is that why we're going north?

Is it all to end in the wastes of Finnmark?

3

The Victims

Svipdag Hathersson hauled his body on to his mount reluctantly. Around him Omund's guards were following suit, stiff and cold after another night in the open. Only the High King, striding about the camp, his eyes blazing with grim determination, showed any sign of enthusiasm as their pursuit entered its ninth gruelling day.

The King's Marshal leaned forward, folding his arms on the horse's neck. The cold had seeped into his wounds, which had not yet healed, and he knew that the torment of another day's riding would weaken his reserves of strength.

During the snowstorm which had begun the previous afternoon they had lost Hather's trail. Now, with a new dawn and no signs to follow, it seemed to Svipdag better to abandon the pursuit and return to the shelter of Dalalven before worse weather closed in around them. But Omund was no longer thinking rationally. Since leaving Uppsala a fanatical gleam had glinted in the High King's eye, a gleam which proclaimed his ambition to fulfil old Skeggja's prophecy to become the last and greatest of the Yngling kings and write his name into the legends of the north.

'Time to go,' Omund ordered suddenly, ceasing his packing and mounting his horse.

Svipdag's smile was closer to a sneer than anything else. 'And which way should we go?' he asked.

Omund's eyes blazed. 'North,' he snapped. 'The way we were travelling yesterday.'

His Marshal sighed. 'With respect, King Omund, we have no trail to follow and we are ill-provided for this weather. Might it not be better to return to Dalalven and equip a proper expedition? It might cost us a week, but there are sledges stored there. We'll make up time by travelling faster than anyone can on horseback.'

Despite his ambition, despite his feeling that Omund's power, instead of strengthening, would wane as a result of this pursuit, Svipdag had no desire to catch up with his father. Such a meeting could force the most terrible decision of his life upon the King's Marshal. To side with Hather would strip him of his office and bring his plans to nothing. To remain at Omund's side, however, would brand him a patricide and rob him of the popular support he would require in order to seize the kingdom. Much better, he decided, if they simply didn't find the fugitives. Hather would turn up again, sooner or later. He wouldn't just simply vanish into the wastes of Finnmark.

Omund shook his head. 'We go on,' he ordered, bringing his horse up beside Svipdag's. 'I want the traitors out of the way, once and for all. We'll soon see to that, and other things as well.'

Clearly the High King wasn't going to explain his last words at that time, the Marshal decided, though he had a fair idea of what Omund might mean. Their route was not altogether unfamiliar to Svipdag. Various landmarks along the way reminded him of the errand he had undertaken for the High King earlier in the year, which had sent him to the circle of the burning stones.

And then it came to Svipdag, just what was really happening. This journey of theirs was much more than just a simple pursuit, and the absence of a trail made no difference to it. If they could not follow Hather, they had simply to travel to the burning stones and await him there. For he would come to the burning stones, as Svipdag knew they would themselves. They would stand before Vultikamian and watch as the prophecy was fulfilled, as Omund became the last and greatest of all the Ynglings.

But what deed of blood would be required? Svipdag

shuddered, seeing the dark red splash and trickle across the destinies of all of them.

Before long they passed the four frozen Danes and their horses, then sighted the figures of Hather and Olaf ahead of them, only to lose them again in the whirling snow.

'To the forest,' Omund called. 'We'll find their tracks again in the shelter of the trees.'

And so they pressed on, Omund and his men cheered and encouraged by even such a brief glimpse of their quarry, Svipdag nursing his doubts in silence as he waited for the fateful game to draw to its end.

For Saeunna's party, some kind of end was already approaching. Bolli's shape had led them into the shelter of the forest. They followed a path which wove and twisted between the trees, as he led them towards the grim conclusion of their journeying. Sheltered from the worst of the wind and snow they made good progress, though the darkness of the day and the snow-laden canopy of branches overhead denied Saeunna any sight of the sun which would have reassured her as to their direction. Yet Bolli, she knew, would not betray them. He had no reason to . . .

Shortly after mid-day, when the snow had all fallen, the trees began to thin. They emerged from the forest and stood looking down across a snow-clad valley. The sun appeared behind them. Saeunna realised that they had continued northwards instead of making their way south as Bolli had said they would.

Bolli's shape smiled at Saeunna and pointed. Across the valley, in the distance, stood more forest. From its depths, rising like a thousand ghostly wraiths from ice-cloaked firs, issued a column of steam.

Saeunna felt her jaw drop. She clutched Bolli's arm. 'What is it?' she asked, her voice awed.

'An ancient site of my people,' came the reply. 'They think it mysterious and forbidden, but it is warm and you can wait for Hather there. Once you are safe there I shall bring him to you.'

Their spirits lightened, they began the descent into the valley. The sky began to darken towards evening as they entered the forest which surrounded the column of steam and, still following Bolli's shape, made their way along the path which Mother Skuld had taken so many months before, towards the circle of the burning stones.

That morning, watching the others leave with the shape-shifter as their guide, Atyl Skin had been thinking more of Olaf's folly in attempting to find his father than of the departing party. He was also thinking about the white shape he had glimpsed amongst the trees the night before, that same shape, he had no doubt, that Bolli claimed to have seen too.

Whatever their watcher was, the Dane decided, he stood a better chance of finding it on horseback and in daylight. Olaf could be traced by the prints his mount had left in the snow. They should last for a while. For now, though, he'd have a look about the steading. Probably there was nothing to see, but there were enough mysteries around without leaving another unexplored when he had the chance to do so.

It might, of course, be foolish to start into the forest alone, especially after hearing the calls of the wolves from its depths. But he had heard at most two of them; they would have to be really starving to attempt to pull down a man on horseback, and the weather had not been bad enough recently to deprive them of more usual game.

He used the reins gently to guide his horse along the path left by Bolli's footprints in the snow. Atyl Skin shivered and pulled his cloak closer about him. It was cold among the trees. They seemed to trap and hold the chill of the ground. Anyone alone out here, unable to move, would quickly freeze to death. Lost in this sombre speculation Atyl Skin did not see the wolves until he was almost on top of them. With a startled cry he lost his seat as the horse neighed in terror and reared up in panic. He landed against a tree-trunk; the impact winded him and sent his sword spinning away out of his reach.

The wolves were lying in the snow on top of something which was stretched by ropes to the nearest trees. Their amber eyes fixed on him as he struggled to fill his lungs again, only his thick Lappish coat having saved him from serious injury.

He cursed silently. His horse had run off and here he was sitting in the snow, weaponless, with two of the largest, fiercest wolves he had ever encountered. If he tried to move they'd be upon him before he gained his feet. And if he sat still on his arse they'd get curious and come over, sooner of later. Well, the Lappish coat would give him some protection against their teeth, and it wasn't unknown for a man to kill a wolf with his bare hands. If you forced the forelegs apart it collapsed the ribs into the heart of the animal. But what was he to do about the other one?

One of the wolves got up. Whatever was stretched upon the ground moaned softly. With a start Atyl Skin realised that it was a man in reindeer-hides. The wolf loped over to the Dane's sword and picked it up in its mouth. With its teeth clamped firmly upon the blade it came close to him and set the weapon down by his right hand. Then it returned to its companion and lay down again on the helpless Bolli.

Slowly, carefully, Atyl Skin reached out and grasped the hilt of his sword. Setting his feet flat against the ground he used the tree to lever his body upright whilst the wolves, their eyes burning, watched his every move, only looking away to follow the sweep of the blade as he severed the nearest rope. Still not taking his eyes from them he cut the next rope as well. Only when the last of the bonds had been slashed through did the wolves rise slowly to their feet, still with their eyes fixed upon him. Then they backed away from Atyl Skin and the groaning Bolli, turned and vanished into the forest.

Atyl Skin's eyes widened with surprise when he beheld

the man he'd just watched lead Saeunna and the others away from the steading.

Bolli clutched his sleeve and he helped the old man to sit up, marvelling at the warmth which his frail body still held.

'A . . . shape-shifter,' Bolli squawked. 'He's taken . . . *my shape* . . .'

'Bolli? Is that you?'

The old man grinned. 'It shouldn't be,' he continued with a struggle. 'He left me here to die of cold or be eaten by wolves. Something went wrong, though. The wolves came, but they kept me warm instead of tearing my liver out. Will you help me up?'

Atyl Skin, in numb bewilderment, assisted the old man to rise. One or the other, the one here or the other with Saeunna and Princess Hanni, had to be a shape-shifter. But which one? The only solution seemed to be to catch up and keep a close eye upon both until one gave himself away.

Yet shape-shifters were sorcerers. No mortal man could use wolves to keep himself warm in the snow, and there was only one set of tracks to and from this place.

'I must try to find my horse,' the Dane said, keeping his sword in his hand.

'It will have gone back to the steading,' Bolli said. 'I should think we'll find it there.' He began to lead the way back.

A man with power over wolves. A man who should be dead, but isn't. A man who shouldn't be here, but is.

Atyl Skin's grip upon his sword tightened. The point came up to the level of Bolli's shoulder-blades. The Dane's muscles tensed for the thrust. And then a well-aimed rock struck his wrist, sending the sword spinning out of his grasp.

Atyl Skin spun round to face the two riders who had appeared amongst the trees. Bolli turned as well, his eyes wary. Immediately he noted the toll of passing years, the lines upon the firm young face he'd last seen, but saw too the strength and nobility which had made those features memorable to him for the better part of half a century.

He then walked over to the riders and stretched up his hand to the nearest. 'Hather Lambisson,' he grinned. 'At last.'

A little snow fell from the branches overhead as a raven relinquished its perch and flapped off untidily. It made its way to the clear air above the treetops, above the snow-whirls which obscured much of the landscape. Its companion hovered there, waiting upon the air-currents, and together they flew across the frozen world to where Allfather was waiting for them, with the two wolves, Geri and Freki, prowling about the hem of his snow-damp cloak. The ravens landed and perched one upon each of the god's shoulders. The wolves stilled their prowling and sat looking up at their master.

Odin smiled.

A little way away a humped, veiled shape, leaning upon a staff of age-blackened yew-wood, was making its slow way towards him. Allfather's smile widened and his single eye glittered with hidden pleasure as he watched. It wasn't often Mother Skuld came to him. Usually he had to go to her.

He waited whilst she completed her approach. Then he spoke firmly and without any preliminary greeting.

'No talk of the making and breaking of rules, Norn,' he ordered, preparing himself for the argument which he felt would inevitably follow.

She shook her veiled head. 'No talk of that, Odin,' she agreed.

Allfather's brows lowered suspiciously. This wasn't the Mother Skuld he knew, the Norn who fought him for every tiny concession. This was another one, one he wasn't sure he trusted, and doubtless as powerful as ever in her own fashion.

'Then why have you come here?' he asked her.

He felt her eyes burning from beneath the wadmal veil. She had something to say, but she wasn't going to be hurried. For a long time, while the ravens Hugin and Munin shifted their grip upon the god's armoured shoulders, and the wolves looked from god to Norn and back with their patient yellow eyes, Mother Skuld said nothing.

'Then there's nothing to be said,' Allfather grunted. He turned away, the ravens still perched, the wolves rising to follow him.

'Odin, wait!'

Allfather turned back to her. Slowly the gnarled hands rose from her sides, the yew-staff standing on its own, stuck firmly into the snow. The hands began, with an almost infinite stealth, to lift the hem of her veil.

'There is something to be said, Odin,' she told him as the veil rose higher. 'And I think I should say it without hiding behind anything, including this veil.'

'Pity for the victims, little mother?' Odin asked, sneering, pressing home what he hoped was an unexpected advantage. 'I only have one eye, you know. Don't make me blind it with tears of laughter at your words.'

She faced him. It was something he had never known her do before in the human world. In their own distant realms, Asgard or Trollheim, or even the giant-land Jotunheim, he had seen her face before. But never here, never upon the snow-bound soil of men in human form.

And Allfather became afraid for the first time in many centuries, feeling her power close its fingers upon his heart, feeling it form itself into a fist which would squeeze the life-blood from his purposes.

Their eyes met. God and Norn stood together, face to face, while the world about them waited for its fate.

'No tears for the victims, Odin,' Mother Skuld began. 'There shall be more before this game is ended . . .'

4

Divination by Death

The forest about the burning stones exuded an indefinable menace, a desolation somehow both physical and spiritual, which bit through their flesh like the cold and then went deeper to fasten its teeth into their very hearts. Their path was uneven, tangled with long-dead vegetation beneath the snow, strewn with fallen branches which could break a horse's legs. Only the shape-shifter's path was clear and even, seeming to smooth itself before him and then renew its dangers the moment he had passed.

Above them the branches swayed and creaked beneath their burden. As the trees began to thin out, the snow grew less and less upon the approach to the steaming runestones. Suddenly a loud cracking sounded overhead. The riders looked up, staring in helpless horror as two icicles, each the length of a man, broke off and hurtled down like falling stakes, each impaling one of Hanni's maids and continuing through their bodies to skewer the horses as well.

'Sorcery!' the shape-shifter screamed. 'Quickly now, ride for the steam!'

Hanni began to cry out hysterically. Flosi, ahead of her, leaned back and seized her horse's bridle, dragging beast and princess after him towards the steam-shrouded clearing. One of the impaled horses, not quite dead, struggled to rise before it crashed over on its side whinneying helplessly, the dead maid held to its back by the monstrous nail of fallen ice.

Somehow they reached the clearing and rode through

the steam into the stone circle. Once there they reined in their horses and dismounted, wild-eyed with the horror of the last few moments.

Saeunna shuddered and placed an arm about her trembling daughter. Thurid's children were huddled to their mother's skirts while the Yngling prince endeavoured to calm the distressed Hanni, now completely alone in a company of strangers. Her guards were gone. Her maids had just died horribly. Even Atyl Skin was missing.

Saeunna and Gudrun went to her, so Flosi could return to Thurid and his little son and daughter. 'Don't be frightened,' Saeunna whispered. 'The others will come for us. At least we will be warm here . . .'

Her voice trailed off as her eyes fell upon the deep, massive slab of the central altar. Her first reaction was one of panic, but Saeunna knew that any display of fear would do nothing for the others and she fought it down. She could taste the bitterness of betrayal in her mouth. For they had indeed been betrayed.

She clutched at the shape's sleeve. 'That stone in the middle, Bolli,' she began. 'I've seen it before, in my dreams. There was a child upon it . . .'

'Is that all you saw?'

Saeunna shook her head. 'No. The child was in danger, terrible danger. There was . . . something . . . above it, something that meant it harm, that meant harm to all of us.'

The shape stepped away from her. Saeunna's hand remained outstretched, as it had been when she touched Bolli's arm. A numb, sick feeling spreading slowly through her, she attempted to move it, to draw it back, and could not.

With difficulty she turned her head. Her eyes could travel no further than the altar before they locked, unable to move further. Those others of her party she was able to see, Flosi and his wife and their children, were also standing motionless, only the terror in their eyes distinguishing them from cunningly carved and coloured statues.

'Was this what you saw in your dream, Saeunna?' the shape which had been Reindeer Bolli asked. Its voice was no longer the high squeak of the ancient Lapp. It had deepened and lessened in volume until it was no more than a harsh whisper, the same whisper that had issued from old Skeggja at the feast, a whisper that could send the most fearsome of chills down any mortal spine.

The thing walked slowly towards the altar, changing with each step. The stoop of age began to melt and dissolve, paling and spreading into something quite different. The reindeer-skins became a loose-fitting robe of sickly, dirty white, taking on the pallor of disease. The head, instead of simply changing into another head, grew long and pointed, stretching into the hood which hid the sorcerer's features as surely as Mother Skuld's veil hid hers.

They tried to move, to call out, to run, but it was useless. They were powerless against the bonds which restrained them, powerless to do anything but stand and watch the transmutation taking place before them. The robe stretched long, hiding the hands, if they were still truly hands, sweeping the ground with a stained and tattered hem to hide the feet.

Vultikamian took his place beside the altar and raised his hidden face to the advancing night. He swept out an arm and the runestones upon the outer edge of the circle began to glow with a faint red light. As they did so the snow about them began to melt and shrink away from the heat.

'Shall we be warm?' the whisper demanded. 'Yesss, we shall be warm. It is so nice to feel a little warmth, and I would not have you await your deaths in too much discomfort. Cold flesh is so . . . *uninteresting*, don't you think?' Saeunna tried to speak, to ask this creature what it was, what it wanted of them, why it should seek to take their lives. This was to be no simple murdering at the hands of a madman. That could have taken place at any time since they left Bolli's steading, as the deaths of the two maids proved. And why bring them here to kill them? Why here, among the burning stones?

She felt the hidden eyes turn towards her. She hadn't been able to speak, but the sorcerer had heard her unspoken questions for all that. The hood nodded.

'I am Vultikamian,' came the hissing reply. 'I am the giver of immortality to the chosen, the one who can blind the eyes of death. Death is my gift. It is mine to bestow or withold as I desire. For you, for all of you here, it shall be my gift. For one who has yet to arrive here the denial of death shall be my gift.'

Omund? Saeuna asked in her thoughts. You're going to fulfil the prophecy, to make Omund immortal?

'How else shall I command the north? I seek my goals, Saeunna. They have been set and they shall be achieved. I seek to hold all the north beneath my power. Yet I am not so foolish as to create a sorcerous empire that would set the hands of every being on this earth against me. Omund shall rule, immortal and unconquerable, as my puppet, until I find another who shall replace him. For one day he will have to be replaced. Men will set their weapons against him because of the immortality I shall bestow, but better against him than against me.

'As for fulfilling the prophecy,' Vultikamian continued, his white robes now showing slightly pink in the reflected light from the runestones, 'it was my own prophecy to fulfil. Would you have me lie to myself?'

As you have lied to Omund?

The sorcerer shrugged. 'How have I lied to Omund? All that I promised him shall be his. All that I promise you shall be yours. He shall be the last and greatest of the Ynglings, but it will take a mighty sorcery to work the rite. That is why I need you here. Your blood will help me in my work.'

She tried to shield all thoughts of Hather from her mind, to prevent Vultikamian reaching out and examining her hopes and fears. But the effort was useless.

'Your husband is still alive,' he told her, 'as is your son Olaf. Yet they will be powerless to prevent me. I am the master of all upon the face of the earth in this place. If any not loyal to Omund, and thus not loyal to me, enter this circle, they will find themselves as powerless as you are at this moment.'

Saeunna felt him smile beneath the hood. If he could hear her thoughts then he could also divine the desperate sinking of her heart.

'You have a little while to make peace with your gods,' Vultikamian hissed. 'To the ends I purpose it suits me to use up these Ynglings first. Thurid, come here.'

Her limbs released from immobility, as though in her sleep, Flosi's wife walked slowly towards the creature by the altar. No one could move to stop her, or find voice to cry out. They could only watch in numb horror.

'Lie down,' the sorcerer ordered her.

Unresisting, doomed as surely as if she were already dead, Thurid stretched her body along the altar-slab. A sharp knife of luminous flint appeared at the folded end of the sleeve of Vultikamian's robe. With a single slash he cut through his victim's clothing, leaving her nakedness exposed upon the altar.

The helpless watchers felt his eyes glittering beneath the hood as he studied Thurid's youthful body. 'One day I shall enjoy such things again,' he whispered, his tone almost wistful. Then his voice dropped again and he began to mutter words mostly unknown to them. One word, however, Saeunna recognised. Svipdag had explained it to her after she'd heard Skeggja say it.

Leib-Olbmai. Man of blood.

The glowing knife of chipped and polished flint struck between Thurid's breasts. She didn't scream, or writhe, or convulse. She simple passed from unmoving life into unmovable death. Her heart's-blood jetted up, hanging like a red mist, coruscating in the air above her as the droplets caught and reflected the light of the glowing stones about them. For an instant the altar itself pulsed with brilliance so powerful that it lit the dead woman's flesh and revealed the dark shadows of the bones within, then the light continued upwards into the fountain which gushed from Thurid's ruined body.

They felt time hanging suspended about them, even as the blood hung glittering in the air. Vultikamian raised his hidden features and stared at it, watching the scene which began to form upon its surface like a reflection in the waters of a lake.

Omund was there, with Svipdag and his men, struggling through the snow-whirls which beset them, seeking for some visible sign which might assist their progress.

The sorcerer chuckled. He turned away from the altar and faced the outer edge of the circle, whispering an invultuation to the night. Behind and above him the vision in the blood began to change. The snow still whirled to either side, but now a corridor began to form, the swirling flakes parting, being pushed aside to admit the sorcerer's power. Vultikamian's prisoners saw Omund clearly as the High King reined in his horse. Then, his face triumphant, the man destined by sorcery to become the last and greatest of the Ynglings waved his soldiers forward and started into the tunnel in the snow. For an instant Saeunna glimpsed Svipdag's face as he rode behind his royal master. Then the image wavered and Vultikamian turned back towards the altar-slab.

Time began again. Thurid's blood, now dull, spattered down like discolouring rain onto her corpse. The rite of divination which had cost her life was over.

'We have some time to wait,' Vultikamian informed his prisoners. 'King Omund will not be here until late tomorrow. I am not devoid of mercy. You will be uncomfortable if you remain in your present condition until his arrival, so I shall offer you some relief. You may move, but you may not approach me or attempt to leave the burning stones or I shall render you powerless once more.'

They felt the rigor leave their limbs. Saeunna opened her mouth but no words came.

She felt Vultikamian smile. 'And you may not speak,' the sorcerer said softly.

* * *

On the other side of the forest, beyond the valley, Hather and his companions were also making their camp. Atyl Skin's misgivings about Bolli, prompted by the wolves, had been quieted by the way in which the old Lapp had welcomed Hather, and the way they had talked of the old days as no shape-shifter could have done.

They travelled through the day, speaking little so that they might make up what time they could. Hather realised that their pursuers might well be hampered by the snowstorm raging outside the shelter of the forest, but he was still conscious that he was both pursuer and pursued, caught up once more in the gods' dreadful game.

Before, with Starkadder, he had simply followed, as he had when the *vargr* had taken Svipdag prisoner. This time, however, he was under threat from both sides. Ahead of him, he was certain, was the evil power of Vultikamian. Behind him, delayed by the storm, came Omund, who by this time must regard him as a traitor to Sweden and all that he had formerly held dear. When at last the day's ride was behind them and they had settled for the night, Hather took the first watch, gazing across the valley at the column of steam which rose from the forest, screened by the snow-weighted trees from revealing its origin.

Bolli had already explained the steam before their camp was made. 'They call them the burning stones,' the old Lapp had said. 'It's a place of legend and sorcery. My people don't go there.'

'What are the burning stones?' Hather asked.

Bolli shrugged. 'It depends upon who you listen to,' he replied. 'Some say that they are nothing more than a circle of runestones, erected many years ago, which draw their heat from some kind of warmth deep in the ground. Others say it is a place of mystery, a place where the world of men meets the world of the gods, where the forces of good and evil meet to do battle.

'Sorcerers have the nine-squared skin,' he continued. 'They use it to place themselves between the worlds. Think of the burning stones as another way of doing the same thing, of standing with one foot upon the earth and the other in the home of the gods.'

'Rather like the sign of Ginnir?' Hather asked.

'Like, yet unlike,' Bolli answered in his high-pitched voice. 'Our wizards set the sign of Ginnir upon their yurts, so that none of my people can be in doubt what may take place within. It's the symbol used to mean a place where good and evil meet, but such a place is made by men. Now, I don't say that the circle of the burning stones wasn't made by men, hundreds of years ago. But since then it has become much more than that. Many say that a sorcerer has made his abode there. Others claim that it is no sorcerer, but one of our gods.'

'Which god would that be?'

'A dark one, Hather,' came the reply. 'The one they call Leib-Olbmai, the blood-man. Now, many Lapps regard Leib-Olbmai simply as a hunting god, a giver of game to those who seek for food other than the reindeer. But he is more than that. My father was a shaman. At one time he hoped that I would follow his calling, so he told me a great deal of secret lore. My skills were insufficient though. That's why I left my motherland, and why, although I returned to Bjarmaland, I was unable to settle there. There's no room for a failed shaman among my people. However, I'm straying from the point.

'Leib-Olbmai, my father said, is more than just a hunting god. He is invoked by those seeking game, those who wish to bring about the deaths of animals, yes. But he's more than that. Those who wish to bring about the death of a rival or an enemy invoke him. He is a bloodman in more ways than just those of the hunter. He is the one who sheds blood to bring death, but also the one who sheds blood to bring life.'

'I don't understand you,' Hather interrupted. 'How can the shedding of blood bring life?'

'You've assumed that the blood being shed is that of the one life is being given to, my friend. That isn't so. The blood is shed in a ritual which can bestow a kind of immortality. I've seen it myself. I knew a man once who was the better part of three hundred years old. Yet he walked and talked as we do. He still enjoyed women though they would scream out in the night at the repulsiveness of his body and what he wanted of them. He lived, though, and he had power.'

'How did he die?'

Bolli smiled. 'You're assuming that he did die. But you're right. He died, and he died horribly. The gods themselves took pity upon those his ancient evil was seeking to corrupt and they destroyed him. He was pursued into the forests by the people he had tyrannised and buried beneath a falling tree. At least, his tracks were seen to go to where it fell, and none were discovered upon the other side. It was thought that the gods had toppled the forest to punish him for his sorceries.'

Hather scowled. There was an old rule about the deaths of enemies. You saw their bodies. If you didn't see a body, then you didn't assume a death. Such an assumption could easily cost you your life. Hather himself had assumed that the *vargr* died at Skroggrmagi, but it hadn't. Only later, when he believed that he had reached safety, had his enemy crawled out of the ruin of the citadel to threaten him anew.

For now, though, there was a watch to be kept, hope to be maintained. The burning stones, so far, were simply the next stage in his journey to recover his wife and daughter and to preserve both Hanni and the surviving Ynglings. They lay ahead, but behind was Omund, seeking the death of the Champion of the Ynglings and the fulfilment of his own dark purposes.

And then there were the dwarfs. What dark terror were they planning, as they pursued underground? The weather and the landscape had slowed both Hather and Omund, once they had entered the snows of Finnmark. Yet Bombor's dwarfs would be scurrying along their tunnels, drawing ever closer, unhampered by storms or darkness.

5

The Burrowers in Darkness

Bombor was grinning evilly to himself. Since going underground to escape the sunlight at the beginning of the first day's pursuit his men had made excellent time. The tunnels of Trollheim extended far in every direction, even burrowing beneath the sea in the south to reach into the Dane-Lands. To the north they stretched several hundred leagues into Finnmark, cutting through the roots of the mountains and winding below the forests.

For the average dwarf to find his way in any part of the subterranean kingdom was next to impossible, but Bombor, knowing the work he would have to undertake, had included among his men an ancient, crabby creature named Thekk. Despite his name, which meant *pleasant one*, Thekk was one of the most objectionable and bad-tempered dwarfs Bombor had ever come across. There was nothing personal in Thekk's behaviour; it was simply his way. Short for a dwarf at just under three feet tall, Thekk was incredibly ancient as well as being dreadfully foul-mouthed. His beard, long since turned white, was always stained a dirty earth hue. His eyes were small and piggy, but very sharp. His hands were enormous and had short, flat fingers terminating in wicked talons. He used them to great effect as either picks or shovels, as the work might demand.

The greatest of Thekk's few virtues, by far, was that he had been born an earth-dwarf, rather than a rock or metal dwarf, and had early shown a great ability at tunnelling. His skills had earned him promotion, and he had been tunnel-master to both Dvalin and Alvis, the last two dwarf-kings to reign before the present anarchy. Consequently he knew almost every inch of every tunnel in Trollheim and, perhaps more importantly, the lie of the land above them.

Travelling as rapidly as they could on foot, Bombor's party had saved hours, perhaps even a day, in their pursuit of Hather's party. Yet they had become confused by the various travellers above them. It was virtually impossible to tell by sound alone which was Hather's party, which Omund's and which that led by the shape-shifter. Indeed, it was this third party which had confused them.

Hather and his companions must constitute one of the three groups of travellers. Probably, Bombor reasoned, Omund had mounted a pursuit. That was two, with Omund's probably the largest-sounding group. But the third? Bombor shook his head. Flecks of soil flew from his discoloured hair. This third party was a mystery he would have to solve if he was to find Hather. He had been puzzling over it as they entered an underground cavern, its roof a tangle of twisted roots from the gigantic firs which comprised the forest overhead, and seen the tall figure waiting for them.

Thekk had turned to him, scowling. 'That's a man,' the old dwarf snapped. 'That's a man-thing, Bombor. You rat. You bucket of dead fish! You've led us here to be betrayed by a man-thing!'

Bombor ignored him. Certainly the figure was man-shaped, but it was not a man. Men didn't enter Trollheim and sit about waiting to be found and torn to pieces. Not with only a long, rune-engraved spear to defend themselves.

The figure removed the shield from a horn lantern, illuminating the cavern. Beneath the hood of its travelling-cloak a single eye burned fiercely. As Bombor saw that evil eye he felt the shivers begin along his spine.

He already knew the answer to his question, but he asked it anyway as his dwarfs advanced to form a circle about him.

'Who are you?' he demanded, mustering a show of fearlessness.

'Come now, little Bombor,' the figure responded. 'After all the time you've spent trying to get my attention you don't know who I am?'

Bombor shuddered. 'Odin? Is that you? Is it really Allfather?'

'But of course, I forget,' the figure smiled. 'You've never seen me before, have you? But I've seen you, of course. I've sat upon my high seat and looked out across the world and seen your work. Its reek of blood has ascended even to Asgard, little dwarf. Had I not been bound by vows you'd never understand I'd have stopped you long ago.'

'Vows? What's he talking about?' Thekk growled. 'What has this to do with him? You there. What's your part in this?' he snapped at Allfather.

Odin's smile widened into a grin. He was enjoying this. 'I have a son called Thor,' he answered evenly. 'Thor's a big lad and very fond of weapons. He has a hammer, Mjollnir, which he uses to kill things he doesn't like. Such as dwarfs. I don't think he'd like you very much, little Thekk.'

Thekk glared. He was about to bellow with rage, then he understood and held his tongue, probably for the first time in his life.

'That's better,' Odin remarked. 'Now, Bombor, I think we should begin to understand one another. You've been killing off my Ynglings. That is hardly the way to endear yourself to me.'

With a determined effort Bombor strove to fight his fear, to present to Allfather a boldness he was far from feeling. He had to use whatever guile he could muster, both to save his life and to retain the respect of his followers.

'Go on, Odin,' he said with apparent calm.

The god nodded courteously. He knew very well what Bombor was doing, and he offered the dwarf his grudging admiration for the attempt.

'You've been doing the work you agreed. Now you want the reward you picked out for yourself. Not the reward Omund promised you; you've enough gold in Trollheim already – yellow shit, I think Dvalin used to call it. No, you never wanted that. What you wanted was to capture Hather Lambisson. Am I right?'

You know you are, Bombor thought. 'Is there a point to this?' he asked, showing a real impatience to have it over and know his fate.

'A most potent point, if you will be honest with me,' came the reply. 'Tell me the truth and I promise you the opportunity to fulfil your ambitions. Now, why do you want Hather Lambisson, Bombor?'

The dwarf swallowed. Odin was the betrayer, the oathbreaker. That's why Bombor had been surprised to hear him speak of vows he was unable to break. He couldn't know that Odin was powerless to betray Mother Skuld, or any of her sisterhood of Norns. Now Odin was making him a promise, challenging Bombor to believe whether he would keep his word or not.

'How shall I trust your promise?' the dwarf demanded.

'By my word. By my written word, if you wish. I shall carve it in runes and obey it. Will that satisfy you?'

'You promise me the opportunity to fulfil my ambitions, and you'll keep your word?'

'I do. I will.'

'And in return you want me to tell you something that you must already know?'

'Your mind is usually quicker than this, Bombor. You're wasting precious time on nothing by this hesitation. A chance for the future or the end of everything now. Which is it to be?'

The dwarf decided. It wasn't much of a choice anyway, he thought. He said: 'I want Hather Lambisson as a hostage. You want to save your Ynglings. To do that you need your champion . . .'

'Perhaps,' Odin interrupted, smirking.

'To get your champion back you'd pay my price for him.'

'Which is . . .?'

'Trollheim is in chaos since Alvis died at Skroggrmagi. It needs a ruler to unite it. I have claimed the throne, but I cannot succeed unless I can show some symbol of authority. There is only one such symbol. The sword which was forged with Alvis' fate. But it's not in Trollheim any more. It was never returned after Svafrlami stole it. For a while it was in Midgard, the realms of men, but you sent Starkadder to steal it away to Valhalla.

'I want Tyrfing, Allfather. Tyrfing will buy me my throne, bring Trollheim under my rule. I'd be a good ruler. What you want for Midgard, I want for Trollheim. That's why I've pursued Hather Lambisson, to take him and use him in exchange for the sword Tyrfing.'

He trembled slightly before the gaze of Odin's single eye, his chest heaving with the effort of his words.

He waited.

Odin sighed. Then he answered: 'That is the truth, Bombor. You've dealt fairly with me. Now I shall bargain fairly with you. You shall have what you want. If you do as I say, I shall give you Tyrfing. Yet as soon as you sit upon the throne of Trollheim you must destroy it and forge a new symbol of your authority. I took Tyrfing into Valhalla to keep it from the realms of men. It is too potent a weapon to return ever again to Midgard. That is why you must destroy it as soon as it has fulfilled its purpose for you. Do you agree?'

The dwarf nodded. In his tiny heart he was beginning to hope again.

'You know that I shall make you work for me before I give it to you?'

'I do, Allfather. What is it you require?'

'Send your followers away for a little while,' Odin ordered. 'Except for that one,' he added, pointing at Thekk.

The old dwarf's piggy eyes widened. As the others left the cavern, leaving Thekk and Bombor with Odin, he attempted to scurry away as well. The problem, he soon discovered, was that he was so frightened that his legs refused to work.

Slowly, carefully, Odin began to explain what he wanted. As he began to outline the way in which it was to be accomplished, Thekk's fear drained away into the earth. This was work he understood. He found himself protesting at certain things, approving others. His protests, instead of being met with the wrath he expected, were listened to and reasoned away, details being altered at his suggestion, or being insisted on by Odin.

When Allfather had finished, Bombor asked Thekk, 'Can it be done?'

Thekk drew a circle upon the cavern floor with one foot, then rubbed it out with the sole of his boot.

'It can be done,' he answered eventually. '*If* what you say is correct. If you're wrong, though, we might as well try to shit in the treetops at noon as do what you want.'

Odin noted the return of the old dwarf's natural irascibility. Bombor he had no love for, but this ancient midget would be a worthy ally in the difficult task which lay ahead.

'I am right,' the god assured him. 'And if any dwarf in Trollheim can do this thing, you can.'

Thekk felt his wrinkled cheeks flush with pride. For a dwarf to be complimented by Allfather!

'You may call your followers back now, Bombor,' Odin continued. 'I trust you both to tell them only what you have to to get the work finished. You must decide for yourselves how best to save yourselves afterwards. If not,' he added with a chuckle, 'I'll have no need to give you Tyrfing.'

'And . . . Omund?' Bombor asked.

'Your bargain with Omund Olisson is void. He'll do nothing for you now. He has his own ambitions to take care of.'

The god smiled. Then, without either Bombor or Thekk seeing how he did it, he simply vanished from their sight.

Thekk shook his head violently, as if to clear away a haze from before his eyes. Then he walked to the tunnel entrance and called for the others to follow them. As they hurried back many were wide-eyed with disbelief and admiration at finding their leader still there after a confrontation with Allfather. Bombor saw this and preened with renewed arrogance. Thekk simply spat and started off into the tunnel ahead of them.

Bombor followed the others through the cavern and into the tunnel. There is hope, he decided, with a smile which eventually became an evil grin. Thekk and the others will complete the work in time. Then Allfather will keep his promise to me. I'll make certain that he does. After all, he still needs Hather Lambisson, and he didn't say anything about me not taking Hather prisoner, once the work is finished, to ensure that he keeps his promise.

He could even see Tyrfing's glittering length in his mind's eye.

Odin had appeared to them about mid-day. They reached the burning stones towards evening, at about the same time as Saeunna and the shape-shifter. As Thurid died above them, Thekk and Bombor explored the torrid, glowing underground chamber from which the burning stones drew their heat. Bombor soon found it uncomfortable, but Thekk, with his greater experience and appreciation of subterranean marvels, was both fascinated and delighted by what he discovered.

'Just as Odin said,' he called across to Bombor, who had now retreated some way up the approach-tunnel. 'And here,' he added, tapping a dull patch on the chamber-wall, 'is what we want. This shouldn't be too difficult at all.'

He looked across to the mouth of the tunnel where Bombor was waiting for him. Between them lay a deep fissure in the floor from which an intense, scorching heat issued. It was surrounded by a gallery of rock which had given Thekk access to the part of the chamber wall Odin had told him to examine. In the gallery the dwarfs would be shielded from the worst of the heat, though it would be difficult to withdraw back into the entrance-tunnel once the work was completed.

Thekk began to climb the wall beside the dull patch. His hands blistered and his boots began to smoke, but he'd endured worse than that during his time with Dvalin. Besides, he was working for their lives now, working to discover a way to complete Odin's work and stay alive to find a way back to Trollheim in the train of their victorious new ruler.

His probing talons found the weak spot in the roof of the cavern. It would be the following night before their task was completed, which was exactly when Odin wanted the work finished. Thekk mentally noted his grudging admiration for the god. He had known exactly what was to be done and had left out nothing. He had even made certain that the job could be done close to a means of escape, a tunnel up to the stone circle above, providing they actually broke through after nightfall.

What they would actually find in the circle after their escape the old dwarf couldn't begin to guess. He assumed from the smug expression Bombor had taken to wearing, that Hather Lambisson would be there. And where there was Hather, there would probably be Omund and more than one or two of Omund's guards. Well, he'd fought humans before, and he'd do it again if he had to. Besides, anything would be better than staying down there in the cavern once their task was finished. Thekk had seen such things before, and the old dwarf would rather face the noonday sun.

'How do we do it?' Bombor called.

'You're not including yourself in that *we* are you?' Thekk growled.

'Of course not. But I think that we should get started.'

The old dwarf felt the heat begin to bite. He scuttled back round the gallery and into Bombor's tunnel. Behind the pretender to the throne of Trollheim several pairs of eyes were glistening in the reflected glow from the cavern.

'Groups of four at a time,' Thekk ordered. 'First, a tunnel to the surface from here, for two reasons. The first is that any man working in there needs to be snow-damped. The second is that we might need a second means of escape. There's nothing to be gained by all being crowded in there when the time comes. Better to get everyone who isn't involved out through here first. I think you'll agree, Bombor?' he added, sneering.

'It's as sensible as anything you've said so far.'

Thekk grunted. Then: 'You four, dig up to the surface and find something to cover the entrance with.' He paced along the tunnel for some distance, then added: 'Dig up here. You'll come out into the shelter of the forest that way. Then you four, as soon as they're through, rub yourselves well in the snow, then report to me and I'll show you what we're going to do.'

His words were followed by some muttering. He glowered at the mutterers with lowered brows and they fell silent.

'If it's any of your business, I don't like it either. Still, if you'd rather go back you're welcome. Personally I don't think I'd like to find out what Allfather has prepared back there for anyone who doesn't carry out his orders.'

Thekk went to stand at the entrance to the glowing cavern beneath the burning stones. Odin had been right about everything, he reflected. So, why was he still uneasy? Yes, the work was dangerous, but he'd done such work before. So, why didn't he want to go through with it here?

The answer came to him. Odin had been right so far. And perhaps, just perhaps, Odin had been *too right*.

And if that was the case it could cost a lot of dwarfish lives.

6

Sorcery at the Burning Stones

With the coming of the dawn, Saeunna and the others found themselves once more tied by the invisible bonds. They had spent a miserable night, Flosi trying vainly to comfort his terrified children for the brutal death of their mother, struggling to behave like the Yngling prince he was, even though he realised his efforts were probably in vain, and that the coming day would add some new and dreadful horror to their torment.

He was right. As Saeunna fought to demand of Vultikamian why they had been ensorcelled again, she saw Flosi begin to walk slowly towards the altar-slab. Inwardly she prayed to Thor and Allfather that her fears might be groundless, but she knew even as she framed the words that the prayer would be futile. Vultikamian turned his hooded features towards her and she sensed the wicked smile behind the mask, a smile which told her that they were helpless now, and would remain so until his purposes were accomplished and they lay dead about him, their bodies littering the snow as she had seen them in her dream.

Flosi died for the purpose of the same rite of divination which had claimed Thurid's life. Vultikamian examined the suspended blood, the smile widening beneath his hood as he watched Omund resume his progress through the calm corridor the sorcerer had created in the snowstorm. Omund was jaunty as he rode, doubtless anticipating the completion of his plans, unaware of the puppet role Vultikamian intended him to play. Beside Omund, his face grave, rode Svipdag Hathersson, perhaps plotting something of his own, something that old Skeggja might have promised in her evil master's name.

The blood spattered down, completing Flosi's death. Saeunna wept inwardly, more for Gudrun and the two surviving children than for herself. She'd seen as bad, if not worse. At their first meeting Hather had rescued her from rape and certain death. The *vargr* had promised a terrible end, but suffered one itself. And the terrors she had witnessed at Skroggrmagi would never be effaced from her memory whilst she lived.

While I live, she thought. How much longer will that be?

I have to live, though. I have to, to save Gudrun and the children. Whether Hather is alive or dead at this moment, I have to do whatever I can for the Yngling children, for his sake.

But how?

Vultikamian turned towards her. 'There is nothing you can do, Saeunna,' he informed her, simply stating a fact. There was no mockery in his voice as he spoke. 'It is decreed that this should be. You may fight the gods at your peril, and even win from time to time. But you may not fight against your fate. It is too potent. It affects too many others for it to be turned aside.'

Then take my life, she willed him. Take my life and let these others go. You don't need them, not a sorcerer as powerful as you.

'Flattery now? I admire your spirit, Mother of Gudrun and Olaf. Yes, I admire you. But I cannot help you or grant what you ask. I have lived too long and seen, and done, too many things for such fine sentiments to bind me any longer. I have my own desires to attend to, and they will obviously come before your own. Such is the nature of power, Saeunna. Give up your hope, for it will serve no purpose. I admire both your strength and your determination, but they will serve you better if you use them to prepare for your death.'

She felt the tears well up, though her bondage would

not permit her to weep, for the others whose doom Vultikamian had pronounced.

I shall not prepare to die, she told herself. I shall go on hoping. Perhaps Hather and Olaf are still alive. Perhaps if they cannot save us, they will at least avenge us.

Vultikamian heard her thoughts. He began to laugh.

Yet as he laughed he knew too that it was only the dawn of the last day, and not its ending. Only with the coming of night could he perform that which he desired. Only then, with darkness upon the earth to hide his deeds of blood, could the final ritual be completed. And in the hours of daylight there was much still to happen. Omund's presence was required for the High King to receive Vultikamian's gift of immortality. There were other uncertainties as well. His instincts should have told him of the deaths of Hather, Bolli, Olaf and Atyl Skin, yet they had not.

Still, it mattered little. The moment they stepped within the circle of the burning stones they would be subject to the same enchantment which bound the other prisoners, so there was no possibility of their interfering with the ritual.

As Flosi died with the flint knife in his heart, while Omund and his men were riding closer through the gap in the snowstorm, Hather and his company broke camp and set off across the valley towards the forest which concealed the burning stones. Bolli peered at the snow, noting the faint traces of the tracks which Saeunna's party had left the day before. Now and then he would pause and stare ahead at the rising column of steam, his face thoughtful.

Hather tried to divine his friend's thoughts. Finally he asked: 'The sorcerer you mentioned, Bolli, the one you said was supposed to have taken up his abode at the burning stones – do you know what he's called?'

The old tracker shook his head. 'It's not wise to enquire too deeply after sorcerers,' he replied. 'I didn't ask his name, nor did any mention it to me.'

'Then you've never heard of one called Vultikamian?'

Bolli's head jerked around to stare, wide-eyed, at Hather. 'What was that name again?' he demanded.

'Vultikamian. He's the one my son Svipdag was sent to the burning stones to see by Omund.'

The old Lapp's thoughts raced. Then, slowly, he nodded.

He should have thought of it himself. It was so clear, so obvious, once Hather had spoken that name. The shape-shifter had only left footprints in the snow when he wanted to. It was a sorcerous ability to be able to do that. His father, one of the greatest shamans in Lapland, had been able to travel across snow without leaving tracks. And so, doubtless, would that ancient being he had assumed to be buried beneath the fallen tree, the one who had compacted with the dark god Leib-Olbmai.

The one called Vultikamian.

'So he's not dead after all,' Bolli whispered, feeling a cold sweat break out upon his brow.

'You know of him?' Hather asked.

Bolli explained. 'He was supposed to have died when I was a child in Bjarmaland. My father was responsible for his downfall, but he only achieved power over Vultikamian by making a compact with the supreme god Jumala, who persuaded Leib-Olbmai to break his agreement with the sorcerer. I did hear that Vultikamian had survived and gone deep into the wastes of Bjarmaland to renew the pact, but I had such belief in my father's powers, that I dismissed the rumour. But now I must believe it.

'Vultikamian's power was in the control of others. He could bind or release them at will, also establish his hold over those he wanted to serve him in some way in the future. You could always tell who they were because there was an outward sign of what he'd done. Their eyes changed colour . . .'

Bolli was interrupted by Hather's groan. At last, after so many years, he had learned the truth about Svipdag's missing days in Bjarmaland, and it was a truth that stabbed at his heart like a falling icicle. It was enough to have Omund and Vultikamian against him, but for his own son to be in the sorcerer's power . . .

Yet he held on to his hope. There must always be hope, he told himself. There was hope when he was a prisoner with Starkadder in Oli's dungeon. There was hope as he entered the citadel at Skroggrmagi with the odds at ten to one against him. Now there must still be hope, for the alternative was the stranglehold of grim despair.

And that could only lead them to their deaths.

During the night, whilst the sun was out of the sky, Bombor's dwarfs had carried enough snow down into their tunnel to last them through the work of the next day. Now, beneath the burning stones, they laboured at the place which Thekk had indicated on the gallery wall. The old dwarf was quite pleased by the way their efforts were progressing, though he would never have dreamed of saying so. Bombor's enquiries were met with sour grunts, sour because the pretender to the throne of Trollheim took no part in the work himself.

'But will it be finished in time?' Bombor demanded.

Thekk scowled. 'Not if we waste time answering silly questions,' he snapped. 'If it is, it is. If it isn't, I'm sure Allfather will be the first to tell us.'

Bombor shuddered inwardly at this dour observation. He didn't like to think about what might happen if they failed. It was bad enough trying to work out ways to ensure that Odin the betrayer kept his promise.

Still, it would be worth it. Even if most of his followers died it would be a small price to pay for Tyrfing. That sword would secure the throne for Bombor without his having to fight even a single rival. There could be no rivals for the dwarf who returned Tyrfing to Trollheim.

The dwarfs worked steadily on in their groups of four; two dug, and two distributed the spoil along the floor of the gallery. Their snow-soaked clothing steamed with the heat from the centre of the cavern, and each group could only work for a little time before they had to be relieved by the next. The hairs on their hands and arms shrivelled away, and more than one reeled away from the digging beating at beard or hair. Still, they knew it had to be done, not just for Bombor to have Tyrfing, but for them all to have a chance of keeping their lives.

With the coming of noon, Omund and his followers noticed the storm which had raged to either side of them subside. The day became clear and still, and the speed of their progress increased. In the distance, showing faintly against the tree-clad skyline, they sighted the steam from the burning stones.

Their progress was witnessed by Vultikamian and his prisoners as the sorcerer sacrificed Thurid and Flosi's little daughter, the elder of the two surviving Yngling children. Saeunna and Gudrun watched appalled, their helplessness beginning to induce a sickening lack of hope. This increased when the picture in the blood permitted them a glimpse of Hather, Olaf, Bolli and Atyl Skin entering the forest which surrounded the burning stone circle.

Vultikamian nodded. 'Good,' he remarked. 'There will be eight of you to die when I bestow his immortality upon Omund. A good number. The ritual should go well.'

If only she could speak, Saeunna thought. If only she could call out to Hather, warn him not to enter the circle of runestones. She could no longer doubt that the moment Hather and the others stepped within the stones they would be held helpless by the same grim enchantment that bound Hanni, Gudrun and herself, and little Omund, the High King's only surviving grandchild.

Omund and his men rode on towards the forest. Svipdag rode beside the High King, no longer aware of the wounds that had plagued him during the earlier part of their journey. They seemed at last to be healing, and he felt himself gaining back the strength which had been taken from him. He realised that some great destiny lay ahead, that Vultikamian had chosen him and prepared him for the completion of a pre-ordained task.

He rode beside the High King as Omund's subordinate, but he knew that he was more than just the King's

Marshal now. His decisions were easier to make than they had been, and first amongst them was the knowledge that he would do whatever Vultikamian demanded of him, without question or dissent.

Even to the murder of his own father.

They reached the edge of the forest by late afternoon. Ahead of them, Hather and his companions had paused in horror as they discovered Hanni's maids, still impaled to the carcasses of their horses and now covered with a frosting of rime that glazed the terror on their features into masks. Summoning their courage, pushing on past the corpses, they saw the column of steam before them.

Atyl Skin glared. 'How do we see through that?' he asked.

'By going through it,' Hather answered.

Bolli clutched at his arm. 'Be careful,' he hissed. 'Remember what I told you about Vultikamian being able to control those around him. If he's there, he's prepared a trap for us.'

'Trap or no trap,' Olaf decided. 'My mother and sister may be in there. And Princess Hanni. We can't just leave them in the clutches of a sorcerer.'

He drew his sword and began to walk towards the steam, but Hather stepped in front of him. 'If it is a trap,' his father said, 'there's no point in us all walking into it. I'll go first, Olaf.'

'Because you're my father?'

'Because it was I who led us into this. If we'd stayed at Uppsala instead of trying to run for Sudrafell we might still be safe. This is my doing, and it's my risk.'

Under the ground Thekk was inspecting the digging. His taloned fingers detected the first signs which confirmed what Odin had told him.

He turned to the dwarf behind him. 'Is the tunnel up from here finished?' he demanded.

The dwarf nodded. 'All but the last foot,' he replied.

'Is there anywhere we can secure a rope?'

'There's a spur of rock projecting from one side. We could tie a rope to that.'

Thekk grinned. 'Then do it. And after that, clear the others out and ask Bombor to come here. As soon as night falls, get up into the forest. Follow the stars through it until the tail-star of Freya's Wagon* is directly overhead. You'll find another tunnel there. It's on a different path to this one, but you should find your way south again if you follow it. Whatever you do, don't come back to this one.'

'And you and Bombor?' the dwarf asked.

'We'll go up here. If all goes well we'll join you in the other tunnel. But don't try to wait for us. It'll be like Ragnarok around here.'

The dwarf left him. Moments later Bombor joined him, frowning. 'The others get out to safety, yet you keep me here? Are you mad, Thekk?'

'You want Tyrfing, don't you? You want Hather Lambisson to force Odin to keep his promise, don't you? Do you think you'll get either by running away with the others?'

Thekk grinned at Bombor's obvious fear. Well, the others will be safe, he thought to himself. I've had a good life, and this one's going to make a dreadful king. If we both die here it won't make that much difference to anything. And in a small way I'll have cheated Odin, if he intends to betray us, by saving the rest.

And there are few enough dwarfs that can be said to have got away with that.

Above them dusk began to wrap itself about the world. With drawn sword and pounding heart, dreading what he might find, Hather Lambisson stepped into the column of steam and passed into the circle of the burning stones. As he blinked and wiped his eyes against his sleeve, he felt the slow lethargy of Vultikamian's enchantment begin to

---

* Ursa Minor, the Little Bear at the end of the Plough.

steal upon him. He saw Saeunna and Gudrun, standing motionless. He saw Hanni, and little Omund.

He saw Vultikamian, the thing that had taken Vermund's body in the mist.

Hather tried to speak, to call out to his men. Instead his voice froze in his throat and his weapon fell from numb fingers.

'So, Hather,' Vultikamian mocked, 'we meet once more. It was so kind of you to come.'

Outside the burning stones the others waited. Finally Atyl Skin called: 'Hather? What's in there? Hather, will you answer me?'

No answer came.

'Hather, can you hear me?'

The silence from within the circle remained unbroken. Bolli was frowning, Olaf hefting his sword.

'Could the steam keep him from hearing us?' Olaf asked.

The Dane scowled. 'It shouldn't.'

'Then we have no choice,' Bolli said. 'We must follow him.'

They heard the sound of riders approaching through the forest.

'You could be right,' Atyl Skin muttered. 'That'll be Omund, so we've no choice at all. Whatever we do has to be done before he gets here, so let's do it now.'

Shoulder to shoulder, weapons drawn, they stepped into the steam and entered the circle of the burning stones.

And froze.

The eight prisoners within the ring of runestones all sensed Vultikamian's smile beneath the hood. 'I have you all now,' the sorcerer smiled. 'Even you, little Bolli, the son of my old persecutor. I'll save a special death for you.'

There was no struggle, no appeal. They heard his words, they heard the sound of Omund and Svipdag and the soldiers approaching beyond the curtain of steam, and they knew, in their hearts, that hope had left them to their fate.

Death by sorcery. Death to give Omund the immortality he craved, even though it was to be as the puppet of a Lappish sorcerer. Poor Hanni had travelled from the Dane-Lands to die like this. Only a little boy remained of the proud Yngling dynasty. And Hather's family, his wife and two children, would die beneath Vultikamian's flint knife.

Hather struggled to think of some means of their escape. There was no point in counting on Odin, after what the god had told him upon Vermund's grave-mound. Nor could he have any faith in Svipdag after what Bolli had told him of Vultikamian's influence. All that remained was Bombor and his dwarfs, and there was no reason, even if they could somehow thwart Vultikamian and take him prisoner, to believe that they would trouble to save humans.

'There is no way out, Hather Lambisson,' the sorcerer whispered. 'I alone am master here. Only my creatures and those who serve them are immune to the enchantment which binds you and your companions. For I am Vultikamian, Hather, who has compacted with Leib-Olbmai. I am the one who blinds death and bestows immortality. I am the master of everything upon the face of this earth.'

As he spoke Omund and Svipdag walked through the curtain of steam. They bowed deeply and he favoured them with a nod of acknowledgement.

'Are you ready, Omund Olisson?' Vultikamian asked the High King.

'I am ready, sorcerer.'

'First, you must acknowledge me as your master, Omund.'

The High King's pale eyes blazed defiantly for a moment. Then their fire went out and he bowed again. 'You are my master, Lord Vultikamian,' he said.

'Once for assent,' the sorcerer remarked. 'Now, again.'

'You are my master,' Omund repeated.

'Twice for confirmation. Now, once more.'

'You are the Lord Vultikamian, master of my fate.'

'The third time for eternity,' Vultikamian sneered. 'That's good, Omund. Very good. We may now begin. Svipdag, bring the child.'

Hather could only watch, immobile and helpless, as his son picked up little Omund, the last untainted survivor of the House of Yngling, and carried the child to the stone altar. His heart was sick with loathing and desperation at his inability to intervene. The sorcerous rite would proceed as Vultikamian had always intended, and all Hather could do would be to watch, to wait his turn, and then to die.

He had failed them all. He had failed his family. He had failed his friends. And he had failed his god. Odin had depended upon him to save the Ynglings. But now, even if Bombor's dwarfs somehow managed to free him, there was no means by which he could do what was expected of him.

'Strip the child,' Vultikamian commanded.

Svipdag obeyed.

Beyond the curtain of steam Omund's guards waited with growing misgivings. They could hear nothing from inside. Nor could they explain the lassitude which had suddenly come upon them; which left them weak and helpless. A figure came among them, its face veiled, and walked unhindered through their ranks to stand before the column of steam as though it had been waiting for a long time for something that was about to happen.

7

The Death-Blinder

'Come here, Omund Olisson,' Vultikamian ordered. The High King obeyed him. 'Now, lie down upon the altar.'

The sorcerer turned to the others. 'There is only one substance which may wash away death,' he began. 'That substance is blood. Yet it cannot be any blood. It must be the blood of the very young, and the blood of the very old, and the blood of others carefully chosen. Only thus can death be blinded and a kind of immortality bestowed upon the chosen one.

'This child is the very young blood that we need. Bolli, you are going to furnish the old, tired blood of age. You shall die last. The order of death will be according to age. After the child you, Gudrun. Then Hanni. Then you, Olaf Hathersson. After Olaf, Saeunna. Then Hather. Then Atyl Skin. And finally . . . I promised you a special death, Bolli. You shall watch your friends dying, one by one, bathing Omund Olisson in their blood, washing away his age, and his time, and his thralldom to the passing years, and know that, once they have been drained and cast aside, your time will finally come.'

The glowing flint knife appeared once more in the creature's sleeved hand, as Svipdag held the little boy who was the only Yngling left besides Omund above the High King's prone body.

'And now that you know your fates, it is time to begin,' Vultikamian concluded. 'Hold the boy still, Svipdag Hathersson.'

Slowly, with an exaggerated stealth which agonised the

helpless witnesses, the flint knife rose above little Omund's throat. Vultikamian's arm stretched high above his hooded head, ready for the fatal blow which would begin the series of deaths to purchase Omund's immortality. Hather tried to will Svipdag to snatch the child away, to run from the circle before Vultikamian could realise what was happening and bind him with the enchantment which held the others, but he knew even as he made the attempt that it was doomed, that those two days in Bjarmaland so many years ago had condemned his elder son to follow the sorcerer's will for as long as he lived. Hather's last hope began to fade.

Beneath him Thekk was scrabbling at the earth with his talons. Bombor, almost through to the ground above, hung from the rope in the tunnel, awaiting what was to come. And as he hung there an idea came to him of repaying Thekk for the insolence he had had to suffer from him over the years.

Slowly, carefully, so that the older dwarf should not see what he was doing, he drew the rope up out of Thekk's reach.

Moisture began to run between Thekk's fingers. He snarled and scowled at the earth he dug as he scrabbled and scraped to work Allfather's will. His hair was mostly gone with the heat and his clothing was starting to smoulder and char. It didn't matter, though. All that mattered now was that he complete his task in the moments that remained.

He chanted his reasoning, struggling to work as he had never worked before. Where there's a dull spot on a hot wall, there's something behind it to cool it down. Where there's a dull spot on a hot wall, there's something behind it to cool it down. Where there's a dull spot on a hot wall . . .

Go on, Thekk. Go on.

'Vultikamian, wait!'

The flint knife hovered. The sorcerer's hooded head turned.

A bent, veiled figure leaning on a blackened yew staff

hobbled into the circle of runestones and stood before the monster by the altar. All heard her words and watched Vultikamian hesitate.

'Have you come to witness the fulfilment of our agreement, little Norn? I had not hoped for such an honour. Still, you are welcome. And you are just in time.'

Mother Skuld nodded beneath her veil. 'Yes, Vultikamian,' she replied. 'You are right. I am just in time. But not for what you think.'

Outside the circle two wolves began to howl. The midnight, tattered shapes of two black ravens flapped through the steam and hovered above the altar.

Now, Thekk, the Norn said silently. *Now!*

Thekk's talons hooked about a stone in the earth. They dragged it away. For a moment there was nothing more than a trickle of moisture, then the flood began, forcing itself through with a strength that knocked the old dwarf away from his digging and pushed him towards where the rope should have been hanging.

It wasn't there.

'You are master of all upon the face of the earth?' the Norn asked Vultikamian. 'Perhaps you are. But are you master of all that is *beneath* it, sorcerer?'

The knife wavered above the child.

'This is no time for riddles, Mother Skuld,' Vultikamian hissed. 'If you have to speak, speak clearly.'

'Then so I shall. I was wrong to make a bargain with you, Vultikamian. I know that now. You seek to face and overthrow the *Hvitakrist*, the new god from the south who will bring us our rest. We cannot permit you to do that.'

'Permit me? *Permit me?* You have no choice. You cannot void my power. I told you when last we met . . .'

Bombor broke through the ground into the circle. He looked about him. He saw Hather Lambisson, standing helpless and immobile, and ran towards him.

Thekk's oath was lost in the rush of water from the underground lake he had breached. He slammed across the gallery before its force, gasping for breath, bruised and battered before the furious jet which streamed and steamed into the cavern beneath the burning stones.

'. . . that I shall never lose my power . . .'

Bombor grabbed at Hather. Omund's face contorted with fear. Saeunna felt the rigor which bound her limbs begin to leave her.

Mother Skuld pointed at the sorcerer with her staff. 'Until the burning stones grow cold,' she sneered.

The water beneath them flooded up, snatching, fighting, biting at the heat which welled from the centre of the cavern. Thekk crashed against the gallery wall on the far side, steam hissing around him, water forcing its way into his nose and lungs.

'Have you felt your burning runestones recently, Vultikamian?' the Norn continued. 'Touch one now. Feel how warm it used to be!'

Bombor paled. The motionless Hather Lambisson had moved, had snatched up his fallen sword.

And rammed it through the dwarf's heart.

The underground lake flooded on, wild with its release from centuries of bondage, waging a terrible battle with the fire which had dwelt beside it. The two elements met with a violence beyond the power of man to imagine.

A runestone cracked. It shattered. It flew apart, never to come together again.

Vultikamian howled. The knife swept down.

Svipdag snatched little Omund to safety and threw him to Saeunna, who caught and held him. Omund saw the flashing, luminous flint above him and rolled away moments before it smashed against the altar-stone, shivering into fragments.

The wolves, their eyes hungry, their mouths slavering, their teeth wickedly sharp, prowled through the steam and slowly, menacingly, advanced towards the sorcerer.

'You are the death-blinder?' Mother Skuld jeered. '*You are the death-blinder?* There is only one Death-Blinder, Vultikamian. And his creatures are here to punish you for your presumption!'

The ravens swooped, stabbing their beaks at the

white-robed figure, drawing blood. Vultikamian screamed and staggered away from the altar, his arms raised in a useless gesture of defence. The wolves sprang.

Another runestone burst into pieces. Then another. A gap appeared in the curtain of steam. Omund rushed towards his men. They stood watching him, made no move.

'Kill them!' Omund screamed. 'Kill them! All of them!'

Nobody answered him.

Svipdag flung himself to the ground as steam began to jet from the base of the altar-slab. With a roar the conflict of water and fire erupted from beneath. The slab shivered and rose into the air.

Lupine teeth fastened themselves into Vultikamian's flesh. Hanni screamed. Gudrun grabbed her and pulled her towards the edge of the circle. Bolli rolled aside as the altar-stone smashed into the ground, crashing through into the cavern beneath.

The ground shook. Hather pulled his sword from Bombor's body. Atyl Skin, pushing Olaf ahead of him, dodged flying fragments from another broken runestone.

Thekk hurtled back through the tunnel on the far side of the cavern. Even as he felt his end approaching he was smiling to himself. The others were safe. His life, and possibly Bombor's, was a small price to pay for that. *Besides, you never intended to keep your promise anyway, did you, Allfather?*

Little Omund bawled in Saeunna's arms as she reached the edge of the forest. Gudrun and Hanni followed her. So did Olaf and Atyl Skin. With surprising strength for one of his years, Bolli pulled Hather to safety as the circle began to fall into the chaos of the cavern beneath.

Omund's guards ran. Svipdag rolled himself clear, inches before the ground collapsed. He struck a runestone. It flew apart and he rolled through to safety, his mind too bemused to wonder at his preservation.

The last of the runestones fell. Where the burning stones had stood nothing remained but a massive crater in the ground, a crater that hissed jets of water and jagged flames. Of the wolves and ravens there was no sign, but tossed upon a towering column of boiling water, scalded and bloody, bobbed the shredded, broken body of the sorcerer Vultikamian.

The wizard who had sought to blind death had been claimed by his ancient foe at last.

Hather looked about, his eyes sweeping the survivors. 'Where's Omund?' he demanded.

The only answer was unspoken by human voice. Instead it was spoken by the hoofprints in the snow.

Still deep in the cavern where he had spoken with Odin, bruised and bleeding, scalded and raw, but somehow still alive, Thekk shook the water from his ears and sneezed it from his throat and nose. Despite the darkness his eyes hurt when he opened them, but he blinked a few times, and slowly began to make out an object which an unseen hand had stabbed into the earth before him.

So there was honour, or at least the possibility of honour, in the dealings between dwarfs and gods after all. He'd never thought it possible, but the proof was there, waiting for him to take it.

He set his hand to the hilt, pulling the sword free. With a new understanding in his heart, and Tyrfing trailing from his grasp behind him, the next king of Trollheim began the long underground journey to the south.

8

Blood upon the Ice

Saeunna, with little Omund in her arms, looked up at her husband and his sons. Beyond them the ruined circle was cooling, the last of the steam from the cavern wisping into the air.

'It's over, Hather,' she pleaded. 'The child is safe. The House of Yngling has survived. It's over. Let him go.'

Hather Lambisson shook his head. 'It can only be over when Omund is dead,' he told her. 'I have to follow him, my love. I've no choice.'

'Yes you have,' she persisted. 'Let him alone. His power is broken. No one will ever let him threaten his grandson again.'

'You know I can't do that, Saeunna. Omund is sly and vicious and devious. While he lives he's a threat to that little one's future, and to the line he's betrayed. That's why I have to follow him. I have to know, once and for all, that his power can never return to haunt us.'

Her eyes filled with tears. Saeunna remembered her dream of the frozen lake. Hather saw, and understood.

And knew.

He leaned down from the saddle and kissed her. 'I've loved you long,' he said gently. 'I shall love you still, whether you ever see me again or not. If this is to be our parting, Saeunna, then wave me good-bye bravely. Believe me, I have no choice. It's Omund's life or mine, now. Or both our lives.'

He set his heels to the horse's flank and rode away, following the hoofprints in the snow which pointed the direction of Omund's flight. Behind him Svipdag and Olaf stayed only to kiss Saeunna and Gudrun, then followed their father in his pursuit of his ancient enemy.

Saeunna watched them go. None of them looked back, but she waved to them anyway, her heart heavy with knowledge of the death to come.

Gudrun clutched her arm. 'Will we see them again, mother?' she asked, her voice weighted with unshed tears.

Saeunna lowered her hand and screened her eyes with it. 'I don't know,' she answered, unable to voice what she knew to her daughter. 'Only their return will tell us that, Gudrun. We'll wait here, and we'll pray for it. With what's behind us, can we doubt the power of prayer?'

'I don't know,' Gudrun answered her. 'Can we, mother?'

Saeunna turned to Bolli. 'You know this country,' she said. 'What will they find that way?'

Bolli shrugged. 'Some forest,' he told her. 'A few hills. And Lake Fikui, which we call *cold lake*, because it remains frozen all the year round.'

Saeunna felt herself grow ice-cold. Once again, as in her dream, she saw Omund's sword impale her husband. She wanted to seize a horse and ride after him, but the impulse passed and she knew that, even with her warning ringing in his ears, Hather would still do what he had to. He had no choice but to follow his destiny, as she had the harder, more terrible task of waiting to hear the news of his death.

'And I shall love you, Hather Lambisson,' she whispered. 'Even though I know that you will never come back to me, I love you now as I have done from the first. Remember that, when Odin takes you to Valhalla.'

They settled down to wait. Five days, Hather had said. 'Wait five days. Two days to pursue. A day to settle the matter. Two days to return. Then, if we've not returned, don't wait any longer. Ride south for Uppsala and hold what order you can in the kindom in the name of the High King. You don't have to say whether the High King is Omund or the child in your arms, Saeunna. Then send to Sudrafell for my men to secure your position.'

Atyl Skin watched them ride off upon their pursuit. He wanted to go with them, to finish the job which Hather had prevented him from completing over twenty years before, the death of Omund Olisson. His place, though, was with Princess Hanni and Saeunna and Gudrun, waiting through the five days with them, ready to offer them his protection on the journey back to Uppsala if Hather and Olaf didn't return.

For Svipdag, riding with his younger brother beside his father, it was as if the weight of mystery had been taken from his life, that weight which had shackled and hampered him through the years, setting him apart from humanity. If he survived this expedition, he knew, he would retain his ambitions to take control of the kingdom. But he would never again raise his hand against those he loved, for Vultikamian's curse was gone with the sorcerer's death, freeing him of another's power for ever.

Hather's face was set as they tracked Omund out of the forest and into the snow-covered hills. From the distance between the hoofprints it appeared the High King was riding his mount hard, more intent upon putting distance between himself and any pursuers than in sparing his horse. Hather had banished all thought of Saeunna's dream, finding fresh strength and comfort in his sons, both riding beside him, with him, for the first time. His suspicions about Svipdag were a thing of the past. His doubts about Olaf had also gone, banished by the young man's courage during the terrible ordeals they had faced together. His sons were men, full men, both of them. Should he fall when he finally faced the treacherous Omund there would be strong brothers, the Hatherssons, to care for the welfare and safety of the one tiny surviving Yngling.

That was for the future, though. Now there was only pursuit.

He searched his heart for a reason to let Omund go, to stay his hand and spare the man who had threatened both his family and the future of Sweden, but he could find nothing. Omund had compacted with the dwarfs to murder his own wife and children and their children. He'd promised himself to the sorcerous service of Vultikamian. He'd lured Hanni from the Dane-Lands to be sacrificed in the wastes of Finnmark. And he'd betrayed his own blood for the sake of greed and ambition. No, Omund had to die. Only then would little Omund be safe. Only then would Sweden be safe from the mad plotting of the High King. The time had finally come when the Champion of the Ynglings had to face and kill his king to protect the Ynglings for the future.

Olaf pointed to a deep impression in the snow ahead. 'There,' he said. 'King Omund's horse stumbled and fell, there. It's tiring badly.'

They reached the crest of a hill and looked down. To either side the horizon was fringed with distant forests. Ahead of them was only the low line of the hills beneath the sky. They were in open country now, where Omund would be unable to find cover and evade them. Some little way away the tracks became badly disturbed. Further on down the slope a dark shape stood out starkly against the whiteness. As they rode closer it revealed itself as the High King's mount, dying of cold and exhaustion. It had been ridden to the point of collapse.

Svipdag'd dark eyes glittered. 'Omund's on foot,' he grinned. 'It shouldn't take us long now.'

Hather's gaze scanned the whiteness of the landscape ahead of them. In the valley below stretched the dull, winding, frozen surface of the serpentine Lake Fikui. Omund's footprints led down to it, then stopped.

Olaf rode to the shore of the lake. Twin swathes ran out upon the ice. 'He's on skates,' he called. 'He must have had some with him.'

Svipdag swore. 'We've lost him now,' he spat. 'We can

ride around the shore, but he'll make better time than we can.'

Hather went to see to the fallen horse. Its eyes were dulling, though its breath still steamed out in rapid snorts. Drawing his sword he slashed the dying animal's throat. Its blood spurted, staining and melting the snow around its head and neck. Then it lay still.

'Get the bridle,' Hather ordered. 'Cut it into thongs.' As he spoke he drew a knife and knelt beside the beast's belly, to rip it open. Its entrails heaved as their weight pushed them out through the wound. Working rapidly, using his gloved hand to pull back the flesh as he cut it, Hather exposed the animal's ribs and broke two free.

Svipdag handed him the thin strips of leather taken from the bridle and Hather remounted, riding down to the shore of the lake. Dismounting again he sat in the snow, binding the rib-bones to the soles of his boots, curve downwards, to form makeshift skates.

'Olaf, you and Svipdag ride around the shore,' he called. Then he stood up to achieve a precarious balance and set off across the ice, sword in hand.

Two bends of the shore ahead of him, his eyes wild and his bones bruised in his stumbling haste, King Omund was picking himself up from a fall. Behind him, loping along in easy pursuit, hands extended and her fingers hooked like talons, the silent figure of old Skeggja, her clothing in flames, her features distorted with vengeance, haunted his flight. Somehow the ghostly creature never came any closer to him, no matter how often he fell, but by the same token it never fell back nor gave him any respite from his panic. Whatever others might be following him, even were one of them Odin himself, not one could be as terrible as the ancient, blazing witch.

I shall see you again, little Omund, she had called to him from the burning tower in the forest. Not in life, but I shall see you again . . .

Too late, the High King realised, he had discovered the truth of the witch's promise. Now she was here, rushing along behind him, driving him on through the ruins of his life towards whatever end was ordained for him. Omund's one regret, now forgotten in his fear, was that his old enemy Hather Lambisson still lived. If there was any wish left to Omund, it was that he might have one last chance to destroy the Champion of the Ynglings.

Mother Skuld stood with Odin. They watched the final stages of the pursuit unfold before them. 'Well, Allfather?' she asked. 'Is it time, Death-Blinder? Is it time at last, Odin the Betrayer?'

Along the shore of Lake Fikui Olaf and Svipdag raced their horses through the snow. Beside them, his progress occasionally hidden by hummocks on the water's edge, Hather was drawing inexorably closer to the ghost-ridden Omund.

Allfather looked at his companion. Mother Skuld had resumed her veil, but the agreement between them still held, even though either could have claimed that it had terminated with Vultikamian's destruction. She had acknowledged her error in supporting the sorcerer, and together, in a rare blending of their separate intentions, they had lent their joint support to the cause of his defeat and death. Now only two Ynglings survived and, by the terms of their agreement, only one could still live by that day's sunset.

For Odin the choice was not as simple as it might have appeared. Omund, if he lived, could father more children. His little grandson, however, was simply a vulnerable child, susceptible to all the diseases of childhood and, during the interregnum which must follow, susceptible also to the daggers of any number of would-be assassins. With Hather and his sons dead Omund could reclaim his throne. And it would only take a little persuasion from Allfather to ensure his behaviour in the future . . .

Omund fled on, still casting desperate glances behind him. Old Skeggja was still there, though the flames about her were subsiding and her hands no longer stretched out quite so cruelly. In fact, that wasn't really her face any more. It was another face, a face he had known for longer, a face he had even more cause to hate.

It was the face of Hather Lambisson.

Ahead, Olaf and Svipdag had overtaken him. As if he had read Odin's mind the thought came to Omund that their deaths would repurchase his throne. Their deaths could save him, could restore to him everything he'd lost . . .

He was tiring, though. The time to stand and fight was now. Hather was closing the distance between them on his horse-rib skates. Omund swung wide, away from his original path. Hather, unable to check his speed, swept past him.

'Decide, Odin,' Mother Skuld hissed. 'If Omund lives I take the child. If Omund dies the child lives. That is the way it has to be.'

Hather's skates sprayed a fine mist of ice as he skidded to a halt and began to push towards Omund. The High King had swung around so that the sun was at his back, stabbing red and brilliant into his opponent's eyes. They were both bone weary from the chase, which had taken up the night before and most of this day. Now the sun was slanting low towards its setting, staining the frozen surface of the lake with its bloody taint and the long, dark slashes of their shadows.

The opponents started towards each other. Their swords met and clashed as they passed, the impact spinning them away to either side. Hather twisted towards the side then skated into the sun, turning to take the advantage which Omund had gained before and wasted.

Svipdag attempted to urge his horse down onto the surface of Lake Fikui. Its hooves slipped and scrabbled on the ice, finding no purchase, and it whinnied and backed up onto solid ground once more. He read an equal concern on Olaf's face, knowing that they were powerless to intervene and help their father.

The swords met again. Omund felt a sudden stinging pain on his left forearm from Hather's deflected blade.

His eyes grew wide and wild with desperation. Close-quarters combat was impossible on the ice. They could only break apart and charge at one another until a death-blow was given or received.

Allfather lowered his head. 'My choice is made, Mother Skuld,' he muttered sadly.

The combatants turned to face each other across the long, narrow lake. For the last time they dug in their skates and pushed out towards the centre, their legs moving in sweeping strides to build up speed. With the distance between them diminishing rapidly one of Omund's skates caught a ridge in the frozen surface. With a scream of fear he crashed to his knees whilst Hather swept towards him, his face a mask of merciless determination.

Omund scrabbled up to regain his balance. With Hather almost upon him he extended his sword, holding it at arm's length

Hather's expression offered no change, no sign of fear, no hint of pain. The point of Omund's weapon tore into his stomach and protruded through the back of his cloak, but it did not check his charge.

He thought of Saeunna. He remembered his daughter and sons. He remembered a dream of dying upon Omund's sword, and he knew that it was now come true.

Olaf began a stumbling run across the surface of the lake towards them. Svipdag followed.

'So you've chosen Omund,' Mother Skuld remarked, her voice slightly surprised. 'Very well, the child is mine.'

'Not yet, Norn,' Odin snapped.

It might have been his death-blow, but Omund's sword hadn't slowed Hather's charge. The weapon was driven deeper into his body as he slammed into the standing Omund and carried him backwards, before him, towards the snow-banked shore.

'You're dead,' Omund howled triumphantly, feeling the hot blood spurt from Hather's belly. 'I've killed you, Hather Lambisson! I've won!'

Hather smiled. A trickle of blood ran from his mouth

onto his chin. He said nothing, but still held his sword. Omund's weapon trapped within his body, he set the point of his own beneath the High King's jaw and began to push. The victory in Omund's eyes faded, replaced by pain and sudden terror. He tried to scream but the point pushed through his windpipe, severing the roots of his tongue. As the two dying enemies struck the bank beside the lake, Hather's sword thrust its way up into his brain.

They lay still, reddening the snow and ice around them. Olaf reached them first and pulled his father away from Omund's body. His hand moved to the hilt of Omund's sword to draw it out, but Hather's hand firmly clamped his wrist.

Svipdag joined them. He glanced at Omund, the discoloured tip of Hather's sword forced through the top of the High King's skull with the force of their impact against the shore, then knelt beside Hather, helping his brother to cradle their dying father's head.

Hather's eyes were calm. They showed tiredness rather than pain as he lay between them. With his free hand he clasped Svipdag's wrist as well.

'Look to the future . . .' he whispered. 'Protect the child. You . . . know I love you both . . . and Gudrun . . . and your mother. Tell them that. Give Saeunna a good account of me . . .'

His eyes flickered closed. For a few moments more his mouth worked, but no words came.

Odin turned to Mother Skuld. 'You will excuse me now,' he said softly. 'I have a duty to perform.'

'A new hero to be welcomed to Valhalla?' she asked him gently.

'As you say, Norn,' Allfather answered her. 'And none has better earned a place in my hall than Hather Lambisson of Sudrafell.'

Epilogue

The Ending of a Saga

No mound would be raised before Uppsala for Omund Olisson. No runestone would be cut to recall his treachery. Olaf and Svipdag buried him where he had fallen, cutting a shallow grave upon the frozen shore of Lake Fikui. Their father's body, though, they set upon his horse and took back to those who waited beside the ruin of the burning stones. There they gave Saeunna and the others the good account of his dying that Hather had asked them to.

'He died with your name upon his lips, mother,' Olaf told her. 'Even at the moment of his death his thoughts were for you.'

She turned away to hide her tears. Oh, but what a man he'd been, her Hather. So good, so fine, so kind and yet so brave and strong. They had met in conflict and he had died in conflict. Still, there were other times to remember as well, times of peace and love, times spent watching their children grow to adulthood. Could she really feel bitter that he had left her now, that he had given his life for the cause in which he believed, to which that life had been sworn?

Through her weeping she glimpsed Gudrun, her daughter, sitting nearby with Hanni's arm about her shoulder. In Gudrun's lap lay a sleeping child, the one surviving member of the House of Yngling. Only time would show what was to happen to that little boy. There was no way for Saeunna to know that he would survive, that he would grow up to become the mighty king Omund Roadmaker, so called from his desire to unite the kingdom by improving the routes between the vassal kingdoms which comprised it. Nor could she know that his son was destined to be Ingjald, sometimes called Ingjald the Bad, sometimes Ingjald Firestarter, who would truly be the very last of the Ynglings to sit upon Sweden's High King's throne.

They carried Hather's body home with them. It rested at Dalalven and Uppsala before its eventual return to Sudrafell, where the Champion of the Ynglings was buried before the gates of his home. It was a sad time for all of them, but even sadness fades eventually, and some happiness was destined for those who had lived through the terrors of the burning stones.

Svipdag resumed his kingship of Tiundaland and, following his ambitions, became leader of the kingdom for the duration of the interregnum. His brother Olaf ruled Ostragotland from his father's capital. He and Hanni married and became Omund's foster-parents as well as having children of their own. Saeunna lived with them, growing old and smiling out her memories, loving the survivor of the House of Yngling as much as she loved her own grandchildren. One day, she knew, she would see Hather again, and it seemed only fair to her that the last day of her life, when it came, would also be the happiest.

Bolli bade them farewell at the burning stones and returned alone to his steading. He lived out the remainder of his years in solitary peace and contentment, pleased to have played his part in the shaping of great events. When he knew that his time was approaching he set his reindeer free and made his way to the ruined stone circle. There he sat, waiting for his dark, Lappish gods to do with him as they willed.

Atyl Skin returned to the Dane-Lands to tell the story of their adventures to his king. Then he returned to Sudrafell and remained there, a friend to Olaf and Hanni, almost a brother to Saeunna, until his death.

Svipdag Hathersson held the reins of power wisely and well for many years. When Omund grew to manhood the eyes of the kingdom turned to Svipdag to see how the regent would behave when called upon to step down. He surprised everyone, even his brother Olaf, by submitting with dignity to the restoration of the House of Yngling. Yet his ambitions remained and, in time, they were to play their part in the eventual destruction of the dynasty.

The duel upon Lake Fikui, and the agreement with Mother Skuld, had won more for Odin than simply another hero to feast in Valhalla. The Norn's testing of the god's power, of his resolution to preserve the Ynglings for as long as he believed it necessary, was never to resume. The two old enemies, never quite lovers, never quite friends, called a truce which would hold fast until the Ragnarok, the Doom of the Gods. And Allfather, his attention no longer diverted by the Norn's scheming, was already beginning to think of a way to preserve his peers from that final, all-destroying conflict.

When he left Mother Skuld to greet his hero upon his entry to Valhalla, Odin was not alone. Others went with him to clasp Hather's wrist, old friends and comrades in arms who had gone before. Vermund Bjarnisson was there, and Thorvald Brotamad and Askel Horsetail. So was Leif Half-Foot, together with many others. Yet Hather's surprise was greatest, and his smile the broadest, for two who held themselves back until the last, two that he had never thought to see standing side by side. The first was his father, Lambi Nef, whom Starkadder had killed so many years before. They embraced warmly, then they stood apart, allowing that last one to join them, to welcome the boy he'd known so long before, the boy who had become the Champion of the Ynglings.

'I've missed you, old Starkadder,' Hather said, extending his wrist. 'I've thought about you long and often through the years. And I have to tell you that I've been proud to say that I played a small part in your saga.'

Starkadder's gaunt features returned Hather Lambisson's smile. 'I'll not argue with you, lad,' he answered, 'but you're wrong. It wasn't you who played a role in my saga at all. It's my turn to be proud, and I am, Hather, I am. I'm proud because you've been true to me all these years, because you've always said that it was Tyrfing which killed me, not yourself. And I'm proud because of what you've been, the best and greatest of us all.

'No, Hather,' Starkadder continued. 'I'm the one who's played the small part in a saga. *Your saga*, Hather Lambisson, not my own.'

They clasped wrists as Allfather approached them. 'I know what you're going to say to us,' Starkadder grinned.

Odin returned his smile. 'You should,' he answered. 'For I've said it to each of you in turn.'

Hather took a last look at the place where Olaf and Svipdag were burying Omund's body on the shore of the lake.

'What are you going to say, Allfather?' he asked.

There was no pain in parting from his sons and his family like this. There was only the peace which followed a life well-lived. For Hather Lambisson there was a seat waiting in the company of old friends, and he would be glad to take his place among them.

'Shall we be going now, Hather?' Odin asked him.

Hather nodded. 'I'd like that, Allfather,' he replied.

VARGR-MOON

BERNARD KING

His King had sent for him. He had long avoided the court and its men of power, for power, he had seen, drove men mad. But now he, fated slayer of Starkadder, was commanded to attend.

Other men were there gathered: warriors, blood-bondsmen, lordly weapon-wielders, mercenaries: summoned for a terrible purpose.

From a midnight-black past of legend and epic, a *vargr* had descended upon the land. Half-myth, winter-haunting, a creature both wolf and man, killer and devourer of all flesh, moon-maddened and growing in strength, it must be destroyed before it destroyed the realm. Now forces beyond the understanding of men were stirring.

Post·A·Book

A Royal Mail service in association with the Book Marketing Council & The Booksellers Association.

Post-A-Book is a Post Office trademark.

MORE TITLES AVAILABLE FROM HODDER AND STOUGHTON PAPERBACKS

		BERNARD KING	
☐	39011 X	Starkadder	£2.50
☐	40848 5	Vargr-Moon	£2.50
		STEPHEN GALLAGHER	
☐	42268 2	Valley of Lights	£2.95
☐	49178 1	Oktober	£2.99
		JOHN FARRIS	
☐	05900 6	Minotaur	£2.95
☐	42644 0	Wildwood	£2.95
☐	40575 3	Son of the Endless Night	£3.50
☐	41729 8	Nightfall	£2.95
		FRANK DEFELITTA	
☐	05533 7	For Love of Audrey Rose	£3.50
☐	38929 4	Golgotha Falls	£2.95

All these books are available at your local bookshop or newsagent, or can be ordered direct from the publisher. Just tick the titles you want and fill in the form below.

Prices and availability subject to change without notice.

HODDER AND STOUGHTON PAPERBACKS, P.O. Box 11, Falmouth, Cornwall.

Please send cheque or postal order, and allow the following for postage and packing:

U.K. – 55p for one book, plus 22p for the second bood, and 14p for each additional book ordered up to a £1.75 maximum.

B.F.P.O. and EIRE – 55p for the first book, plus 22p for the second book, and 14p per copy for the next 7 books, 8p per book thereafter.

OTHER OVERSEAS CUSTOMERS – £1.00 for the first book, plus 25p per copy for each additional book.

NAME ....

ADDRESS ....

....